SIN
FOR ME

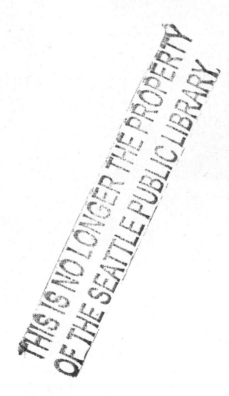
11/14

The Motor City Royals Series by Jackie Ashenden

Dirty for Me

Wrong for Me

Sin for Me

Published by Kensington Publishing Corporation

SIN FOR ME

Jackie Ashenden

KENSINGTON BOOKS
www.kensingtonbooks.com

KENSINGTON BOOKS are published by

Kensington Publishing Corp.
119 West 40th Street
New York, NY 10018

All Kensington titles, imprints, and distributed lines are available at special quantity discounts for bulk purchases for sales promotion, premiums, fund-raising, educational, or institutional use.

Special book excerpts or customized printings can also be created to fit specific needs. For details, write or phone the office of the Kensington Sales Manager: Kensington Publishing Corp., 119 West 40th Street, New York, NY 10018. Attn. Sales Department. Phone: 1-800-221-2647.

Kensington and the K logo Reg. U.S. Pat. & TM Off.

eISBN-13: 978-1-4967-0395-8
eISBN-10: 1-4967-0395-2
First Kensington Electronic Edition: April 2017

ISBN-13: 978-1-4967-0394-1
ISBN-10: 1-4967-0394-4
First Kensington Trade Paperback Printing: April 2017

10 9 8 7 6 5 4 3 2 1

Printed in the United States of America

To all those who told me I couldn't.

I did.

SIN FOR ME

Chapter 1

Zoe sat on one of the coveted corner couches in the darkest part of Anonymous, sipping her frozen blackberry margarita and nodding her head up and down in time to the hard-thumping bass that vibrated through the nightclub.

Anonymous had only been going a year, but its gritty, industrial atmosphere—the huge vaulting space used to be some kind of factory that had been abandoned along with seemingly half the buildings in Detroit—was a major draw for the young, cool, and often tragically hip.

It was Saturday night, which meant the place was packed with miles of tattoos, more piercings than a death metal concert, and so many beards and man buns she may as well have been in Portland. Not that she minded any of those things.

In fact, it was the whole reason she was here in the first place. By herself. Without anyone cramping her style.

Anyone being Gideon Black.

She sat back on the couch, surveying the heaving crowd on the dance floor in the middle of the club, then checking out the long metal length of the bar on the other side of it, just to be sure a familiar tall and hulking figure wasn't lurking around.

But no, seemed he'd believed her when she'd told him she was joining Tamara and Rachel for a girls' night at Rachel's place.

Excellent.

She picked up her margarita and took another hefty sip, scanning around for any likely looking dudes.

There were lots of guys, obviously, and more than a few who were her kind of tall, dark, and handsome. Lots to choose from, in other words. But she wanted her first one-night stand—her first anything, really—to be with someone she kind of liked.

What does it matter? It's only one night.

She wasn't there to pick someone to have a relationship with. She only wanted someone hot who could make her forget her stupid, goddamn unrequited love for Gideon. A love that wouldn't ever be returned, at least not in the way she wanted it to be. Because he pretty much saw her as a little sister and nothing more.

Well, you are his little sister.

Not technically. She was his little *foster* sister. And she'd only been that for a year when they'd lived in the same foster family. Then he'd turned seventeen and aged out of the system. So really it didn't count.

It still pissed her off that he refused to see her as anything different, though.

No, scratch pissed. She was fucking *furious*. Furious at him, somewhat unfairly, but mainly with herself. Because she'd felt that way about him for ten years, and nothing had changed.

Oh no, wait. Something had changed. He'd told her a couple of weeks ago to stop following him around all the time. Like she was some kind of stupid, eager puppy.

You are *a stupid, eager puppy.*

Zoe swallowed half her margarita, balefully looking at the crowd around her.

Ever since they'd first come to Detroit from Chicago, she'd been at his side, living in their apartment above the garage while he'd protected her, looked out for her, made a family for her with Rachel and Zee and Levi. And she'd been happy. Safe, protected. Being near him, knowing he was there, had been all she'd wanted.

But lately she'd started to find that safety and stability a little too stifling. A little bit too much like a cage. She'd started to think about what she wanted to do with her life, about the direction she was headed. And after watching Zee find Tamara, and Rachel and Levi find each other again, she'd begun to think about her own love life—which was nonexistent.

Currently you are headed to Nowheresville via Viriginforever Town.

Zoe glowered.

The leash Gideon kept her on was short and feeling shorter by the day, especially in the past month or so. And his getting pissed off with her for following him around and daring to ask questions about her future, hurt.

Something needed to change.

Hell, she hadn't been a rebellious teenager, not with Gideon being a very strict big brother stand-in, so maybe she was due a little rebellion time. Like now.

Attention-seeking much?

Zoe sniffed and drained her margarita, putting the glass back down on the low metal table in front of her with a click.

She wasn't seeking attention; she was just trying to do what any twenty-five-year-old woman would. Have a normal damn life, and part of that normal damn life included going out to a nightclub, getting drunk, then getting laid.

Not necessarily in that order.

Across the dance floor, over by the bar, her attention snagged on a tall guy with broad shoulders and dark hair. Pretty hot-looking. No tats, but then you couldn't have everything. He made eye contact with her, and she found herself blushing and looking away, which was super annoying.

Her experience with men amounted to checking out hot dudes on Tumblr, and talking to her friends in a few of the online forums she frequented. Though really, who knew what sex they really were? She was assuming guys, but on the Internet it was never safe to assume anything.

Her experience with actual men in real life was nil. If you didn't count Zee and Levi, which she didn't.

Maybe she should have brought Rachel or Tamara along with her as wing women. Then again, they probably wouldn't approve of what she was doing, and she'd prefer to keep it on the down-low anyway.

It was bad enough *everyone* knew about her stupid Gideon crush. Having other people witness her general man-ineptness would be a blow to her pride she didn't think she could take.

She glanced back at the bar again, to see what the guy who'd looked at her was doing, steeling herself not to look away this time. And her heart gave a small hop inside her chest.

Because he was coming toward her.

Holy shit.

She reached out for her margarita but sadly there was no more left, so she had to fiddle awkwardly with the empty glass as the guy came closer. She tried not to blush or grin at him like a lunatic.

Man, he was pretty nice-looking. Didn't have Gideon's air of gentle but firm authority or his compelling charisma, but there was something about him that she liked anyway. He was certainly approachable. At least, he was approaching her.

He wasn't a local, that was for sure, since locals knew who she was and who was protecting her and liked their balls to remain in place. So obviously this guy had to be from somewhere else. Which was fine. In fact, better than fine. It suited her purposes nicely.

She swallowed as he came up to the table, suddenly aware that she was pushing herself back in her seat. Stupid. She needed to chill the hell out.

"Hey," the guy said, giving her a very direct smile. "Looks like you're all out of . . . whatever was in that glass of yours."

"Blackberry f-frozen margarita," she said, the words coming out in a helpless, stammering rush. "And . . . uh . . . yeah, I am."

"Can I get you another?" His eyes were blue and they roamed over her with disconcerting frankness, as if he was sizing her up.

Okay, this is your moment of glory. Do it.

Zoe returned what she hoped was a natural-looking smile and not a fixed rictus, which is what it probably was. "Um, sure. That would be great."

Gideon was not happy. Anonymous was the last place on earth he wanted to be at one a.m. on a Saturday morning, but unfortunately, since Zoe had not in fact gone to Rachel's for a girls' night like she'd told him, he was going to have brave the revoltingly hipster crowds in order to check it out.

It wasn't that he didn't like nightclubs. He just didn't like them with Zoe in them. On her own.

Normally he was a chilled out guy; never let his temper rule him. Was calm and considerate and patient. But right now he didn't feel very fucking calm. Or considerate or patient.

Right now, he felt fucking pissed.

The line outside the door to the club was insane and the bouncer was new, which meant he didn't know Gideon and didn't realize that Gideon basically ruled Royal Road—a fact that should have granted him automatic entry without any dicking around.

Sadly for both Gideon's temper and the new bouncer's reputation, there was dicking around.

Eventually, after a tense five-minute standoff, Gideon cowed the bouncer into submission with a promise to report him to Jimmy, the guy who owned Anonymous, before banging open the doors and stalking into the club.

The noise and heat of well over a hundred people all dancing, drinking, and doing various other and probably illegal things hit him like the front of a particularly violent thunderstorm, fraying the already tenuous grip he had on his temper.

He didn't know if she was here or not, but he was hoping for her sake that she was, because he was coming to the end of his considerable patience.

The past few weeks had been a real fucking trial, what with Zee and his goddamn father threatening them all, and then Levi getting out of jail and having a few issues adjusting. Which in turn had unfortunately attracted the attention of the very last person on earth Gideon wanted attention from. The person Gideon had been protecting Zoe from for the last ten years.

It hadn't been Levi's fault. Levi didn't know Zoe's or Gideon's background, or what had gone down with Zoe's mother. But still. Oliver fucking Novak was now sniffing around Royal because of Levi's development plans, which meant Gideon didn't want Zoe going AWOL, and certainly not at night.

Yeah, she better be here. He didn't know what had gotten into her, whether it was some kind of late puberty/rebellion thing or what, but that shit was getting old and she didn't understand the danger she was in.

Which means you have to tell her.

Gideon glowered at the crowds on the dance floor, scanning around for a small, delicately built young woman with black curls, big golden eyes, and glasses.

He had his reasons for not telling her, the main one being that he hadn't wanted her living her life in fear. Then again, if she was going to pull this kind of shit, then clearly they were going to have to have a discussion. Novak hadn't taken on Levi's plans purely to shine up a down-and-out neighborhood for his senatorial bid. He'd chosen Royal for a reason and maybe that reason was Zoe.

Gideon moved around the dance floor, trying to spot her. It didn't look like she was there, though it was a little difficult to tell what with all the writhing bodies. Lights were flashing, sparkling off sequins and sliding over glistening skin. A woman ran a hand along his arm on her way toward the dancers, giving him a suggestive look.

He shook his head and, ignoring her pout of disappointment, shifted his attention over to the long metal, industrial-looking bar. No sign of Zoe there either.

Last place to look was the seating area at the back of the massive space and if she wasn't there, he was going to have to figure out just where the hell else she might be, because there weren't many other places in Royal she would have gone to.

Worry began to thread through his anger and he had to fight the very real urge to start picking people up and flinging them out of his way.

He'd protected Zoe ever since she'd been a kid and he'd be damned if he failed in that duty now just because she was having a teenage tantrum.

The seating area in Anonymous was composed of black leather sectional couches and small metal coffee tables. The lighting consisted of exposed, old-fashioned filament bulbs and glass light shades. There was graffiti on the exposed brick walls, all adding to the gritty, industrial vibe of the place.

He checked out the huddled groups around the tables, and then, his anger beginning to flex like a bodybuilder on steroids, the pairs entwined in the darker areas toward the back.

Not that it should matter to him either way whether Zoe was with anyone or not, but still. He didn't like the thought of it. She was too young for that kind of stuff, too innocent. Jesus, if some fucking asshole had picked her up, there was going to be hell to pay.

But Zoe wasn't part of any of the entwined couples, which made him feel relieved and yet even more worried. Because if she wasn't here, then where the fuck was she?

He turned and made another circuit of the entire club, just to be sure.

But it wasn't until he'd turned to head toward the exit, his worry deepening into genuine fear, that he caught the sound of a familiar laugh. It was husky and warm and infectious, and it felt like he hadn't heard it in far too long.

Zoe.

He whipped his head sharply toward the sound, narrowing his gaze down a long corridor that led to the club's bathrooms.

A couple stood together, the woman against the wall, the man in front of her. She had her head tilted back so she could look up at him, her black curls tied back into a thick ponytail that fell to the middle of her back, her glasses pushed up her nose. In the darkness it was difficult to see the expression on her face, but then came the sound of her laughter. The man bent his head and kissed her, stopping the sound dead.

For a second Gideon just stood there staring, relief holding him motionless. Then he saw red, his anger smashing right through that relief like a wrecking ball through an old brick building, propelling him toward them before he was even conscious of doing so.

Taking a fistful of the guy's T-shirt, Gideon yanked him away hard. "Oh no you fucking don't."

The man stumbled back a few steps while Zoe's eyes went wide with shock.

"Gideon?"

"Hey! What the fuck?" the guy cried.

Gideon stepped in between them, putting his back to the asshole behind him, meeting Zoe's big gold eyes. He didn't waste time with niceties. "Where the fuck have you been?"

"What? What the hell is wrong with you?" The shock twisting Zoe's fine, delicate features began to fade, morphing into anger. "I've just been having a night—"

"You lied to me," he interrupted, not sure what he was most furious about: the fact that she'd worried the hell out of him, had told him she was somewhere else, or that he'd caught her kissing some random asshole.

Why should that bother you?

He ignored that thought. "You told me you were at Rachel's."

"Zoe?" The random asshole was standing behind him and no doubt spoiling for a fight since Gideon had interrupted him in full seduction mode. "Who is this guy? Is he bothering you?"

Not happening. So not happening.

Gideon spun around, met the other man's eyes. "Get the fuck out of here. If I catch your hands on her again, I'll pull your spine out through your neck."

"Oh my God, Gideon!" Zoe's husky little voice practically vibrated with rage. "You're being a giant dick!"

But he paid that no attention, keeping his gaze on the man in front of him, staring him down. "Make a good decision." He kept his voice hard. "If you want to come back to this club again, you'd better leave now before I change my mind and start making life difficult for you."

The guy scowled. "You and whose fucking army?"

Obviously, he wasn't from around here. Because if he was, he'd have shut up and done whatever Gideon said because no one screwed with Gideon or one of his crew, and especially not with Zoe. Not if they knew what was good for them.

Gideon wasn't a violent man. Oh, he'd done violence in his past and once had even made a living out of it. But he didn't relish it and preferred to handle situations in other ways. Still, he had a line and that line was the little family he'd created here in Royal Road. Most especially Zoe.

Anyone crossing that line was going to find himself without an important part of his anatomy.

"I don't need an army," he said coldly. "Now get out of here before I lose my patience and get security to throw you out."

The guy spat a few curses, but it turned out he had some brains after all because he stalked off into the crowd, giving Gideon one last baleful look.

Which Gideon ignored.

"You asshole." Zoe's voice was low and fierce. "Thanks for ruining a perfectly good night."

He swung back around to meet her furious gaze, conscious that he was pretty fucking enraged and that there was no good reason for it. Though on second thought, it was probably due to the relief that she was okay. Definitely nothing to do with that bastard and the fact that some stranger had been kissing her.

Was that her first kiss?

Jesus Christ, what was with him? With an effort, Gideon closed off that part of his brain and concentrated on her instead. "You're coming home," he ordered. "Now."

Zoe's chin firmed, becoming stubborn in the way he'd gotten far too familiar with over the past few weeks. The way she did when she wasn't going to do what he told her, come hell or high water. "No." There was now a mutinous look on her face. "I just wanted a night out like any other twenty-five-year-old and I'm going to damn well have it."

Ah, fuck. Her getting willful was the last thing he needed, and now wasn't either the time or the place to explain things to her, especially when he didn't have the patience to be his usual understanding self.

"The hell you are," he snapped. "If you don't come with me

right now, I'll throw you over my shoulder and carry you out myself."

Her chin stuck out even more. "Yeah? Try it, asshole. Go on, I dare you to."

Abruptly, Gideon came to the end of his patience.

She was going to regret that.

He reached out, grabbed her by the hips, and lifted her up, flinging her over his shoulder exactly as he promised.

Zoe went rigid and utterly silent. Which was probably shock, but at least it gave him a couple of peaceful seconds to turn and start making his way to the exit.

The crowds only gave them a cursory glance. For some of them a man with a woman over his shoulder was nothing out of the ordinary, and for others, they either simply didn't care or they knew him.

Zoe herself remained quiet for the first couple of steps, then she made an outraged squawking sound and began to wriggle out of his grip, beating her fists on his back.

It didn't hurt but didn't make his temper any better either.

"Stop it," he growled. "Or I'll spank you."

For a second there it looked like he might have to make good on that promise. Then the fists on his back fell away and she stopped struggling. "I hate you," she muttered bitterly.

"What are you? Sixteen? Grow up, Zoe."

She gave a disgusted snort. "What the fuck do you think I've been trying to do?"

He brushed past a couple of the security staff, both Royal Road locals. They gave him a nod as if it was perfectly normal for him to be hauling Zoe out of a nightclub over his shoulder.

She gave a groan. "I feel sick."

He sighed, shoving open the nightclub doors and stepping out onto the pavement. The line outside had doubled, some of the people laughing and shouting encouragement as he strode past. Fucking idiots.

"You better put me down, otherwise I'm going to puke down your back," Zoe said grumpily.

Of course. She was drunk on top of it all. Could this goddamn night get any better?

Rounding the corner of the nightclub to get away from the crowd, Gideon finally lowered her to her feet. But he didn't move away. Instead, he slapped his hands to the rough brick on either side of her head and pinned her to the wall with his gaze.

"So what the fuck do you think you were doing?" he demanded.

Zoe blinked at him, then lifted her chin the way she had done back in the club, shoving her glasses up her nose with a prominent middle finger. "Like I said, I was having a night out. Why are you being such an asshole about it?"

"You lied to me. You said you were at Rachel's."

"Yeah, because I knew you weren't going to let me go anywhere."

"There's a reason for that—or had you forgotten?"

Her amber gaze was belligerent. "Oh, you mean the whole 'there's bad things out there on the streets, Zoe' threat? The one that prevents me from going out and doing anything? From basically having a goddamn life? You really think I'd have forgotten that?"

Christ. She had no idea and if he had his way, she never would. But the time for keeping her in the dark was clearly over. They were going to need to have a serious talk once she sobered up.

"I'll discuss that later. Right now, the issue is you lying to me about where you were going. I need to know where you are, Zoe. How can I look out for you otherwise?"

Her lower lip was stuck out in a pout and it was red from where that asshole had kissed her. Though why the fuck he should be noticing that, he had no idea. "I don't want you to look out for me," she said flatly. "You told me you were sick of me hanging around you twenty-four seven? Well, that makes two of us."

Guilt twisted in his gut. Because beneath the current of anger in her voice, he heard the echoes of hurt. Could see it in her eyes, too, though she was trying her level best to hide it.

"You know I didn't mean that."

The past few weeks had been tough on all of them, Zoe in particular. She didn't do well with change—the legacy of too many foster homes in too short a space of time—and hated it when things were unsettled with her surrogate family.

It didn't help that he'd been worried too, first about Zee, then about Rachel and Levi. And although things were sweet now, Novak's sudden reappearance had made him even more on edge.

They'd argued—he couldn't even remember what about—but he'd ended it with him telling her to quit following him around twenty-four seven. Afterward, he'd apologized, but she'd only shrugged as if she didn't care.

She was a terrible liar, though. He'd hurt her and it looked like she was carrying that hurt around with her still.

She lifted a shoulder. "Whatever. You were right. Now get out of the damn way and I'll go back to not following you around, okay?"

"I'm not going anywhere." Too bad about what he'd told her. He was *not* letting her out of his sight. Not tonight. "And you're coming back home with me."

Another flare of anger lit her eyes. She took a step forward, getting right up in his face, and he could smell tequila and blackberries and the subtle lavender scent from her favorite soap. "No way. I want a night out. I want to have just one fucking night as a normal woman, where you're not looming over my goddamn shoulder or telling me what to do. Where you're not here!"

Life as a normal woman? What the hell was she talking

about? She made it sound like she was a prisoner and he was her jailer, which wasn't the case at all. She could go out whenever she liked and he wasn't *always* there.

Sure, he didn't like her to go beyond Royal too often, especially not now, but it wasn't like he'd stuck her in a tower and thrown away the key.

"You are a normal woman." He stared at her, scanning her fine, delicate features. Trying to figure out where all this was coming from. "And you can go out whenever you like, I'm not stopping you."

"Oh, sure. Like you're not stopping me now."

"It's different now."

"How?"

Because you found her in a nightclub kissing someone?

The thought was in his head before he could stop it.

Ridiculous. It wasn't the kiss or the asshole kissing her that was making him stop her. Sure, he was concerned about it but only because she was drunk and by herself, and who knew what kind of moves that prick would have pulled?

"Because you lied about where you were. And then when I got there you were drunk and letting some asshole feel you up."

Her smooth, coffee-colored skin flushed a deep red, the look on her face outraged. "I was *not* letting him feel me up! It was just a kiss!"

"And what if he'd wanted more?"

"Maybe if he'd wanted more I'd have let him," she shot back, fury sparking in her eyes. "At least that's what normal women do at nightclubs. Normal women who aren't still virgins at twenty-five."

Jesus, was this what it was all about? Zoe wanting to get laid? The thought made him feel unsettled, though he couldn't think for the life of him why. He'd talked to her about plenty of embarrassing stuff over the years. Sex was the least of it.

"Christ, is that all you wanted to do? If that's the case then going to a club by yourself, getting drunk, and picking up a guy is not the way to do it."

She scowled. "Then how else is it going to happen? When no one in Royal will touch me because of you?"

Oh, he was *not* having this discussion here with her. Not when she was drunk and he was at the end of his patience. "We can talk about your love life later. Right now, it's time to go home."

"But I don't want to go home and I don't want to talk about it later." Fury made her eyes glow behind her glasses, the beautiful gold color molten. "I want to go have a good time, go get drunk, and then go get laid. So far, I've managed the first two, now I just need the third." She gave him a challenging stare. "So get out of my way unless you're planning on doing the honors."

Chapter 2

Oh shit. Why the hell had she said that?

Zoe clamped her stupid, drunken mouth shut, but it was too late. The words were out there, echoing off the walls beside them and going around and around in her own head.

Was it just her, or could he hear the slightly desperate tone in them, too?

She could feel her cheeks flaming and she wanted to look away so she wouldn't have to see the instinctive disgust or rejection on his face. But she'd been stupid enough to say it out loud, which meant she needed to see his reaction. Even if it wasn't one she wanted.

He was a man who didn't let any emotion he didn't want show in his face, so it was a testament to how badly she'd taken him by surprise that she read shock in his eyes, loud and clear.

Then it was gone, his black gaze as direct and as level as it usually was. "I'm gonna pretend I didn't hear that," he said in his deep, rough voice.

Embarrassment mixed with the frustration and the anger

churning in her gut, along with the tequila that was already there. And the fact that Gideon was standing with his arms on either side of her head, his body right in front of hers, his posture almost mirroring that of the guy who'd been in the process of picking her up, didn't help.

Her mouth was tingling from the effects of her first kiss and she was absolutely furious with Gideon for pussy blocking her. If that was even what you called it when your older foster brother, protector, guardian, or whoever Gideon was stopped you from getting laid.

It had been a nice kiss, too, and she'd just been getting into it when Super Dick here had jerked whatever his name was—he'd told her, but she couldn't remember—away.

And not only that. Gideon had picked her up and tossed her humiliatingly over his shoulder like a sack of potatoes. Then he'd started throwing around spanking threats and her stupid, traitorous body had wanted to struggle harder so he could make good on them.

God, could she be any dumber?

Now here he was, standing in front of her, and she was caged against the wall by six foot four of solid, male muscle. He was a virtual wall all by himself, what with his height and the width of his powerful shoulders and broad chest. A mechanic with the body of a gladiator. A body she wanted to touch with every breath in her.

She stared up at him, trying to mask her reaction to his physical closeness. It should have gotten easier over the years, but it hadn't. She still blushed like a fool whenever he was around and her heartbeat still raced whenever he got close.

His eyes were deep set in his rough, bluntly handsome face, and so very dark. Like the water of a quiet black lake she wanted to dive into to check how deep it went.

Over your head, idiot.

Zoe swallowed. He was so very familiar to her, the way he towered over her, somehow making her feel safe. The warmth of his body. The engine oil and leather scent of him, the one that always reminded her of home.

She knew him so well and yet there were parts of him she didn't. Parts he never showed her that she was terminally curious about and wanted to explore.

The parts of himself that made him a stranger.

"Why not?" A stupid comeback, but she said it anyway. He was so calm and so goddamn patient with her all the time. As if she was a child to him.

You are a child to him.

Great. Like she needed the reminder.

"You know why not."

"No, I don't." She was pushing him, which was probably a dumb thing to do, but she couldn't help herself. "Tell me."

Back in the club, she'd certainly gotten a reaction out of him that hadn't been either calm or patient. In fact, he'd been downright furious with her. Sure, she'd lied to him, but was that the only reason? Or did it have something to do with what's-his-name?

Wishful thinking, girl.

Gideon's expression became set, in the way it did when he'd made a decision and didn't want to be pushed about it. "Like I said, I'm not having this discussion here." He stepped away from her. "Time to go, Zoe."

She folded her arms and cocked her hip, angry and stubborn as hell. "And if I don't? Are you going to pick me up and toss me over your shoulder again? Spank me like a kid?"

His straight, dark brows descended. "Don't tempt me."

"Maybe I should," she said recklessly, on a roll now and unable to stop. "Maybe you could use a little more tempting."

Something flickered in his eyes, something that was gone too fast for her to identify. "If you don't come now, I'll cut off your Internet connection for the next week."

"I could get around it!" She really should stop poking at him, she really should. But what the hell—what could he do to her that he hadn't already done? Lock her away for the rest of her life? No matter what he said, she was kind of locked away already.

The look on his face became even harder. "No rides on the Harley for the next month."

Oh, low blow. Really, really low.

She loved it when he took her out on the back of his Harley and he knew it, the bastard. They never went anywhere in particular, just drove. But it was the only time she felt free, holding on to him as they raced along the freeway, the wind in her face and grabbing at her hair.

On the Harley she could pretend to be someone else. A woman who wasn't his much younger former foster sister. A woman whom he loved and who loved him. Not that she had to pretend about her own feelings—it was his she had to fill in.

"Asshole," she said bitterly.

He didn't even look satisfied, merely giving a curt nod, then turning on his heel and starting in the direction of the apartment they shared. Part of her wanted to tell him to stick his stupid Harley where the sun don't shine and that she didn't want to ride on it with it him in any case. But that would have been too petulant, even for her, so she forced herself to follow him, trailing along behind, full of frustrated anger.

The apartment above Gideon's garage was about a ten-minute walk away, and she was proud of herself that she managed to maintain her aggrieved silence the whole way, not saying a word as Gideon unlocked the front door of the building and held it open for her. She brushed past him, ignoring him completely as she went up the stairs to the apartment itself.

It would have been much better if she could have let herself in and then stormed off to her bedroom, slamming the door behind her, but unfortunately she'd left her keys behind and had to wait for him to unlock that door as well.

He took his time, like he was deliberately provoking her, and when she made to go inside, he suddenly put his arm across the doorway, causing her to come up short instead.

She glared at him. "I thought you wanted me to go home?"

"I do. But if you're gonna be sulky, think again."

"And if you're expecting me to thank you for dragging me home like a sixteen-year-old, you can think again too," she said tartly.

"Stop acting like a sixteen-year-old and I won't have to."

"I'm not acting like a sixteen-year-old." She stared at him, furious with him for not only treating her like a kid, but for not understanding when he should have understood. "I'm acting like any twenty-five-year-old woman trying to have a good time out at a club."

He glared back. "You shouldn't have lied to me."

"Oh yeah? And what would you have done if you were me?"

That flickering look moved in his eyes again, the expression she didn't know how to interpret. "But I'm not you, Zoe."

"That's not what I meant."

"I don't care what you meant. My job is to protect you whether you like it or not, and that's what I'm gonna do, understand? If you wanna discuss it when you're not drunk and behaving like a sulky teenager, then by all means we can discuss it. But not here and not now."

She wanted to argue with him, have it out right here, right now, no matter what he said. Force him to listen because every time she'd tried to bring it up with him he'd either avoided the subject, brushed her off, or told her he was too busy. She was getting tired of it.

For thirteen years she'd been happy with the status quo, with wanting everything to stay the same. Not anymore. Everyone around her was settling into a new phase of their lives—when would it be her turn? When would she be able to get some of the things she wanted? Hell, she didn't need all of them, just a couple.

"You don't want to discuss it," she snapped. "You *never* want to discuss it."

Gideon let out a breath and abruptly lifted his arm from the doorway, stepping back to run a hand through his shaggy black hair. "Fuck this. Just go to bed, okay?"

Zoe bit her lip, her anger ebbing whether she wanted it to or not. He sounded tired, and she hated it when he sounded tired. In fact, he'd been tired a lot the past few weeks. She knew; she'd noticed the dark circles under his eyes. They were there right now, small black shadows, as if he hadn't been sleeping very well.

Guilt gave a sharp, unwelcome twist inside her. She shouldn't have been such a pain in the ass. It was late and since she'd told no one where she was going tonight, he must have looked all over the neighborhood for her before eventually finding her in Anonymous. No wonder he was angry.

Oh, harden up. You'll never get what you want if you keep being such a pushover.

But the rest of her anger was already leaking away like water out of a cracked bucket, leaving her feeling dizzy and a bit sick. Yay for alcohol.

"I'm sorry," she said miserably. "I didn't mean to lie to you. I just wanted . . ." She trailed off. What was the point of explaining? If he didn't understand now, he wouldn't.

He shook his head, his hand dropping. "Just . . . go to bed, Zoe."

This time she did what she was told without a word.

* * *

Gideon flipped the pancake with casual expertise and stared at it as it landed perfectly back in the pan.

Sunday morning pancakes were kind of a tradition with him and Zoe. He'd started making them for her back when she'd first come to live with his last foster family. He'd been sixteen, trying to coax the silent Zoe out of her shell and hoping that pancakes would do it. She hadn't talked quite then, but she'd eaten the pancakes he'd put in front of her. Every last one.

He'd been making them almost every Sunday morning since. Though, given the probable hangover she'd no doubt be nursing this morning, she may not want any.

He wasn't feeling all that shit-hot himself and he didn't even have alcohol as an excuse, just a lack of sleep. It wasn't anything unusual—he hadn't been sleeping well for the past few weeks, his head too full of what was happening with his friends. But what bothered him about last night was the fact that it hadn't been Zoe lying to him or even concerns about Novak that had kept him up.

It was the kiss he'd interrupted.

He couldn't seem to get it out of his head. Zoe with her head tilted back as the guy had leaned in and covered her mouth. Her eyes had fallen closed as if this had been something she'd been waiting for all her life.

What would have happened if he hadn't turned up? Would they have gone further? Would Zoe have actually gone home with the guy?

Gideon scowled at the pancake, the memory replaying in his head yet again. Why the fuck did he keep thinking about it? His interest in Zoe's love life was less than zero.

Sure. That's why you went ahead and hauled that prick off her like he was touching a holy relic.

No. He'd only been protecting her, that's all.

The smell of burning pancake filled the little kitchen and Gideon cursed, snapping himself out of it. Grimacing, he slid the pancake out of the pan and onto the stack he had keeping warm in the oven, then ditched the pan in the sink.

At that moment his phone in his back pocket vibrated with an incoming text.

He pulled it out and glanced at the screen. It was from Rachel.

You track down Zoe?

Quickly he sent her a text back. *Yeah. She was at the club. By herself.*

Rachel's reply was to the point. *What's with her?*

No fucking idea.

There was a brief pause, then: *You want me to talk to her?*

A burst of annoyance went through him. He'd never had any issues with talking to Zoe, and she knew she could come to him if there was a problem. Talking to her was his job, not anyone else's. *No,* he texted back. *I'll figure it out.*

Scrubbing a hand through his hair, he checked the time, then stuck his phone in the back pocket of his jeans. It was ten o'clock. Normally, Zoe would be up by now, especially seeing as it was pancake day. That was unless she was either still asleep, avoiding him, or feeling lousy.

He was betting he knew which it would be. Too bad. Time to have this out with her, see what the hell her problem was.

"I want to go have a good time, go get drunk, and then go get laid."

The memory of her defiant words did not improve his temper as he stalked down the narrow hallway toward Zoe's bedroom door.

If all she'd wanted were a good time and a few margaritas, then Jesus, he'd have been happy to go with her out to the club.

That wouldn't have been a problem at all. But the getting laid part?

"Unless you want to do the honors?"

That unsettled feeling twisted again inside him at the memory of what she'd said. At the belligerent look in her golden eyes, as if she was daring him.

It was never a good idea to dare him.

Why not? You thinking about taking her up on the offer?

Shock like an electric current ran straight down his spine and he stopped dead in the middle of the hallway, trying to figure out just what the hell it was. Because by rights the thought of helping Zoe out with that particular problem should have either disgusted him or amused him. Yet that feeling wasn't either disgust or amusement, which was a real fucking worry.

He shook himself, ignoring the feeling. Maybe he'd been too long without a hookup. Maybe that's all it was. And it had been a long time, what with everything that had been going on. He didn't do girlfriends, not when keeping Zoe safe, the garage, and looking out for the rest of his little family took up most of his time. But he did have a woman he saw on occasion, whom he had an understanding with. Tori, who was happy not to have anything demanded of her the way he was happy to have nothing demanded of him.

Yeah, maybe it was time to give Tori a call.

Moving on down the hallway, Gideon paused outside Zoe's door, listening. There was no sound from inside. Raising a hand, he knocked quietly. No response. He knocked again, louder this time, but got nothing but silence.

So he opened the door and glanced in.

The room was small, only enough room for a double bed and a desk that had Zoe's computer and various other things scattered on top of it. The chair pushed into the desk had clothes dumped on it, and there were other clothes lying in piles on the floor. Opposite was a dresser with a mirror above it, the top of the dresser covered with toiletries and makeup and other sorts of female paraphernalia. Necklaces and other things dangled from the corner of the mirror, tiny jewels glinting in the sunlight coming through the gap in the faded blue curtains.

The sunlight that also illuminated Zoe, lying facedown on the bed, her arms and legs spread out like a starfish, the sheet wound around her waist. Thick black curls covered her pillow and most of her face, so he couldn't tell if she was asleep or not. He thought she probably was, certainly given the deep, even sounds of her breathing.

"Zoe," he said, keeping his voice low. "Your pancakes are going to get cold."

She didn't move.

It was probably an asshole thing to do to wake her up now, but there was some stuff they needed to get straight between them and he wanted to get it sorted out as soon as possible.

"Zoe," he said, louder this time. "Wake up."

She let out a tiny snore.

Irritated for no good reason, he went over to the bed and crouched down beside it, pushing away some of the hair covering her face. She was fast asleep, her lashes lying thick and silky on her cheeks.

He sighed, his irritation draining away. Jesus, she was so young. At least it felt that way to him. Far too young to be going out and getting drunk and picking up random guys to get laid. Especially when it seemed like only a few years ago she'd been that quiet girl, the one no one could get anything out of. No one except him.

She's twenty-five, remember?

He blinked, something inside him lurching at the thought. Which was odd because he knew how old she was; of course he did.

Zoe sighed and shifted on the bed, rolling over onto her back, and he rose to his feet, vaguely unsettled again with no clue as to why.

She was wearing a light blue tank top and a pair of tiny little black shorts that left a lot of smooth, coffee-colored skin on display. The top also seemed to be very tight-fitting, clinging to a pair of small, high, and perfectly rounded breasts.

A strange shock hit him. Like he'd accidentally brushed against a live wire or an electric fence.

Why the fuck was he looking at her tits? He'd never looked at them before so why he was looking at them now, he couldn't think. Zoe was a child and he'd never seen her as anything but, more like a little sister than anything else. Certainly not as a woman.

Yeah, but she's not a kid anymore.

Gideon shoved his hands into the pockets of his jeans and shoved that particular thought right out of his head. Tonight. He was going to call Tori tonight. "Zoe," he said, her name coming out a lot grumpier than he'd intended. "Wake the hell up."

Her face scrunched, then her lashes fluttered and lifted, a flash of amber catching the sunlight. She groaned and flung an arm across her face. "Is it morning?"

"Yeah. Ten a.m."

She gave another groan and rolled over onto her front, burrowing into the pillow. "Leave me alone. I want to die in peace."

He would have been amused if he hadn't been so fucking unsettled. And he *still* felt fucking unsettled.

Because now she was lying on her front and the sheet had pulled away and those little shorts of hers did nothing to hide the rounded curves of her ass. One side had pulled up, exposing more satiny, brown skin.

Had that guy last night touched her there? Had he cupped her butt in his palms? Squeezed it gently?

Gideon blinked as he realized the direction his thoughts were taking. Holy shit, what the *hell* was wrong with him this morning?

"I've got pancakes." His voice sounded rough as cheap bourbon, yet he couldn't seem to tone it the fuck down. "You'd better get up if you don't want them cold."

Zoe turned her head, looking at him with one slightly blood-shot amber eye. "Pancakes?"

"Yeah. It's Sunday, in case you'd forgotten."

She pulled a face. "I don't know if I can eat anything."

Well, that was unsurprising. "Serves you right."

Her mouth turned down. "Gee. Thanks for the sympathy."

"Well, what do you expect? You wanted to get drunk and so you did. There's always a price to pay for the good times, Zoe."

She turned her head a little more, pushing her hair back out of her eyes. "At least I had some good times. Until you came along."

He let out a slow, silent breath. Christ. He'd handled the whole situation badly the night before, he knew that. Allowing his worry to get to him, then Zoe being so goddamned stubborn. That wasn't how he usually dealt with problems.

He liked to keep things calm, be the cool head. Be rational and understanding. He was the still point for everyone else, the calm that made everyone feel safe, and it was concerning that Zoe's telling him a stupid lie about where she was and one kiss should have wound him up so damn much.

Novak. That was the real problem.

Gideon came over to the bed and sat down on the side of it, leaning his elbows on his knees and interlacing his fingers. Then he glanced at her. "What's up, little one?" He kept his tone gentle, using his usual endearment, a reminder to himself of who she was to him. A reminder to her, too.

At this point, Zoe would normally stop being mad at him and tell him what the problem was.

Instead, her gaze narrowed and her mouth went flat. "So we're heading into patronize Zoe territory, are we? You should have brought some Advil with you. My head hurts enough as it is."

His patience—usually limitless—felt thin and frayed this morning, eaten away by lack of sleep and worry, and definitely not up to the task of dealing with Zoe being stubborn.

Still. He tried.

"I'm not being patronizing. All I'm trying to do is have an adult conversation with you about what was going on last night."

She shifted onto her side and propped her head on her hand, a position that did not make his unsettledness any better. Not when it pulled her tank top tight across her tits, making it very obvious that she didn't have a bra on underneath it. "An 'adult conversation,' huh?" That belligerence was back in her voice again, the way it had been last night. "Like we don't normally have adult conversations or something?"

He kept his gaze on her face, trying not to let the strange awareness of her progress any further. "Now you're the one who's being a dick," he said. "You know that's not what I meant."

Color crept into her cheeks. "Is there really any point in us having a conversation? You don't listen to me anyway."

"That's bullshit."

"Is it? I've been trying to talk to you for weeks, but you keep putting me off. Telling me you're busy or that we'll talk at some other time. But you never do. How is that anything but not listening?"

He shifted on the bed, uncomfortably aware that's exactly what he'd been doing. He'd had his reasons of course, but she wouldn't know that and he hadn't wanted to tell her. Because it was all big stuff. Frightening stuff. Stuff to do with her mother.

He hadn't wanted to bring all that old, bad shit back up. He'd been trying to protect her, just as he always did.

You can't protect her if she's going to keep pulling stunts like she pulled last night.

No, he couldn't. Which meant he was going to have bring all that old, bad shit up again whether she liked it or not.

"Okay," he said slowly. "So I'm listening now."

Chapter 3

Zoe gave him a narrow look. The expression on Gideon's face was neutral, his black eyes giving her nothing but his usual endless patience.

Normally, she would have found that comforting, but right now, for some reason, it irritated her intensely. She didn't know what she wanted from him, but this quiet acceptance wasn't it.

You know what you want. You want a fight.

Maybe she did. Maybe she was sick of him looking at her like a parent trying to understand his difficult teenager. Sure, she hated it when they argued, but it was better than this . . . insufferable patience. Like she was a child or a small dog.

She wanted a reaction. She wanted him to stop being so fucking calm.

Like he was last night?

Zoe swallowed. She had a headache, and her mouth felt drier than Death Valley, but the thought of how he'd been last night still made her whole body shiver.

He definitely hadn't been patient then. Especially the way he'd hauled what's-his-name off her. Like a jealous lover, almost. And then the way he'd picked her up and thrown her over his shoulder. Okay, it had been humiliating, but part of her had found it thrilling, too, the fact that she'd finally gotten some kind of reaction out of him that wasn't just . . . this.

Now he was sitting there on the edge of her bed, with his hands laced together, looking all calm and rational and so very Gideon it irritated the crap out of her. It didn't help that he was wearing one of her favorite T-shirts of his—a deep blue one that provided perfect contrast to his bronze skin, black hair, and dark eyes. She wanted to lift it up, look for the edges of his tattoo—the Japanese cherry blossom that spread its branches up his side and over his chest and back. A strangely delicate tattoo for a hard-edged guy like him. But she knew what it meant—it was for his mother.

She'd seen it a lot over the years and had always loved it. But to be able to touch it, trace the branches with her finger . . .

"I'm listening, Zoe." His voice, deep and slightly gritty, almost made her jump.

She scowled, hating the direction of her thoughts. They were pathetic, truly pathetic. He'd never shown any interest in her whatsoever, so why she kept letting her brain go there was anyone's guess.

"Too bad," she said grumpily. "Because now I don't want to talk."

The calm expression on his face wavered a second. "Fine. If you don't wanna talk, you don't have to. But I have a few things I need to say to you." He unlinked his hands and stood up. "Get dressed and come get your pancakes."

He didn't wait for her to agree, striding toward the door as if he suddenly had somewhere he needed to be in a hurry, closing it with a thump after him.

She sighed and rolled over onto her back, directing her scowl at the ceiling instead.

Maybe it was time to face the fact that he was *never* going to see her as anything more than the little foster sister he had to protect. It wasn't what she wanted, no, but wishing things were different wasn't going to make it happen. And this continual mooning after him was only making her miserable. Not to mention it was embarrassing, since the others had noticed the bad case of hero worship she had going on.

Which meant that she had to deal with it. Push it to one side and move on. Like, really move on, not just pretend.

She had been trying the night before, of course. At least until Gideon had shown up. And she could kid herself all she liked about the fact that he'd been angry because he was jealous, but the most likely scenario was the one he'd told her. He'd been angry because she'd lied to him. End of story.

So yeah. She had to move on. Put an end to her crush. In fact, there were a lot of things she had to put an end to. Gideon wasn't going to like them, but that was too bad.

She was twenty-five years old and she wasn't going to let him dictate the course of her life anymore.

Galvanized, Zoe slid out of bed, debating the merits of a shower, then deciding it was probably a good thing given how vile she felt. The hot water made her feel marginally better, as did a clean pair of jeans and a tee. At least enough that when she finally arrived in the kitchen, the smell of frying bacon didn't make her want to hurl.

Gideon glanced at her as he stood at the stove pushing bacon around in the pan, then jerked his head toward the tiny kitchen table that stood against the wall. "Pancakes are there. You want bacon?"

"I don't know. . . ."

"If you're hungover, you'll want bacon."

She wanted to protest that she wasn't hungover, but that would be a lie he definitely wouldn't believe. So she shut up and went over to the table, sitting down and reaching for the pot of syrup and pouring a liberal amount over the pancake stack sitting on her plate.

There was coffee and orange juice already set out—Gideon did like to make sure everything was there when it came to pancake day.

She began to eat, watching him as he came over with the pan and slid a couple slices of bacon onto her plate before doing the same for himself. Then he ditched the pan in the sink and came and sat down opposite her.

Goddamn. Why did he have to look so sexy in old jeans and that blue T-shirt, doing stupid, mundane tasks?

Maybe it was a case of finding someone else who was just as sexy. Maybe if she did that, she wouldn't find Gideon so hot anymore.

Any more lies you want to tell yourself this morning?

No, she had to believe she'd find someone else. She *had* to. Otherwise what else would there be for her? A life of loneliness because she couldn't move on from a man who wouldn't ever see her as anything more than a child.

She wanted more than that. Being lonely sucked.

"So what did you want to tell me?" she asked around a mouthful of pancake.

Gideon poured himself some coffee and sat back in his chair, holding his cup between his palms. Normally his long, blunt fingers were covered in engine oil, but they were clean today, the scars from all the cuts and scratches he'd gotten while fixing cars and bikes over the years showing white against his skin.

Another thing she adored about him—his large, battered, capable hands. She'd really like to know what it felt like to have those hands touch her. . . .

Fuck.

She dragged her brain from its usual Gideon love track and forced it to examine the pancakes instead of him.

"I didn't wanna tell you actually," Gideon said. "But after last night, things have changed."

"That sounds serious." With extreme deliberation, she cut herself a square of pancake.

There was a small silence.

Zoe looked up and met his gaze, and her heart missed a beat. There was no lightness in the look. Whatever he was going to tell her, he was deadly serious.

"It's about your mother, Zoe."

Her headache thumped, the nausea in her stomach getting worse. Her mother? What could he have to tell her about her mother? There wasn't much to say, surely? Claire James had gone away on drug charges when Zoe had been six, spending four years inside. Zoe had gone back to live with her after she'd gotten out and the courts deemed it was safe for Zoe to do so, though Zoe wasn't sure which she'd preferred: her angry, spiteful mother, who clearly resented every second of her daughter's existence, or yet another foster family who didn't much care what happened to her? Whatever, she hadn't been given the choice, sent back to the crappy, run-down apartment where her mother lived, though not for long. Three years later, she'd left Chicago with Gideon, her mother dying of an overdose about six months after that.

She hadn't thought about that woman in years and she'd been quite happy with that. In fact, she'd be quite happy to continue never thinking of her again, so why Gideon was bringing her up was anyone's guess.

"What about her?"

"It's about your father as well."

Shock made her stare. "My . . . father? But Mom didn't know who he—"

"She knew exactly who he was," Gideon interrupted, his black gaze very direct.

Zoe's stomach went into free fall, the shock making her feel suddenly cold. Once, when she'd been small, just before her mother had gone to jail, she'd asked her about her father. Claire had gotten angry and told her never ever to mention him in her presence again. So Zoe never had.

"But . . . I don't understand," she began, struggling to make sense of it. "If Mom knew . . . I mean, how do you . . ." She stopped, pushing her plate away, not hungry anymore. "What are you trying to tell me, Gideon?"

His black gaze was unwavering. "I'm trying to tell you that I know who your father is."

A little jolt of what felt suspiciously like excitement shot straight through her. Just because her mother hadn't wanted her to talk about it didn't mean she hadn't thought about him, hadn't wondered who he was. Hadn't hoped, in some forgotten place in her heart, that he would one day come and find her . . .

But he never did, did he?

She swallowed. No, she wasn't going to ask. She didn't want to know. Because not only was it better to imagine her father could be anyone rather than him finally being "someone," but it would also lead to questions such as how the hell Gideon knew about him. Which in turn would lead into the black hole that was Gideon's own past. The past he never talked about and that she never asked about.

You want to grow up? Then you need to deal with difficult stuff. Stuff you'd rather avoid.

Zoe gritted her teeth and reached for the coffeepot, taking her time with pouring herself a cup, mainly so she could gather her courage. "And?" she asked, splashing some milk in and adding at least three teaspoons of sugar because hell, she was going to need the hit.

"And he's been sniffing around Royal."

She paused in her stirring, staring down at the brown liquid in her cup. Oh God, had he been trying to find her? Only now? After all this time?

A bitter disappointment threaded through her shock and she took a huge sip of her coffee, hoping the scalding liquid might make her feel better. But it didn't.

Gideon watched her for a moment, then he leaned forward, putting his cup down and his elbows on the table. "I've known for a while, but I didn't tell you earlier because I didn't want you to worry or to be afraid. But last night changed a few things. You're not safe. Not until I know why he's hanging around here and what he wants."

Her heartbeat sounded loud in her head, the coffee bitter on her tongue even with all the sugar in it. She took another sip of coffee, then put the cup down hurriedly when her hands started to shake.

"I'm confused," she muttered, still trying to get her around what he was saying. "I mean, sure, Mom never spoke about him and he's never tried to contact me before, but . . . Why does him hanging around mean I'm not safe?"

Gideon's expression's closed down. "He's a powerful guy, Zoe. Whatever it is he wants, it won't be something good."

"How do you know that?"

"Because what men like him want is never good."

Her heart clenched tight in her chest. "But, I'm his kid, right? I mean—"

"I know you had your fantasies about him," Gideon interrupted flatly. "But none of those are gonna happen, understand me? When I tell you that you're not safe, you're not safe." There was nothing but hard certainty in his dark eyes.

Come on, it's been twenty-five years. If your dad had really wanted you, he would have come for you by now.

Yeah, but would he really . . . hurt her? Forcing away the strange lump in her throat, Zoe met Gideon's steady black gaze. "How do you know it's him?"

"I have my sources."

Of course he did. Gideon had many "sources." She hadn't ever inquired too deeply about any of them, because quite frankly she didn't want to know.

There's a lot of stuff you don't want to know.

The thought was uncomfortable. She wasn't a coward—at least, she didn't think of herself as one—but it was true that she hadn't ever pestered Gideon for answers about certain things.

Such as why he'd suddenly turned up at her house without any warning the night he'd taken her away. Or how, as a dirt poor twenty-five year old, he'd managed to buy his garage outright from the old man who'd sold it to him. Or why, even though Royal had been rife with crime, he'd never been hassled for protection money the way other businesses used to be.

Little things like that.

She looked away, busying herself with trying to cut up some more pancake. Not that she was hungry. Somehow her appetite seemed to have vanished entirely.

Thirteen years ago, Gideon had turned up unexpectedly at her house, a wild look in his eyes. She'd been so pleased to see him since it had been at least two months since he'd visited and he never usually left it that long. Then he'd told her that he was in trouble, that he had to leave Chicago, and did she want to go with him. At that stage he'd been an older brother to her, a person she'd felt safe with—at least safer than with her mother. Claire had discovered the joys of heroin and the kinds of people who'd started calling at the house since had frightened Zoe.

She hadn't thought twice about leaving.

She'd walked out of that house with Gideon without looking back.

He'd represented safety and love, and after all the years in foster care and subsequently with her angry, bitter mother, feeling safe and loved was what she'd wanted most in the world.

You can't ask him about his sources. You can't ask him how he knows what he knows. Because you don't want anything to compromise that feeling.

"So what's he doing here?" She kept her gaze on her breakfast, pushing around some pancake on her plate.

"He's here because of Levi's development plans. At least, that's his ostensible reason."

Zoe blinked, staring at the smear of syrup on her plate. "You mean he's one of those suits Levi was showing around a couple of weeks ago?"

"Yes."

A shiver went through her, coming from somewhere deep inside. Levi, only recently released from prison, had been trying to get financial backing for some property development, and had met with a couple of guys who'd apparently shown some interest in providing financing for him. That he'd ended up subsequently dropping those plans should have meant those guys were no longer in the picture though.

Apparently not. Apparently at least one of them is still around and Gideon didn't tell you.

She looked at him. "You knew even back then?"

His expression was calm, his black gaze steady. "Like I said, I didn't want to tell you because I didn't want to scare you."

"No, you only snapped at me instead."

There it was, a tiny flicker in his outward calm. Good. "Yeah, I admit I've been on edge more than I normally am. But that's only because I don't know why he's here."

"But you just said he was here because of Levi's plans."

"Sure, but a guy like that doesn't just decide to invest in some random development. There's a reason he's been particularly interested in Royal, especially now that Levi dropped him as a financial backer." Gideon's tone gentled. "That reason could be you, little one."

That gentleness, like the endearment that had never bothered her before, seemed to slip under her skin like a splinter, needling her.

She tried not to let it, tried to ignore it. Because what he was telling her was way more important than that. Her dad was here in Royal and he was obviously some kind of hotshot investor.

"But . . . why? After all this time?"

"I don't know for certain." Gideon's dark eyes were inescapable. "I'm going to get my contacts to investigate. But like I said, whatever it is, it can't be good, Zoe. Not with men like him."

She swallowed. Okay, this was serious, which meant that maybe it was time she stopped running away from stuff she didn't like or was afraid of. Maybe it was time she learned who her father actually was. "Men like who?"

The look in Gideon's gaze softened. "You don't have to—"

"Tell me."

He raised a brow. She never interrupted him. No one did. In fact, she was a little surprised she'd done it herself. Then again, she was never going to move on if she didn't start changing stuff up. Gideon would just have to deal.

He shifted, leaning back in his chair and crossing his arms. "Men like Oliver Novak."

Holy shit.

Zoe stilled. She didn't know much about Novak, only that he was a high-flying businessman who came from one of Michigan's richest families, and currently had his eye on becoming a senator. Definitely a hotshot business type.

And your father.

Her mouth felt dry, even after the coffee, and the food she'd eaten was sitting uneasily in her stomach. "You're sure it's him?" Because really, it might not have been. Gideon was seldom wrong but there was a first time for everything.

"It's him." There was no hesitation. Apparently, he wasn't going to be wrong today.

"But how do you know?"

Something in his gaze became harder. "You're not gonna want to know the answer to that and I'm not gonna tell you."

She could push him if she wanted to and part of her *did* want to. But shock was still echoing through her and her gut felt unsettled, and she didn't know if she could really handle any more surprises today. So all she said was, "And you think he's definitely here for me?"

"There's nothing else here for him. So logically that makes the most sense."

She wrapped her fingers around her cooling cup, finding the fading warmth comforting. "Why though? What does he want with me?"

Gideon had that terribly patient look on his face again. "Zoe, you're the bastard kid of a powerful man who's gonna run for senator. So my guess is that he's here to figure out what you know." He paused. "And make sure you never tell anyone who your father is."

Her face had paled and he hated the flicker of fear in her eyes. He knew she'd cherished secret dreams about her father's identity because she'd told him a couple times, years ago, and he certainly didn't take any pleasure in dashing her hopes of a loving reconciliation.

It had to be done, though. She had to know what and who she was dealing with, especially if she was planning on more repeats of the night before. He wouldn't tell her everything—there were some things that needed to remain secret because they would only hurt her if she knew—but she needed to understand the danger at least.

"So what you're saying is that he might be here to . . . what? Kill me?" she asked.

Gideon didn't know this for sure, obviously, but in his experience Novak didn't have much in the way of family feeling. What he did have was the kind of ravenous ambition that simply smashed through anything standing in its way. And if that someone just happened to be Zoe . . .

Cold slithered down his back. "That would be difficult," he replied, trying to ignore the sensation. "Or he could be wanting to buy your silence somehow. But make no mistake, Novak's sketchy as fuck and I don't want you taking any chances."

Her jaw had gotten that familiar stubborn cast to it. "How do you know he's sketchy?"

"I've heard things." Things he wouldn't be telling her about anytime soon. Mainly because they touched on a past he wasn't proud of and didn't have anything to do with now. A past he didn't want Zoe connected with in any way.

A past that included being hired by Novak to "deal" with her mother due to her mother's blackmail threats.

No, she really didn't need to know that.

"He's not the guy he makes himself out to be, trust me on this."

She gave him a narrow look as if debating whether or not to actually trust him on that. Then, clearly deciding to drop the matter, she lifted a shoulder. "Well, if he does get me alone and asks me if I'm his daughter, I'll just tell him I don't know anything. Then he'll leave, right?"

Christ, if only it were that simple.

But it wouldn't be. Not with a guy like Novak.

No, there would be no negotiating on this. She wasn't going to like it, not one bit, but her safety was more important to him than anything. The whole of the past thirteen years was built around it, the decisions he'd made the night he'd picked her up from her mom's shitty Chicago house, all for the sake of it.

Nothing was going to happen to her. He wouldn't allow it.

"No," he said. "It would be better if he doesn't even know you're here."

"Sure, but—"

"Which means you'll be lying low for a while."

She blinked at him. "Lying low as in . . . ?"

"Staying here. Not going out like you did last night. In fact, not doing pretty much anything that will draw his attention."

Zoe had gone very still. "Not going out," she echoed. "Not going out of Royal. . . . ?"

He held her gaze, because he wasn't going to be moved on this, no matter how much of a fuss she kicked up or tantrums she pulled. "I mean not leaving this apartment."

Her mouth opened. Then shut. Her amber eyes looked huge behind the lenses of her glasses. "Not leaving this apartment? Are you freaking kidding me?"

Yeah, well, he knew she wasn't going to like it. This wasn't surprising. "No, I'm not kidding you. You're staying here, Zoe."

Her expression suddenly became fixed. "And for how long do I have to stay here?"

"As long as it takes to get rid of Novak." He wasn't sure how long that would be. He had some contacts currently investigating what was going on with the guy, but so far he had no answers. With any luck, once Novak had determined Zoe wasn't here, he'd maybe fuck off back to where he came from.

But if that prick found evidence that she was here and it was, actually, Zoe he was after, then . . . Well, Gideon would have to figure out a plan about what to do when the time came. Until then, though, she was staying here. Out of sight.

Zoe rested her hands lightly on the edge of the table, the

fixed expression on her face telegraphing her emotions loud and clear. As predicted, she was not happy. "So let me get this straight. You want me to stay in this apartment, for however long it takes for Novak to get out of Royal."

"Yes."

Little golden sparks of anger sparked in her eyes. "What if it takes a week? What about a couple of weeks? Are you saying I have to stay in this apartment the whole time?"

Jesus Christ. She was arguing with him about this now?

He frowned. "You do understand how serious this is, don't you? Oliver Novak is trying to make a bid for senator. Do you really think he won't try to follow up any loose ends that might jeopardize his chances? Such as silencing his bastard kid?"

It was a low blow, he knew that, and may not even be true. But shit, if it scared her into doing what he told her then that was probably a good thing. There was more at stake here than her feelings. Novak was a ruthless son of a bitch—as Gideon had good reason to know—and maybe the guy would have drawn a line at getting rid of his own daughter, but maybe he wouldn't have. And that wasn't a gamble Gideon wanted to take, not if it meant putting Zoe at risk

And shit, if Zoe thought her life was in danger, then perhaps she'd think twice about running around Royal by herself.

The sparks of anger leapt into flames. "But like you said, silencing me could mean just paying me off. It doesn't necessarily mean he's going to kill me, Gideon. Or is this what your stupid 'sources' say?"

He should tell her the truth, he really should. But that would involve revealing things about her mother he didn't want her to know, not to mention things about himself he'd been trying to leave behind for years.

So all he said was, "You'll just have to trust me on this." He pushed back his chair and got to his feet, starting to gather up all the dishes. "Anyway, what's the big deal? It's not like you go out a lot as it is anyway."

Zoe gave him a bitter look. "Yeah, and who's fault is that?"

"Don't tell me." He reached for her plate. "It's mine."

"Of course it's yours. I'm not allowed to leave Royal without you. I wasn't allowed to go to college because you couldn't be sure of the campus security—in fucking Princeton! And then I wasn't allowed to get a job anywhere but at your freaking garage because of the same thing." With a sudden, sharp movement, she shoved herself away from the table, making the cups rattle and the saltshaker and syrup pot fall over. "And now you making it so I'm not allowed to leave the apartment at all. What's next? A collar and a leash around my neck so you can tie me up?"

Still holding their plates in his hands, Gideon stared at her. There was fury in her eyes and frustration, too, like there had been the night before. "What's going on, Zoe? Where's all this coming from? We talked about all that stuff."

"No, *you* talked about all that stuff. I didn't. You told me what was going to happen."

"And you agreed."

It had been years ago, once he'd bought the garage and things had settled down. Zoe was fiercely intelligent and her grades at school had been extraordinary given her background. She was interested in just about everything, but her strengths were definitely math and most of the sciences, and her teachers had been keen to find a scholarship for one of the prestigious universities.

But he'd blocked it. He didn't want her going out of state, didn't want her drawing the wrong kind of attention—*any* attention, to be honest. Still, she'd needed more in her life, an outlet for all her bright intellect, so he'd gone to the local community college and made a few inquiries about what sort of courses they offered.

It was clear, though, even then, that Zoe needed more than a struggling community college in a run-down neighborhood in Detroit. That her teachers had been right, she should be applying to places like Princeton or MIT, where there were world-class facilities and teachers who could challenge and stimulate her. Money wasn't the problem—he could have gotten it, if she'd needed it. The problem was her not being with him. Her not being safe.

According to his contacts, Novak had already tried once before to find her, though why, Gideon didn't know. Not for anything good, he'd lay money on the fact. Whatever, it had only cemented for him that she had to stay where she was, not draw attention. Let him protect her.

It had been a hard decision to tell her that college would have to wait. That her job would be working for him in the garage's office for the foreseeable future. It felt like instead of opening doors for her, he was closing them.

But he'd had no choice. Until the issue of Novak was dealt with, Zoe had to remain off the radar.

Understandably, she wasn't looking very happy about that right now. "Yeah, I agreed, but it wasn't like you gave me a choice."

He frowned. "You didn't seem to find it a problem back then."

"Well, maybe it's a problem now." Her jaw was jutting mutinously, those flames of anger leaping higher.

Fucking great. She would pick the worst possible time in the world to start questioning things.

With an effort, Gideon kept a grip on his patience. "And why is it a problem now?"

"Oh, I don't know." Her chin had come up, her eyes glittering. "Maybe it's because I'm twenty-five and I have no career and no boyfriend. I haven't been anywhere or done anything. I live in a stupid apartment with my stupid foster brother and work in his stupid garage office, and I'm still a stupid virgin!"

The words echoed around the kitchen and for some reason, the only one he seemed to be able to focus on was *virgin*.

"Perhaps you could do the honors?"

Jesus. What the hell was his brain doing repeating the question she'd asked him the night before? And why the hell did he keep thinking about it?

Zoe's virginity or otherwise had nothing whatsoever to do with him.

Are you sure? She's yours, isn't she? All of her . . .

He turned abruptly and strode over to the kitchen sink, dumping the dirty dishes on the counter beside it.

"So?" Zoe demanded from behind him. "You've got nothing to say to that?"

"What do you want me to say?" He pulled open the dishwasher and began loading the plates, because concentrating on that was better than concentrating on memories of the night before and what she'd said. "You want to change that, you'll have to change it after this shit with Novak is over."

There was an outraged silence behind him, but he didn't stop what he was doing and he didn't turn around. His patience was fraying like it had the previous night, a pain in the ass since he'd never had any problems with it before.

Then again, he'd never had Zoe act like a spoiled brat before, so maybe that was the issue.

"You're an asshole," Zoe said, her voice unsteady. "You don't give a shit about what I want."

A flare of anger did further damage to his patience, because that was so much bullshit he didn't know where to start. Everything he'd done for the last thirteen years was about protecting her, keeping her safe, and now she was having a fit about her goddamn feelings?

He gritted his teeth. "If you're going to act like a sulky teenager, I'll treat you like one."

"Oh really? Am I grounded then? No, wait. I already am."

A cup wouldn't sit right on the dishwasher shelves so he shoved it in way too hard, the fucking thing coming apart in his hands.

"Fuck's sake, Zoe. I'm not having this argument with you." He straightened, tossing the bits of broken china onto the counter. "My decision is final. You stay here in the apartment or, if you wanna go out, you go out with me. Just until this situation with Novak is finished. Understood?"

If looks could kill, there would have been a huge crater right where he was standing.

"No," she snapped. "It's not understood. If it was Rachel instead of me, would you say the same things to her?"

Of course he wouldn't. Because Rachel was a friend in the same way Levi and Zee were friends, part of the small family he'd created all those years ago at the Royal Road Outreach Center. Lost teens who had nowhere to go and no one to help them. The same kind of teen he'd once been.

No, he'd wouldn't say these things to Rachel, because Rachel wasn't his the way Zoe was his, and he hadn't dedicated the last thirteen years of his life to making sure she was safe.

"Like I said." He kept his tone hard. "I'm not having this argument with you."

Zoe's fingers curled into fists. "I thought you said you'd listen to me."

"And you told me you didn't want to talk."

Her chin jutted mutinously. "Maybe I changed my mind."

"Yeah, well, it's too late." He kicked the door of the dishwasher shut. "Now, if you want something to do, you can clear up the rest of the breakfast things."

Zoe stared at him a long moment, her amber eyes glowing with anger. Then suddenly something changed in her face. She looked calm, as if she'd decided something. Which instantly put him on edge.

Without a word, she turned and strode out of the kitchen.

Ten seconds later, the front door of the apartment slammed shut.

Fucking hell. The little brat had walked out on him.

Chapter 4

Zoe was almost shaking with anger as she slammed the door of the apartment behind her and headed down the stairs to the street entrance.

She couldn't think of why it had come up on her so suddenly either. Maybe the shock of finally knowing the identity of her father and the realization that he might be here to find her. Or maybe it was the knowledge that only now, when she'd finally figured out that she wanted her life to be different, did Gideon seem hell-bent on keeping it the same.

Whatever; she was sick of being told what to do all the time, especially by him. And she wasn't staying in that goddamned apartment, not when she'd finally made the decision to move on with her life.

What about Novak? What if Gideon's right?

Well, what if he was? What if Oliver Novak was actually her dad and he was in Royal looking for her? Hell, she only had Gideon's say-so that there was something shady about him. He might actually be a nice guy desperate to get in touch with his long-lost daughter and not apparently bent on "silencing" her like Gideon seemed to think. In which case there was no reason for her to stay inside, no reason at all.

She heard the apartment door bang open again behind her.

"Zoe!" Gideon's voice, heavy with authority, echoed down the narrow stairwell. "Get the fuck back up here. Now."

Her pulse kicked up a couple of notches, but she didn't stop going determinedly down the stairs. He was overreacting, and she was sick of it.

Actually, she was kind of sick of him and this entire situation. Which was why she was getting out of it and heading to Rachel's. Because that's what she needed, some girl time with her friend. Where she didn't have Gideon the Dick hanging over her, taunting her with his hotness, telling her what she could and couldn't do.

Yeah, he could suck it.

At the bottom of the stairs she reached out to grab the door handle. Only to have Gideon's warm, strong fingers wrap themselves around her wrist. "Oh, no you don't," he said roughly in her ear, and pulled her hand away from the door.

Holy shit, how had he managed to get down the stairs so fast? Sometimes the guy moved like Zee, all fluid, silent grace, except she was pretty sure Gideon didn't do MMA like Zee did.

Doesn't it make you wonder what he does do?

But she had no time to think further, because Gideon was hauling her around to face him, his fingers tight around her wrist. All traces of his usual infuriating calm were gone. His rough, handsome features were set in hard lines, dark eyes glittering with fury.

Her stupid heart gave a little kick in her chest. Well, she'd wanted some kind of reaction out of him, hadn't she? Looked like she had it.

Unfortunately, though, it didn't change anything.

She tried to jerk her wrist out of his grip but it was like it was stuck in concrete. "Let me go, asshole."

"Didn't I just tell you that you weren't to leave the apartment?" he demanded, ignoring her. "Didn't you listen to a fucking word I said?"

Her heartbeat was thumping weirdly. His fingers on her skin were hot and though he wasn't hurting her, the pressure was firm. Enough to remind her she wasn't going to be getting away in a hurry.

She liked it. Crap.

"And didn't I just tell you to let me go?" She tried pulling her hand away again, but again, there was no moving that grip of his.

Gideon gave her a narrow stare. "If I let you go, will you try to leave again?"

He smelled good, of oil and wood smoke and leather, making her mouth go dry, making her feel slightly panicky. "God, I'm just going to Rachel's. Chill out."

"You're not going anywhere, I told you."

An intelligent woman would have bowed to the inevitable and accepted that. But it turned out she wasn't very intelligent where Gideon was concerned.

She took a step forward instead, getting right up in his face. "Go to hell," she said through clenched teeth.

His sensual mouth flattened in response, a hard light glittering in his eyes, tripping her pulse into overtime. God, was she insane?

You know why you want to test him.

Okay, yeah. So she did. She liked seeing his usual calm disturbed, liked making him lose his vaunted patience. He affected her so badly, why shouldn't she affect him for a change?

"You really don't wanna push me on this, Zoe." His voice had gotten an edge of darkness to it, an authority that reached right inside her and squeezed tight. Making her even more breathless.

"Why not?" She couldn't help herself. Needling him like

this felt like being stuck on a roller coaster, unable to get off. Scary. Exhilarating. Thrilling. "What are you going to do to me if I do? Spank me like you promised last night?"

The hard line of his jaw got tight. "You've got no fucking idea what you're talking about."

"Sure I do." There wasn't much space between them, only inches. Yet she took another step forward anyway. "But maybe it doesn't matter when you clearly don't have the balls to do it."

It was a stupid thing to say and she knew it. But she was on this damn roller coaster and the adrenaline was surging in her blood, making her feel a little crazy. A little wild.

And he was so close now, towering over her the way he always did, the broad width of his shoulders and chest making her very aware of his strength. Of his power. Of the firm pressure of his fingers wrapped around her wrist. Normally it made her feel safe and protected, but not now.

Now she felt like she'd put herself into the path of an approaching hurricane.

The dense black of his eyes held hers like a magnet. "And maybe little girls should be seen and not heard."

A thrill bolted straight down her spine, sending another surge of adrenaline through her system. She lifted her chin. "I'm not a little girl, asshole."

"Yeah, you are. A little girl who doesn't know what she's doing." He jerked her wrist all of a sudden, pulling her so she was right up against him. "You're poking a sleeping tiger with a stick, Zoe, and if you're not careful, it's gonna wake up and bite you."

The breath had locked in her throat, the heat of his body making her want to melt against him. "Maybe I want it to wake up," she said recklessly, her voice all husky. "Maybe I want it to bite me."

He was very still, a hard, hot wall blocking her path. "No, you don't."

"Bullshit." She was totally out of control now, but she didn't care. "Everyone thinks you're some scary dude, but I know the truth. You're not a tiger, Gideon, you're a damn pussy cat." She met his gaze, challenging him. "We both know you'd never do anything to hurt me, so how about you stop all this stupid crap about tigers and start treating me like a responsible adult."

"A responsible adult, huh?" His voice was quiet, level. Which in itself should have been a warning. "And how exactly should I be treating you as a responsible adult?"

Zoe swallowed, trying to ignore the quiver right down deep inside. The one that knew this was the calm before the storm. "Well, you could start by letting me go."

"And then?"

"And then you'll let me go out to see Rachel."

There was a silence, the air getting thick, the way it did before a heavy rainstorm.

Then Gideon let go of her wrist.

Oddly deflated, Zoe absently rubbed at it with her other hand. "Thank you. I guess you—"

But she never had a chance to finish.

He reached out, grabbed her, and tossed her over his shoulder the way he had the night before. Then, carrying her as effortlessly as if she weighed nothing, he strode back up the stairs.

Zoe blinked, momentarily confused by just what the hell had happened, staring at the stairs receding below her. She was upside down and the heat of Gideon's shoulder was pressing against her stomach, one strong arm wrapped around her thighs, holding her in place.

"This is getting old," she muttered.

"If you don't like it, stop being such a brat."

They were at the top of the stairs, Gideon pulling open the door to the apartment—or rather, the door to her prison.

Jesus, this was such bullshit.

As he stepped into the hallway, she twisted violently, trying to get away. Only to have his hand come down on her butt. Hard.

All the air rushed out of her lungs in a startled gasp, the sound of his palm smacking down on her echoing in the narrow space.

Holy shit, had he really just spanked her?

"Try that again and you'll see how much of a fucking pussy cat I am." There was a rough edge to his voice, one she'd never heard before. "And I guarantee you won't like it."

She blinked again, staring sightlessly at the floor in shock, struggling to process what he'd just done. Her heart was racing, one ass cheek stinging from where he'd smacked her. It hurt and yet . . . it felt good, too. How did that work?

She sucked a harsh breath. Oh, she was *not* going to put up with that.

So she twisted again.

Gideon cursed, his arm tightening around her thighs so she couldn't move. Then he brought his palm down on her butt a second time.

There was a sharp crack of sound, then the sting, drawing another gasp from her and this time making tears start in her eyes. Because he wasn't holding back. He was honest to God spanking her.

Stupid. She really should stop this right now.

There was a hot, raw feeling, a pulsing ache between her thighs. Making her increasingly aware that the hard ridge of his shoulder was pressing onto the zipper of her jeans. That all she needed to do was wriggle down a little farther and the pressure would be right . . . *there.*

This wasn't stupid. *She* was the one who was stupid. Because she had to be. There was no other explanation for the urge that filled her. The one that made her wriggle again against his shoulder as if she actually wanted more.

He didn't say a word, his palm coming down even harder this time.

Zoe jerked, the pain fading quickly, leaving behind the sweet burn that had her shifting her hips, searching for the pressure that would ease the ache, make everything better.

But Gideon's palm didn't lift this time, staying firmly on her butt, and as her hips moved, he pressed down, his fingers giving her ass one hard squeeze.

She caught her breath, because that hurt too, yet it also increased the nagging ache. Trying to keep the groan of frustration inside so he wouldn't know, she bit her lip instead, tasting blood.

He said nothing, keeping his palm exactly where it was as he resumed his journey down the hallway, pausing only to kick open the door of her bedroom before stepping inside.

Zoe barely had a moment to catch her breath before he shifted her off his shoulder, dumping her back down on her bed.

She sat there a second, feeling dizzy and her butt stinging, the remains of anger and thwarted desire churning uncomfortably in her gut, realizing with a cold shock that her performance in the hallway had probably revealed something she would have rather kept hidden.

She didn't want to look at him, to see whatever expression was on his face—probably disgust because hell, she'd virtually begged him to spank her and then wriggled around like a fish on a line. He'd know what was going on, he wasn't stupid.

"Are you going to tell me what the hell that was all about?" Gideon's voice was hard.

Zoe reluctantly lifted her head and looked at him.

He was standing in front of her, his arms crossed, staring down at her, his expression absolutely neutral. As if he hadn't just spanked her on the butt in the hallway.

But she could see something in his black eyes. Something

that hadn't been there before. God . . . was that . . . ? No, it couldn't be. She'd been looking for a response from him for years and had never seen any sign of one. It had to be wishful thinking to imagine he'd found that as affecting as she had.

"Sure," she said slowly, her heartbeat thumping hard in her ears. "As soon as you tell me why the hell you hit me."

That something—a spark, a flame, she wasn't sure which— leapt again in his gaze. Then he blinked and it was gone. "Consequences," he said, his tone flat. "You don't get enough of them."

Yes, she'd imagined it. Or maybe it was only temper she'd seen.

A disappointment she didn't want to feel curled through her.

Slowly she put her hands on the bed and leaned back on them. If he looked farther down, he'd see what she wasn't able to hide. That her nipples were hard. Not that it mattered. He didn't see her that way and no amount of wishing it were otherwise would change things.

Maybe you should ask yourself why he put his hand on you in the first place.

Zoe swallowed as the realization hit. He'd never touched her before, not like that. Hugs, yes, plenty of those. Spanks on the butt? No, definitely not.

She looked at him, staring at the familiar lines of his face. Straight black brows. The sharp blade of his nose. His beautifully carved mouth. Eyes the color of darkest obsidian.

Was she wrong? Had there actually been something there? After all, he'd put his hand on her and something felt different now. Changed in some way. As if a line had been crossed. A line she didn't want to cross back over again.

"Consequences, huh?" she said, unable to keep the husky edge from her voice. "Sorry, but if you want to teach me a lesson, Gideon, you'll have to do better than that."

* * *

Gideon kept his arms folded, mainly because he didn't know what would happen if he didn't.

Zoe was sitting on the bed, leaning back on her hands as if it didn't matter to her that he'd just spanked her ass like a naughty kid. Her cheeks were red and her amber eyes were dark, a smoky, slightly glazed look in them.

All of which were enough to make him conscious of something he didn't want to be conscious of.

But that wasn't the worst part of it.

The worst part of it was the heat from her denim-clad ass lingering on his palm, her gasp of shock replaying itself over and over in his brain, and the feel of her lithe, slender body shifting around on his shoulder as if she was searching for something.

He knew what she was searching for. He knew why she'd gasped. And now he knew why she'd been pushing him, inciting him.

Like it's such a shock? You've always known about her feelings for you.

Yeah, he'd known. He'd only thought it was a giant case of hero worship that if he ignored, she'd eventually grow out of.

Didn't look like she'd grown out of it.

Christ, he should never have put his hand down on her. Never. He'd just lost it, which was ridiculous given the fact that he *never* lost it and certainly not with her. But if she wasn't going to do what he said, then he'd have to make her. How else was he going to protect her?

You put your hand on her. You smacked her ass.

His anger shifted and changed, turning inward, on himself. He'd have punched anyone who'd done that to her, punched them right in the mouth. So why the fuck had *he* done it to her?

He couldn't think of one good reason. Only that she'd dared him, goaded him, told him he didn't have the balls. Then she'd twisted like an eel on his shoulder and he'd just... brought down his palm. And not just once. He'd done it three times.

Because you liked it.

The thought stuck in his head like a thorn.

Zoe was staring at him, her cheeks pink, her eyes full of a very specific kind of challenge. A very feminine challenge.

Fucking hell. This was bad, very bad. Did she even know what she was doing? No, of course she didn't. She was an innocent, a goddamn virgin and no matter how much she threw herself at him, it wasn't going to happen.

Zoe was Zoe and he'd never looked at her that way in his life.

Except you did like it and you are looking at her that way now.

No, he wasn't. Good God, she was a child. A kid. His little foster sister. And wherever the hell these thoughts were coming from, they could fuck right off again.

Gritting his teeth, he kept his gaze on hers and tried to ignore the fact that her tight white T-shirt did nothing to hide her hard nipples. Or how her worn skinny jeans outlined the long, slender shape of her legs. Her hair was thick and curly, and he knew if he sank his fingers into it, it would feel soft. . . .

"No," he said, both to her and to himself. "I'm not gonna do anything of the kind. The only lesson you need to learn is that you're staying in this apartment even if I have to lock you in myself."

"Is that so?" She shifted on the bed. "You know what? You're a hypocrite, Gideon. You were such a prick to Levi about how he treated Rachel at first, and yet you apparently don't have any problems with shutting me in my bedroom, or spanking me in the hallway." She tilted her head, the thick dark curls drifting over her shoulders. "I wonder what the others would say if I told them that?"

His anger twisted again, at her for being so goddamn stubborn. At himself for not being able to deal with this the way he normally would.

So she wanted to play hardball? Well, maybe that was the answer. He knew how to play that game—he'd once made a living out of it after all. But he'd never played it with Zoe; he'd never needed to.

Seemed liked he needed to now.

He had to make her back off before this hero-worship shit she had going on for him did some real damage, and the only way to do that was to show her he wasn't the hero she thought he was and never had been. Hell, maybe even frighten her. He didn't want to do it, but he would. For both their sakes.

He even had an idea about how. The little virgin needed to see exactly what she'd be getting herself into with him, and he was betting she wasn't going to like it.

Gideon straightened, locking gazes with her, concentrating the entire force of his stare on her. Men had once quailed when he'd done that to them, mostly because they all knew what it meant.

That it was time to pay.

Zoe didn't know that though and she didn't quail. She only raised that chin of hers in defiance.

"So, you liked that, did you?" he asked softly, putting a certain amount of menace into his tone. "You liked me spanking your ass?"

She blinked and the color in her cheeks deepened. "Maybe."

"I think you did." He let his gaze dip very pointedly to her chest. "At least, your body did."

She shrugged, obviously trying to be cool and just as obviously not doing a very good job. "Yeah, and?"

"Did it make you hot, little one?" He kept his voice soft, kept his gaze on hers. "Did it make you wet?"

Uncertainty flickered in her eyes, her blush deepening even more. "Well I . . . liked it. So?"

He moved forward, keeping his arms folded, slowly closing the distance between himself and the bed. "Did you want me to keep going? Pull down your jeans and put you over my knee? Spank that sweet ass of yours until it was bright red?"

Zoe's soft mouth dropped open, her cheeks crimson. "I . . . I . . ."

"But you wanted more than that, didn't you?" he went on. "You wanted to be taught a real lesson."

"What lesson?" She was trying to pull herself together, he noticed. Trying to pretend that this wasn't affecting her in the slightest, as if men dirty-talked her all the time. "If you're talking about more spanking then sure, why not?"

He bent and put one hand flat to the bed on either side of her hips. Then he leaned forward so they were almost nose to nose. "I don't think you want me as your teacher, little one. In fact, I'm pretty fucking sure of it."

Her throat moved as she swallowed. "W-why not?"

Jesus, she could give a mule a run for its money.

"Because when you're over my knee, I'd tie your hands behind your back so you couldn't move." He leaned forward even more, making her rear back. "Then I'd spank your ass red for being such a fucking brat."

Her eyes widened. "Oh? Well, I could—"

"What? You think a spanking is all I'd give you?" He didn't take his gaze from hers as he began to move forward, steadily forcing her backward. "I like dealing out punishment. It's my favorite. It's what I'm good at and spanking that ass is not the only way to do it."

Zoe had pushed herself away from him until she was in the middle of the bed, but he didn't stop. "I'd hold you down, spread your legs, play with your pussy." He leaned over her, forcing her onto her back. "Make sure you were dripping wet and desperate to come. But I wouldn't let you."

Her mouth was open, a look of open shock on her face, her blush fire red.

"I like a woman to beg and I'd make you beg for me, Zoe," he went on relentlessly, because giving her a glimpse of the kind of man he was, the kind of man he'd been hiding from her, was the only way to make her understand. "I'd make you beg for my cock and if you were a very good girl, I would fuck you with it. If you were a very bad girl, I'd make you suck it instead." He paused, staring down at her, holding her there with the sheer force of his gaze. "Think you can handle that?"

She said nothing, staring up at him as if she'd never seen him before in her life.

It hit him then, like a blow to the head, that he basically had her on her back, right underneath him. That he could smell the sweet lavender scent of her, tinged with feminine musk, and feel the warmth of her slender body. That the hard tips of her nipples were almost brushing his chest, and the pulse at the base of her throat was racing.

That he wanted to put his mouth over it.

A kick of desire punched right through him, stealing his breath.

All those things you told her, you actually wanted to do them to her.

He couldn't move. For some reason he was caught there, holding himself above her, looking down into her familiar, delicate face, watching the ebb and flow of color in her cheeks, the shock and confusion in her golden eyes.

This is Zoe. She's your foster sister. And you can't do any of those things to her.

No, he couldn't. So why the *fuck* was he hard?

"Gideon?" Zoe said hoarsely.

He shoved himself off the bed with a sharp movement, his heartbeat hammering in his ears, his stupid dick like iron in his jeans.

What a fucking dumb idea that had been. He'd only wanted to put her off, scare her. He hadn't wanted to be turned on by it. Christ. Clearly, all those mornings spent jacking off in the shower weren't enough. He needed an actual woman, not his own palm.

He turned toward the door. "I wouldn't tell the others, if I were you," he said, unable to keep the harsh note from his voice. "And you won't be leaving this apartment again, not without me."

There was a silence behind him.

"If you try and keep me here, I'll call the police." Her voice sounded as thick as his, but there was no hiding the stubborn anger in it.

"They know me, Zoe. That won't work." And it wouldn't. He'd gone to some lengths to keep the chief sweet, make sure they were on his side. They kept a lookout for anyone who might be a threat to him, while he passed on any info that they might need to keep the place safe. It was an understanding that worked very well for all concerned.

She made a soft, frustrated noise. "Okay, look, give me one thing and I promise I'll stay here. That I won't give you any grief."

His inconvenient hard-on fading, he swung around. "What do you want?"

She was sitting back up again, her arms folded over her tits, hiding those pretty little nipples. Which was probably a good thing. "Take me to Anonymous."

"Why?"

"You won't let me get a different job and you won't let me go to college. You want me to stay inside for God knows how long. . . . The least you can do is help me get laid."

The words made him feel like someone had taken a defibrillator and applied it directly to his chest. "Jesus, Zoe. I'm not—"

"Yes, you fucking will," she interrupted fiercely. "I have *never* asked you for anything. Not one single thing. You can damn well give me this."

Anger hooked into the remains of the desire still pulsing inside him, and he had no patience left with which to fight it. "If you think I'm taking you to that fucking nightclub and leaving you there for some asshole to pick up, you're wrong."

"I'm not asking you for that." There was a familiar, determined light in her eyes. "You can help me choose the guy, vet him for me. And then, I'll bring him back here and—"

"Oh, fuck no."

"If you don't do this then I'm leaving." A thin thread of hurt wound through her voice. "And I won't ever come back."

She meant it, he could see that. She meant every word.

Of course, he could lock her in, tie her up. Watch her twenty-four seven. But he had a suspicion that would break something fundamental between them. A trust they'd always had.

He'd already put a crack in it with that performance he'd given just now. Could he really break it entirely?

Stupid question. Of course he couldn't.

But her life is at stake.

However, there were other ways to skin a cat. Such as doing something he almost never did. Compromise.

He dredged up a last shard of patience. "You're seriously asking me to me to find you a guy to take home?"

"Yes."

A baser, more primitive instinct inside him growled at the thought of anyone else touching what was his. But no, he was a different man now and anyway, Zoe wasn't his. Going out to Anonymous with her wouldn't be the smartest thing to do, not when Novak was hanging around, possibly searching for her. Then again, at least if he was with her, he could keep the chances of her being discovered low. And hell, if it meant she'd stop all this rebellion crap and do as she was told, then wouldn't it be worth it?

"Okay," he said flatly. "I'll find you someone."

Then he turned around and left before he could change his mind.

Chapter 5

Zoe sat on the comfortable, old, blue velvet couch in the living room and reached for the stretchy red dress that sat on top of the pile of clothing Rachel had brought for her. "What about this one?"

Rachel, sitting at the other end of the couch, frowned at the dress. "Sorry, but you might need more tits for that one."

Zoe looked down at her admittedly not very well endowed chest and wrinkled her nose. "Good point. Would a push-up bra work?"

"It could. But I'd go for something more like this." Rachel held up a narrow band of leather.

Zoe blinked at it. "Is that a . . . skirt?"

"Yeah. You could wear it with . . ." She reached out and unearthed something else from the clothing pile. "How about this?"

It was a simple top made out of black lace. Zoe was vaguely disappointed. She'd asked Rachel that morning to come around with a selection of clothes that would be good for looking hot in a club, because God knew, she didn't have any. Rachel had duly brought some with her, but Zoe had been expecting something eye-poppingly sexy, not a plain leather skirt and lace top.

Rachel, spotting her lack of enthusiasm, raised an eyebrow. "You wear a sexy bra underneath it and nothing else. I guarantee it'll look amazing." She waved the clothing at her. "Try it, go on."

Zoe pulled a face, but took the clothes.

She trusted Rachel's judgment on this, because Rachel took the hot-but-tough look and basically made it her bitch. Zoe wanted it to be her bitch too.

Gideon had promised to take her to Anonymous tomorrow and she was pretty sure he'd only give her one shot at this. Which meant she really needed to not screw it up. It was either that or she was stuck in the apartment like Rapunzel in her tower until Gideon told her it was safe to come out. If indeed those threats he kept talking about were true, and since he seemingly wouldn't give her any reasons to back up his suspicions, she was doubtful.

At the thought of Gideon, a pulse of something distinctly warm shot through her and she had to busy herself with the laces of her sneakers in order to hide her hot face.

The past couple of days had been hell, no two ways about it.

After he'd proved his point in her bedroom, she'd pretty much stayed in there the rest of the day, too embarrassed and shocked to leave. She hadn't wanted him to know how much he'd affected her, but looking him in the eye would have given herself away as bad as avoiding him. So avoiding him it was.

She'd sat in her room, distracting herself playing computer games, trying not to replay every word he'd spoken to her over and over again. Trying not to remember the heat of his body or the way it had felt to be on her back with him over her, his arms on either side of her head. Staring down at her with that unfamiliar hot darkness in his eyes as he'd said those . . . things to her.

Shocking things. Terrible things.

Sexy things.

Because yes, despite herself and her efforts to be cool, they'd shocked her. They'd also turned her on.

With every word Gideon had said, an image had popped into her head. Of him doing those things to her. Of being turned over his knee and having his hand on her again, this time without her jeans on. Without anything on.

"If you were a very bad girl, I'd make you suck it instead."

Clearly she was insane or some kind of masochist, because he'd obviously been telling her that stuff to scare her off. And sure, it *was* scary. In fact, come to think of it, *he'd* suddenly seemed pretty scary himself, which was weird since she'd never felt afraid around Gideon. In fact, it had all sounded pretty intense and she wasn't sure she was ready for any of that.

Yet it had also been intensely hot, and part of her had been panting for it.

Not that he's ever going to do any of that to you.

Yeah, well, exactly. So why she kept thinking about it was anyone's guess.

Gideon was a lost cause. Far better to go for a guy who actually wanted her.

Zoe kicked her shoes off and stood up, shucking her jeans down and reaching for the skirt. She pulled it up and fastened the zipper, staring down at herself. "Seems to fit."

Rachel gave her a critical look. "Top."

Yanking off her T-shirt, she grabbed the lace top, tugging it down. Her bra was an attractive flesh shade so not particularly sexy, but that could be fixed.

She held her arms out. "Well?"

Rachel got up off the couch, surveying her from a couple of different angles. "What's the purpose of this again?"

"I want to find a guy."

"Why?"

Stupidly Zoe felt herself blushing. "Because I'm sick of being a virgin."

"Nothing wrong with virginity."

"Sure. When you're not the one who's the virgin." She couldn't keep the sharp sound out of her tone.

Rachel's gaze narrowed. "Ah. It's like that, is it?"

Defensive, Zoe scowled. God, was she destined not to be taken seriously by anyone? "Like what? I'm twenty-five, Rach. I'm the oldest virgin in the entire world."

"Uh-huh." Rachel stopped in front of her and folded her arms. "And that's not dramatic at all."

It was. Kind of. But when you were virtually a prisoner in your own apartment, everything was dramatic. Still, she wasn't going to tell Rachel that. She'd briefly toyed with the idea of complaining to the others about what Gideon was doing, but she had a feeling that Zee and Levi would be in agreement with him, while Rachel . . . Well, Rachel had crossed to the dark side with Levi. She'd probably agree too, dammit.

Besides, if she told them about Gideon's massive safety overreaction, she'd then also have to tell them about her father, and she really didn't want to get into that yet.

"I feel dramatic," Zoe said lamely. "Maybe it's PMS."

Rachel's expression softened. "Or maybe it's something else?"

Oh great, she knew that look. If her friend mentioned Gideon, she was going to walk right out of here. She did *not* want to talk about her crush on him with anyone. Especially when what had happened two days ago had only shown her how woefully unprepared she was to handle any guy like him.

"It's nothing else," she said, knowing she sounded bad-tempered and yet not really sure how to deal with it.

Rachel's expression said it all though. She knew Zoe was full of bullshit. "So how are you and Gideon?"

Zoe looked toward the door. Would walking out be rude? It probably would be, especially considering Rachel had come over with the clothes. "It's fine," she lied, forcing herself to smile. "It's all good."

Rachel cocked her head, her dark eyes searching. "If you don't want to talk about it, that's okay."

Zoe could feel herself coloring yet again. But at least her friend had offered her an out. "I don't think I want to talk about it."

"Fair enough." The look on Rachel's face was sympathetic, which was horrible. "But you know, if you do . . ."

She bit her lip. Normally she had no issues with talking to her friends about anything, but this thing with Gideon was different. In fact, Gideon was the first person she went to whenever she had a problem, and the fact she couldn't do that now was unsettling.

Maybe you could talk to her?

What would she say though? Rachel knew already she was crushing majorly on Gideon, and there was nothing to be done about that. No one could make people's feelings change, not hers and certainly not Gideon's.

So no, talking didn't help.

"Thanks, Rach," she said, because she needed to say it. "I appreciate the offer, I really do. Right now, though, I'm moving on, if you know what I mean. I just want to find a hot guy and have some fun for a change."

Rachel grinned, and it was good to see her smile. Things hadn't been so great with her and Levi a few weeks back, but now the two of them were together and she looked like a weight had been lifted from her shoulders. Levi, too, had lost that frightening, menacing look he'd been carrying around when he'd first gotten out of jail.

They'd definitely found something good together, something that made the two of them very, very happy.

A shard of jealousy stuck in Zoe's heart. She wanted that with someone. She wanted that sense of having someone to call her own. Of someone calling her his, too. Oh, she had the little family of friends Gideon had formed when they'd first settled into Royal. Levi and Zee and Rachel. But now they all had someone special. Everyone except her.

And Gideon.

"Zoe?" Rachel's smile had faded. "You sure you don't want to talk about anything?"

With an effort, Zoe dismissed her pathetic thoughts. "No, it's okay." She took a breath. "So what do you think of this outfit? Will it do?"

Rachel gave her another once-over. "You got a nice bra to wear under that?"

She had one item of sexy lingerie. A gold lace bra she'd bought online a year or so ago, when she'd thought seducing Gideon might work. It had been a stupid idea and, even despite the bra, had only ended up giving her more grief.

She'd found a cheap dress that looked more trashy than sexy, put it on over the lingerie, and had followed Gideon to Gino's, Royal Road's local bar not far from the garage, intending to get drunk and seduce him there.

But he hadn't been inside. She'd gone out the back in search of him, only to find him in the alley behind the bar with one of the waitresses. He hadn't seen her, but she'd seen him. He'd been up against the wall with the waitress and there had been no doubt about what they were doing. The waitress's skirt was up around her hips and Gideon's jeans had been undone. . . .

She shouldn't have watched, but she hadn't been able to stop herself, mesmerized by the fierce pleasure on his face. It was an expression she'd never seen before, and it had felt like she'd glimpsed a secret, hidden part of him.

A part of him she'd never seen again.

She'd abandoned her seduction plans after that and had gone home alone, because obviously there was no point. He'd wanted the waitress, not her. But in her bed, much later, she'd reached for the toy she'd bought secretly online and kept under a pile of tampon boxes in her nightstand. And she'd imagined herself as the waitress.

"I have something," she said thickly, pushing away the memories.

Rachel said nothing, only looking at her.

"What?" Zoe asked, trying not to sound defensive and failing. "It's gold and it's—"

"Don't throw it away, Zoe," Rachel interrupted quietly.

Zoe blinked at her. "Throw what away?"

"Your virginity." The other woman's gaze was very direct. "Don't give it to some guy just because you don't want it anymore. It's precious. It's a gift."

Her cheeks felt hot and she had to look away, fixing her attention on the leather skirt, smoothing it down. It wasn't bad advice. Except the problem with it was that there was only one man she wanted to give that gift to.

And he didn't want it.

So what else could she do? Keep saving it until she finally found someone she wanted as much as Gideon? Or find someone who was hot and wasn't a douche bag and give it to him instead?

Fact was, she wasn't going to find anyone she wanted as much as Gideon and she was done waiting. Which left her with the hot douche bag option.

"I'm not giving it to 'some guy,'" she muttered. "I'm going to find someone I'm attracted to and hopefully he'll know what he's doing."

Rachel sighed. "I'm not saying this to bring you down. I just know from experience and I don't want you ending up regretting it like I did."

Zoe finally looked up and met the other woman's gaze. "I won't regret it. The only thing I'll regret is not doing something about it when I had the chance."

But there was too much knowledge in her friend's eyes. "I know who you're waiting for."

"Rach, please don't—"

"Sometimes when they're that blind, you have to make them see."

Zoe swallowed, her throat feeling tight. Easy for her to say. Levi wasn't her foster brother. "Like I said, I don't want to talk about it."

Rachel lifted a shoulder. "Suit yourself. You want to try anything else? Because I seriously think you should go with that."

Gideon leaned his hip against the workshop counter and looked down at the plans Levi had spread out on them. They were from the architect they'd hired to draw up some concept ideas for the Royal Road development the six of them were planning, and Levi had only just picked them up today.

"I showed them to Rachel before," Levi was saying. "She really likes what the architect's done with her building. Especially getting rid of the parking lot beside it and turning the space into a park."

Gideon stared at the plans. The development project he'd encouraged Levi and Rachel to start on was something he'd often thought about himself. This neighborhood and the people in it meant a lot to him. It had been his shelter, his refuge. His home for over ten years, and he was fully invested in the place. Certainly more so than he'd ever been in Chicago.

The development they'd planned wasn't of the blind, knock-everything-down-and-let-God-sort-it-out school of development that shitheads like Novak were graduates of, but of a more careful, thoughtful sort. They wanted to be true to the neighborhood and its people. It was about making a more pleasant and safer environment for them, not for rich yuppies looking for less expensive housing options.

It was going to cost them shitloads of course, but Levi had money from his investments and Gideon had cash from . . . other things. Things the rest of them didn't know about and that he wasn't going to tell them.

No one needed to know about his past. Especially since it was over and done with.

Not as over and done with as you thought, with Novak hanging around.

Gideon's jaw hardened.

He'd had some contacts keep their eyes out for Novak, but so far the guy hadn't shown his face in Royal for a couple of days. Didn't mean he'd gone, though, and Gideon wasn't stupid enough to believe the guy had suddenly lost interest. Assholes like Novak didn't do anything without calculation, so there was something going on, Gideon was positive.

He kept his gaze on the plans. "Looks good," he said, and it did. The architect Levi had hired had done a great job. "And I'm with Rachel. Royal could use a nice park."

Royal didn't have one at all and that had probably been for the best, considering the drug dealers and gangs that used to plague the neighborhood. However, Gideon had dealt with that issue over the years, and these days the dealers and the rest steered clear of Royal, going for easier pickings farther out.

He hesitated. "You know if Novak's still keeping tabs on this?"

Levi shrugged one massive shoulder, the late afternoon sun coming through one of the garage's grimy window panes, making the ring in his eyebrow glint. "I don't think so. Any reason he would?"

Gideon debated what to tell him. He hadn't spoken to any of the others about Zoe and he planned on keeping it that way. She was his concern, end of story. "He was pretty pissed you cut him out of the project though, right?"

Levi's eyes, one dark and dilated, one silver-blue, narrowed. "He wasn't happy, yeah. But I told him I'd had a better offer. It's just business and he said he understood."

"You think he might hang around here to keep tabs on what's happening?"

A look of surprise crossed the other man's face. "Why? Has he been hanging around Royal?"

There was no reason for Levi not to know so Gideon merely nodded. "Just figuring out if you knew anything."

"No, got no idea." Levi frowned. "Novak needed a project for his senatorial bid and maybe he's still trying to find one."

"Well, he won't find one here." Gideon picked up the wrench that was lying on the counter beside him. "If you see him, find out what his deal is. I don't like assholes hanging around our neighborhood, especially when I don't know what they want."

Levi gave him a speculative look. "Why? You got something going on?"

"No. I just don't like assholes hanging around our neighborhood."

Levi's expression told him the other man knew he was hiding something.

Too bad. That's how he handled shit. Especially when shit like his past came rolling unexpectedly into his present.

"How are you and Rachel?" Gideon asked, changing the subject gracelessly.

One corner of Levi's mouth turned up. "Pretty good." Which was obviously a massive understatement, given the way his expression softened at the mention of Rachel's name.

Gideon turned away to hide his own smile, heading over to the vintage Harley he had up on a stand. He was deeply glad his two friends had finally found each other after all this time. God knew, Levi deserved it after spending eight years in prison, and Rachel deserved it too, because she'd had it pretty rough herself.

Anyway, the two of them were made for each other. Gideon had known it the first time Levi had brought her along to the Royal Road Outreach Center all those years ago. It had just taken them longer to realize it themselves.

Yeah, it was good to see Levi and Rachel settle down, like it had been good to see Zee and Tamara do the same.

Zoe needs to find someone too.

The thought had him scowling at the Harley before he'd even realized what he was doing. Did Zoe really need a boyfriend right now? She was young, she had plenty of time for that kind of thing.

Don't kid yourself that it's about her being too young. You just don't want to lose her.

Gideon stared hard at the engine he was overhauling, doing his best not to listen to his overactive brain. Because it didn't make any sense. Even if Zoe did find herself a boyfriend, losing her was something that would happen eventually. He couldn't stop it. And sure, there would be a period of adjustment since he'd had her all to himself for so long, but he'd deal with it.

He wouldn't ever stand in the way of her happiness.

"I'm going to take these round to Zee's," Levi said, pausing beside the Harley, the plans tucked beneath his arm. "See what he and Tamara think. You want to come along?"

"Can't." He placed the wrench on a particularly stubborn bolt and gave it a sharp twist. "Promised Zoe I'd take her out tonight."

There was a silence.

"Don't you ever get tired of playing watchdog?" Levi's tone was neutral, but Gideon didn't need to see the other man's face to know that the question wasn't actually neutral at all.

Levi had remarked on Zoe's hero worship–crush thing before and Gideon had not appreciated the implied accusation. That he was somehow fueling it by keeping watch over her.

He didn't look up from the engine, trying to loosen the fucking bolt. "Was there a point you wanted to make, Levi?"

"Not really. Just wondered when you're going stop playing the overprotective big brother." There was another pause. "Especially when Zoe doesn't see you as a big brother."

The words fell into the silence like stones, and Gideon wanted to pick each one up and hurl them back.

He's right. Maybe giving her space is the answer, let her do her own thing.

Sure, that might be the answer, but right now, given the situation, it was a shitty one. Zoe needed protection. That had been his job ever since she was six years old, and he wasn't giving it up now just because she had an inconvenient crush on him. Maybe he'd reconsider after the Novak threat was gone, but until then, it was going to stay as is.

"Butt out," he said flatly, twisting hard on the wrench again. "Zoe and I will sort it out ourselves, okay?"

Levi shrugged. "Just remember you want to do what's best for her, not what's best for you."

Oh, fuck no. That was below the belt.

Gideon looked up, giving the other man a hard stare, ignoring the painful place he'd hit. "I said butt the fuck out, Levi. I know what's best for her, not you. Understand?"

Levi held up his hands in a gesture of surrender. "Hey, I didn't mean anything. It was just a statement." But the look in his eyes was skeptical, as if he thought Gideon's protests were bullshit.

Of course they're bullshit.

Jesus, now he wanted to tell Levi that in fact the whole reason he was taking Zoe out *was* for her. Because finding her a lover wasn't exactly his idea of a great night out.

But he stayed silent. He wasn't going to justify himself

to anyone. For ten years he'd protected her and if that didn't prove he only had Zoe's best interests at heart, then he didn't know what did.

Besides, he didn't want a fight, not now.

"Then how about you take your statements elsewhere," he muttered, looking back at the engine. "I got a bike that needs fixing."

Chapter 6

Zoe sat on one of the barstools watching the heaving Saturday night crowd at Anonymous. The dance floor was even more packed than it had been a few nights ago, nothing but a wall of writhing bodies.

She really hoped no one was going to ask her to dance because she didn't think they could physically fit any more people on there.

"See anyone interesting?"

Gideon's deep, rough voice was loud in her ear, and she had to repress the usual shiver that went down her spine at the sound of it.

Somehow it had gotten even worse after that thing in her bedroom last Sunday, which would have worried her if she hadn't been here, looking for something that the club already was starting to get a reputation for.

They didn't call it Anonymous for nothing; hookups were what it was all about.

The awkwardness she felt around Gideon now was reaching record levels, and she didn't think she'd be able to stand it for too much longer. The thought of spending God knows how long stuck in the apartment with him was hideous, and the fact that he didn't seem to find it a problem only made things worse.

"No," she shouted back, since the noise made talking normally next to impossible.

It was kind of disappointing. She hadn't gotten anyone's attention either, which was also disappointing. She'd been hoping Rachel's skirt and lacy top, her gold bra and motorcycle boots would have been the perfect combination of tough yet unbearably sexy and impossible for any guy to resist.

Apparently, though, plenty of guys had been able to resist. *Gideon didn't even look twice at you.*

She scowled at the crowd in front of her. No, her big entrance had been a bust. She'd nervously sidled out of her bedroom as he'd waited in the hallway for her, but apart from an expressionless once-over, he hadn't even blinked at her outfit.

It had made her stomach lurch. Made her feel like going straight back into her bedroom and changing.

He, on the other hand, looked to die for all in black. Black T-shirt, black jeans. Heavy black boots. Radiating a tough menace that he didn't have to work at to project, unlike so many of the other guys. That menace, that rough danger, it was a part of him. It was innate. It was also as hot as hell.

She tried not to look at him, since when she did the thought of finding someone else she wanted as much seemed an impossible task. Especially when a lock of black hair had fallen forward over his forehead, making her want to push it back. He'd muttered something about a haircut a week or so back and she'd told him it was fine. Meaning she loved his hair a little shaggy.

It reminded her of when she'd first met him back when she'd come to live with her first foster family. She'd been scared and he'd seemed so intimidating. Until he'd said, "Hi, Zoe. I'm Gideon. Pleased to meet you." Then he'd held out his hand, his black eyes gazing directly at her, and she'd felt, for the first time ever, as if someone was actually talking directly to her instead of about her.

She still remembered the feel of his warm fingers enveloping her much smaller hand as they'd shaken on it.

A handshake and pancakes. That was all it had taken for her to decide that Gideon Black was her friend and he always would be. That was fine back then, but she wanted more than friendship from him now.

"You should dance," he said. "Get in the crowd."

"I don't really want to dance. In fact, I hate dancing."

"Well, sitting here isn't drawing any attention to you."

Yeah, and he wasn't helping.

He was sitting on the stool next to hers, leaning back against the bar with his arm outstretched behind her, making it look like she was his. And even though she liked that very much, it wasn't exactly sending out *I'm single* signals.

If she was going to find herself a hookup, she was going to have to ditch Gideon.

She turned, reaching for the frozen margarita—not blackberry this time—sitting on the bar top. "I'm going to go sit somewhere else."

He frowned. "What?"

"You leaning over me like a jealous boyfriend doesn't help, Gideon."

His brows lowered even more, making him look dark and saturnine and even hotter than normal. "I'm not leaning over you like a jealous boyfriend."

She didn't bother to reply to that, merely glancing at the arm he'd stretched along the bar behind her.

His mouth hardened, and for a second she thought he wasn't going to do anything about it. But then, slowly, he removed the offending arm and sat up on his barstool. "There. Happy?"

"No. You're still right there."

He stared at her. "I'm not letting you out of my sight, if that's what you're thinking. Not when I can't be certain some contact of Novak's isn't hanging around here looking for you."

Ah yes, that stupid Novak threat.

Perhaps it's not stupid. Perhaps he's right to be concerned. Ever think of that?

Zoe shoved the thought away. "Well, can't you not let me out of your sight a little farther away?"

He gave her another long look, then got off the stool and held out his hand. "Come and dance with me."

She eyed the proffered hand. "But I don't want to dance."

Muttering something she didn't catch, Gideon reached out, took the margarita out of her hand, and put it back on the bar before she had a chance to protest. Then he laced his fingers through hers and pulled her off the barstool, leading her into the heaving crowd of dancing bodies.

Zoe resisted the urge to dig in her heels since obviously doing so wouldn't get her any more attention than sitting on the barstool had. Still, she wasn't a fan of dancing. Then again, if she was dancing with Gideon then that might make it worthwhile.

You're supposed to be moving on, not thinking about Gideon all the time.

Good point. She really needed to find someone who would grab her attention, though, and so far that hadn't happened.

Music thumped in her ear, bright lights and neon flickering over the crowd, shining on sweat-slick skin and glinting off jewelry and sequins. It was hot, nearly suffocating. People hemmed her in on either side, forcing her to move with them or else she'd stumble and probably fall.

Then Gideon's hands were on her hips, pulling her close, holding her up. Her breath caught, her mouth going dry as the heat of his body pressed suddenly against her.

She tipped her head back to look at him, but his attention

wasn't on her. He was gazing around at the rest of the crowd, his rough, handsome face set in hard lines, like a soldier scanning the area for threats. It made him look dangerous, made her heart turn over inside her chest.

This was not going the way she'd hoped, not at all. But that was her fault. She'd stayed too close to him all evening, because staying close to Gideon was her default position. It made her feel protected, safe. It was also easy.

Getting away from him now would be stupid if what he'd said about Novak and the threat her supposed father presented was true, but she didn't believe it was. Not when he didn't have any proof and refused to discuss it.

And that didn't leave her with many options. Because if he was serious about keeping her chained to the apartment, it meant that tonight was going to be her only chance to find a guy who could help her with her virginity problem. Yet she couldn't do that with Gideon looming over her like a dragon over its hoard.

If she was going to move on from him, she had to stop settling for safe and easy.

Zoe reached down and pushed his hands off her.

That got his attention. He glanced down at her, his brows lowering even more.

It was too crowded and loud to have a discussion or offer him any explanations, so she didn't say a word. She merely grinned, and before he could respond, turned and slipped through a gap in the dancing bodies.

Half of her hoped for a hand on her elbow or an arm around her waist, pulling her back to him, but then she heard some woman yell, "Gideon!" from behind her and she knew that wasn't going to be happening.

She didn't turn, sidling through the dancers until she found a space for herself. There were a couple of attractive guys nearby and one of them, tall, dark, and handsome, just the way she liked, smiled at her.

Okay. It was time to get this devirginizing show on the road.

As Zoe disappeared into the throng of dancers, someone called Gideon's name and a pair of slender arms slid around his waist. Irritated, he almost pushed them away, every instinct he had urging him to go after Zoe. Which was a stupid idea since it was unlikely anything would happen to her inside the club.

He'd already done a scan of the whole place and hadn't spotted any of the shady types whose presence usually meant some criminal underground business was going down. That could mean nothing, though. He hadn't been part of that scene for a long time, and keeping tabs on it from his garage wasn't the same as actually being in the thick of it. He had his contacts, of course, and they kept him up-to-date with what was really going on in the city, but there were a lot of new faces in town.

If Novak wanted Zoe, there were plenty of ways to get her, hired muscle being one of them. Again, something that Gideon would know all about since Gideon had once been that hired muscle, back when he'd been a lost teenager burning with anger at the death of his mother. And a murderer for a father. When the only thing that mattered was getting enough money to carve a life for himself, have something that was his any way he could get it. And if someone got hurt along the way, that was too bad.

Novak had been a gift from the gods, offering him more money than he could ever make in six months of doing the building laborer's jobs that were the only legal work he could get. So he'd done the things the guy asked of him, become his enforcer, supplementing that with money from the illegal street fights he sometimes took on to hone his physical skills.

He'd never questioned whether what he was doing was the

right thing, because right and wrong hadn't mattered to him back then. He was the son of a prostitute who'd been murdered by the man who was supposed to love her, and there was nothing right about that so why bother worrying about it? Look after number one because no one else sure as hell was going to, that was the most important rule he'd learned.

Until Zoe. Until she'd shown him that there were other important things too. That people mattered.

So let her go. There's no threat here. You're overreacting.

"Gideon," the woman whispered huskily in his ear, the arms around him tightening. "I've been wondering where you'd gotten to. What are you doing here? I didn't think you liked nightclubs."

Cursing under his breath, Gideon turned around, meeting the woman's familiar blue eyes.

It was Tori, the woman he'd been seeing off and on for the past few months—or rather, having sex with off and on since he didn't do relationships. She was small and curvy and sensual, dark hair piled on top of her head, her hips moving in time with the music. Her wide mouth was turned up in a suggestive smile and there was definite interest on her lovely face.

Hell. Zoe could get some and so could you.

Except suddenly he didn't have any interest in dancing.

Still, he liked Tori and there was no need to be rude, so he slid an arm around her, bringing her up close so they didn't get in the way of the other dancers. Her body was very warm and she smelled good, and yet for some reason his dick just wasn't interested. "I don't like nightclubs," he said. "But Zoe does."

Tori put her arms around his neck, her breasts pressing up against his chest. "So you're here on guard dog duty? That's a shame. She's a big girl, though, she can look after herself, can't she?"

It was too noisy and there were too many people, and he couldn't see where Zoe had gotten to. His irritation wound tighter. "Come on," he said shortly, letting Tori go. "I'll buy you a drink. Can't talk here."

She seemed quite happy with that, following him off the dance floor and back over to the bar, where he bought her a glass of wine and found them some seats at a table that gave them a good view of the dancers.

Couldn't spot Zoe, though.

"When are you coming to see me again?" Tori asked, crossing her legs so the hem of her little black dress rode up her thighs. "I missed you."

Gideon leaned back in his chair, watching the dance floor over Tori's shoulder. "Was thinking of calling you this week, actually. You free?"

She gave him a smile. "For you, baby, I'm free anytime."

The crowd behind her swirled, flashing lights illuminating faces and skin and teeth. The music was a deep vibration in his chest, making him feel restless and on edge.

He really didn't like this place. Didn't like that he couldn't see Zoe. And just because he hadn't spotted any familiar faces didn't mean they weren't there.

"Gideon?" Tori was looking at him, clearly expecting some interaction, which was a pain in the fucking butt when he had other, more important things on his mind. But clearly Tori already knew what was on his mind, because she said, "She's not a toddler. You don't have to keep her in eyesight all the time, you know that, right?"

Except Tori didn't know what Zoe was here for. It wasn't only a dance and a good time. It was to find a man to screw.

Gideon tried to make himself smile, pretend it was all cool. "Yeah, but you know me. I like to make sure she's okay."

"I'm sure she's okay." Tori sipped at her wine. "And I'd rather be talking about us."

"There is no us, Tori. Remember? Fuck buddies only."

"Sure. And it's the *fuck* in fuck buddies that I'm worried

about. We're in danger of becoming just buddies, and no one wants that."

The lights on the dance floor changed, bright light pulsing in time to the beat, and he saw Zoe all of a sudden. She was dancing with two men, one right in front of her, while a second was pressed against her back. The guy in the front was holding her by the hips, while the guy at her back had his hands on her bare thighs. She had her head tipped back, her palms flat against the chest of the man in front of her, and her eyes were closed. She was smiling, a full-on sensual smile that hit him in the center of his chest like a speeding train.

His breath caught, a sudden and violent rage filling him. That someone else's hands were on her smooth skin, touching her as though she were his.

She's not theirs. She's yours and she always has been.

When she'd come out of her bedroom earlier that evening, he'd almost ordered her back inside to go change. Her skirt was so fucking short it was more like a bandage than anything else, and the black lace top she wore was completely see-through. That she was wearing a pretty gold bra that cupped her little tits beautifully made no difference. In fact, if anything, it only drew attention to them.

It was ridiculous. He shouldn't have had any reaction at all to what she was wearing because he never had before. Yet tonight, he found he was definitely having a reaction. It pissed him off.

He'd said nothing earlier, hoping that if he didn't make a big deal out of it then it wouldn't be, but right now, it was a fucking big deal. All those guys had to do was push her skirt up, take her top off, and she'd be on the dance floor in her panties and bra, and nothing else.

For everyone to see.

A deep surge of possessiveness went through him, the kind

of raw, basic need he'd thought he'd put behind him a long time ago, and he started pushing himself out of his seat, responding to that need before he'd had a chance to think about it.

And then he froze, noticing something else. Both men had tattoos at the base of their necks. Tattoos Gideon recognized. Three stars for three brothers, the sign of a Russian gang Gideon knew for a fact had dealings with Novak.

Fuck.

How had he missed spotting them?

"Gideon? Are you okay?"

Tori was looking at him, wide-eyed, and he realized he was half out of his seat, clutching the arms of the chair in a white-knuckled grip. "I'm fine," he forced out.

But he wasn't fine. Every instinct he had was screaming at him to hurl himself into the crowd to get to Zoe. Pull those bastards off her and then blow them the fuck away before they hurt her.

Except that wasn't exactly a smart move in the middle of a crowded club.

Sure, he owned this neighborhood and the police chief was on his side, but even he couldn't get away with murder. In any case, it would alert Novak to the fact that Gideon suspected he was after Zoe, and Gideon didn't want to give himself away like that. It was better if Novak thought him complacent, especially if that led to Novak's getting overconfident and fucking up in some way.

No, he had to be calm and get Zoe out of here without fuss. Or at the very least without killing the men who were touching her.

Gideon finished pushing himself out of his chair.

Tori stared at him in surprise. "Hey? Where are you going?"

But he ignored her, already walking, shoving his way through the crowd around the dance floor, approaching Zoe and the two assholes on either side of her. She was grinding her hips against them and looking pretty happy with where she was at. She wasn't going to be pleased with what he was about to do.

But he didn't give a shit. She didn't know who these guys were and he did.

Not wasting any time, Gideon gave the man pushing against her a hard shove, while he elbowed the guy in front of her. The two men were obviously not expecting it, stumbling away and cursing as they knocked into other dancers.

Zoe's eyes flicked open, and she frowned in puzzlement. Then her frown deepened into a scowl as she realized who it was putting a stop to her fun.

Gideon closed a hand around her elbow and gripped her tightly. "Say good-bye, little one. It's time to go." He didn't look to see what Novak's men were doing, turning in the direction of the exit and dragging her off the dance floor without a backward glance.

"Jesus Christ, Gideon!" Her voice was loud in his ear. "What the hell are you doing? This shit is getting really old." She tried to pull her elbow from his grip, but he was having none of it.

Second time in a week he was pulling her out of this club. It wasn't happening again.

As he went by, he caught a glimpse of Tori staring at him as if he'd lost his mind, but he ignored her. It probably meant calling her for a friendly hookup later wasn't in the cards, but too bad. Zoe's safety was the only thing that mattered.

Fuck, he'd been a fool to let Zoe talk him into bringing her here. He should never have done it, never have said yes. If he hadn't been watching her like a hawk, those pricks would have taken her and God only knew what would have happened after that.

No, *he* knew. He knew exactly.

"Stop!" Zoe dug her heels in, bringing him up short.

He turned around sharply.

They were in the narrow concrete corridor that led from the club to the exit. A blue striplight ran down the walls on either side, bathing the corridor in an eerie glow. People were pushing past them, most going toward the club rather than leaving it.

Zoe had planted her feet in that stubborn way she had, her skin darker and burnished with sweat in the weird blue light. Through the black lace of her top, the gold bra she wore gleamed, drawing his gaze helplessly.

She had no idea, Jesus Christ. In her little skirt and top, with her black hair like a cloud around her head and sweat on her skin, her glasses pushed firmly up her nose, she looked like some hipster's perfect sexual fantasy.

Except the expression on her face wasn't seductive in the slightest. It telegraphed *mad as hell* loud and clear.

Her golden eyes glittered, her mouth set in a hard line. She raised a hand and there was a moment when he had not the slightest idea what she meant to do with it.

Until she slapped him across the face.

The blow turned his head to the side, the sound of her palm against his cheek echoing in the corridor, making people turn to stare at them.

Shock pulsed through him.

Fucking hell. She'd hit him. She'd actually hit him.

He turned his head back to face her. She'd lifted her hand again, but this time he didn't leave anything to chance, reaching out and grabbing her wrist before she could hit him again, holding on tightly to it.

His cheek stung, the shock beginning to ebb. Deep inside him something grew very still, very quiet.

"Have you finished?" he asked, his voice deceptively calm.

"No!" Her chin was sticking out, fury in her eyes. "I wanted to stay and dance, you asshole!"

If he hadn't known her, he would have thought that this was

purely a tantrum. But he did know her and he could see what was beneath all that boiling rage. Fear. Of him.

She'd never looked at him like that before and he didn't like it. He was the one person she should never have to be afraid of, not ever. Yet for some reason, she was afraid of him now and he didn't know why. He'd pulled her off that dance floor to protect her and no, he hadn't had a chance to explain that yet, but surely she knew that he would never hurt her?

After you spanked her in the hallway?

That quiet, still part of him shifted. This had to stop. Whatever it was that was changing things between them had to be dealt with. And soon. Before it broke the relationship they had entirely.

You know what it is, don't kid yourself you don't.

Yeah. He did.

"Zoe," he said. "We need to talk."

Chapter 7

Zoe's hand hurt and she was almost shaking with rage. The last thing she felt like doing was talking. Yet again. Especially when he hadn't listened to her the first time around.

But, oh God, she'd hit him. Which was stupid and wrong and she hadn't meant to at all. She'd just been so . . . angry.

She'd been enjoying dancing with those two guys. Only, in the privacy of the darkness behind her closed lids, it hadn't been two strangers she'd been dancing with. She'd been dancing with Gideon.

It had been his hands she'd imagined on her skin, his heat at her back, or her front, it didn't matter which.

He was her go-to fantasy. And when he'd ripped those guys away from her, she'd realized that actually, he would *always* be her go-to fantasy. That it didn't matter who she was with or what they were doing, in her head it would always be Gideon.

Everywhere she went, he was with her, she'd never be able to escape him, and *that* had been why she'd gotten so angry. She would always want a man who didn't want her.

So where did it leave her?

Nowhere. The same place you've always been.

It went out of her then, all her anger and outraged pride. Because it didn't matter what she did or how angry she got, nothing changed. So what was the point getting upset about it? What was the point fighting against it?

Arguing with him only made things worse and certainly made her feel terrible, and after the uncertainty of the past month, with Zee and his father coming down on them, then all this crap with Novak, terrible is not what she wanted to feel.

So now you're just going to accept the status quo, like you've been doing for years. Nothing will change if you don't change it.

Zoe swallowed. Changing it was too hard. Things were better when she didn't rock the boat.

His fingers were warm around her wrist, making her feel all kinds of things she didn't want to feel, so she pulled against his hold. "Let me go."

That hard look was still in his eyes, the one that had gathered there when she'd slapped him, making her afraid. Not that he'd hurt her, because she knew he never would, but afraid she'd crossed a line. Broken something that couldn't be fixed.

"Are you going to hit me again?" There was no expression in his voice.

People were walking by, staring at them, and without the anger pumping through her, she was beginning to feel self-conscious and stupid, and a bit shaky.

"No," she said thickly. "I'm sorry, I didn't mean—"

"You wanna know why I pulled those guys off you?" He didn't wait for her to reply. "They were Novak's."

She blinked at him in shock, the last glowing remnants of her anger flickering, then going out. "W-what?"

"I think you heard me."

Her dance partners were Novak's men? Surely not. They'd seemed like . . . well, like guys who'd wanted to dance with her, not thugs who'd wanted to hurt her. "How do you know they were Novak's?"

"I just know." There was something unfamiliar in his gaze, something dark and cold and utterly certain.

She swallowed, not wanting to believe him, a part of her wanting to cling to not knowing, wishing she'd never pulled away from him back there on the dance floor. Wishing she'd stayed at his side. Stayed where she was safe and where nothing had changed.

But it was too late for that.

"So you know that like you know Novak's my father and that he's potentially out to kill me?" She tried for sarcastic yet it came out sounding anxious instead.

Gideon's expression betrayed nothing at all. "Here's what's going to happen," he said, ignoring her question. "We're going home, Zoe. And then we're going to talk about what the fuck is going on. Understand?"

A little thrill of fear went through her, though she tried not to show it. "Which particular thing are we going to talk about then? This crap about Novak or . . ." She stopped, suddenly not wanting to say it out loud.

Gideon clearly had no such issues. "You and me. We're going to talk about you and me."

Shit. Talking about "you and me" was the last thing she wanted to do, but it looked like he wasn't going to give her any alternative.

"What about those guys I was dancing with?" she asked, in a last-ditch effort to distract him. "Shouldn't we be talking about them instead?"

"No."

"No? Just . . . no? After you said I was in danger and that—"

"Zoe."

It was only her name, spoken quietly. Yet there was so much authority in the word, she fell silent.

He released her wrist and she let it drop, rubbing at it with her other hand.

"I'm sorry," she said after a moment, wanting to offer an apology at least. Because if he was right and those two guys had actually been Novak's men, then he deserved one. "I didn't mean to hit you."

In the weird blue light of the corridor, he looked even darker and more menacing than he had on the dance floor, the blackness of his eyes like the night itself. "You can explain that when we get home."

"Gideon, I'm kind of tired and—"

"Now, Zoe."

Without waiting for her to respond, he reached out and grabbed her hand, his warm, strong fingers lacing through hers. Then he turned and began to walk to the exit, leaving her no choice but to walk with him.

The line outside the club was long and full of yuppies and hipsters all hoping for a gritty night out on the mean streets of Detroit. The neon painted their excited faces in different colors, picking out the broken pavement under their feet, and illuminating the graffiti on the abandoned building across the street.

The signs of a city that had hit rock bottom and yet was on its way up again. Trash and graffiti and broken buildings, but there was life and color and people having fun all the same.

It was a pity she couldn't take part in any of it.

She followed Gideon down the street, his hand tight around hers, pulling her along. He didn't speak, keeping his gaze forward, not turning to look at her even once.

Clearly, he was really pissed with her.

Is it any wonder? You kicked up a giant tantrum, then

slapped him like an outraged virgin. Face it. You're exactly the child he thinks you are.

She bit her lip, hurrying to keep up with his much longer strides, trepidation tightening inside her at the thought of their impending "you and me" talk. God, she'd much prefer to push him on how he knew all this stuff about Novak, get some answers at least, not talk about why she'd hit him. There was obviously a reason he refused to tell her how he knew, and she had a feeling it wasn't good. But hell, she'd rather push that than have to give him the pitiful truth about her own feelings for him. About why she'd hit him and why she was afraid. It was too painful, not to mention pathetic, and she didn't want it out there. Especially not if he was going to use the same scare tactics on her as he had the last time, up in her bedroom.

The memory made heat prickle over her skin and her breath catch. Oh hell, she really needed to stop thinking about that.

Ten minutes later, they were outside the entrance to their building and Gideon was unlocking the doors, pulling her inside. He stayed silent as they went up the stairs to the apartment, but there was an air of intentness about him. Okay, so there was probably no point repeating the fact that she was tired and wanted to go to bed, and could they talk in the morning?

Sure enough, when they got inside, Gideon pushed her firmly in the direction of the living room. She went with a heart slowly sinking right down into her platform motorcycle boots, her gut churning with a fear she didn't want to examine too closely.

Sitting down on the blue velvet couch under the windows, Zoe put her hands in her lap, watching as Gideon came into the room after her, stopping right in front of where she sat and folding his arms. He looked down at her, making her feel even more like a child with his height and the sheer weight of his presence.

There was a tense silence.

Then he asked, "Mind telling me what the hell was going on back there?"

She tried to moisten her dry mouth. "What? With those guys? I was dancing."

"I meant you slapping my face."

"I'm sorry."

"Not good enough."

She clasped her hands together, her knuckles white. "Well, if you won't tell me how you know all this stuff about Novak, even though it's apparently a life-or-death situation, why should I tell you about what happened back at the club?" It was a stupid thing to push him, especially when he was in this mood, but she couldn't help herself.

His expression hardened. "You really wanna push me on this, little girl? Because you might not like it if I push back."

No, she had a feeling she wouldn't. "Okay, okay. I slapped you because I was angry with you for pulling me away from that dance. I was enjoying myself."

"Angry enough to hit me?"

She didn't know how to answer that, not without exposing herself, so she bit her lip and tried to think of a reply that wouldn't.

He stared at her, a strange intensity in his dark eyes. "What's going on, Zoe? You're pissed with me but you won't tell me why."

I want you, that's the problem. I want you and you don't want me.

She bit her lip harder, trying to keep the truth safely inside. "I told you why. If you have to keep asking, then perhaps you're not listening."

But he only frowned. "You were afraid of me back there, weren't you?"

"I hit you. I wasn't sure what you'd do."

"Bullshit. You know I wouldn't hurt you, Zoe."

"Are you sure? You hurt me last week." The words came out without her meaning to and as soon as she'd said them, she wished she could take them back. Because now it was out there between them, the moment he'd spanked her butt and then she'd . . .

She stopped the thought dead and looked down at her hands since that was easier than looking into his strong, dark face. But it didn't help. She could feel his gaze on her, boring into her with the intensity of a laser beam.

There was another long, hideous silence.

"I know what you want, Zoe." His voice was quiet, all the hard edges softening. "I know why you're so pissed with me. I was just hoping you'd tell me yourself."

She closed her eyes, her heart squeezing tight in her chest. *Please don't say it. Please don't.*

"It can't happen—you know that, right?" He sounded sympathetic and gentle and in that moment she didn't know who she hated more, him for saying it or herself for not hiding it well enough.

"What can't happen?" Even now she couldn't bring herself to acknowledge it to him.

"You know what I'm talking about."

"No, I really don't—" A finger caught her beneath her chin, tipping her head up and there he was, crouched down in front of her, the look in his dark eyes inescapable.

"You and me, Zoe," he said, his voice still impossibly gentle. "I'm talking about you and me."

The lump in her throat swelled up so it felt like she couldn't breathe, let alone speak. But she had to say something. "I know." It came out sounding petulant and not at all cool and calm liked she'd hoped. "Anyway, you don't need to worry. Maybe I had a crush on you a while back, but it's over now, okay?" She swallowed and pulled her head away. "Are we finished? I'm tired and I really want to go to bed."

"No, we're not finished." He didn't move. "We need to sort this out, because I can't afford for us to be fighting all the time, not with Novak possibly looking for you. We need to be working together on this."

"Which really means you telling me what to do."

The look on his face hardened again. "Zoe. This is the sort of shit I'm talking about. You treating this situation like it's something I'm doing to you personally. This isn't about me telling you what to do, this is about keeping you safe, for fuck's sake."

Anger and a kind of despair turned over inside her. "You always say that. You always say it's about keeping me safe. But you won't tell me how you know I'm in danger and I don't understand why *you*. Surely you've got better things to do than to keep watch over me?"

"I'm watching over you because you're my kid sister. Because I'm responsible for you."

Kid sister. Yeah, he had to say it, didn't he? Had to rub it in, make it worse. And of course he didn't answer the other question either, the question as to how he knew she was in danger from Novak.

She looked away again, unable to bear the expression in those dark, magnetic eyes of his. "Fine," she said dully. "I'll stay here. Be a good little girl and do everything you say."

Another silence, even more tense and full of frustration than the last two had been.

"I'm sorry," he said, as if that made it all better.

"Don't say that." Her voice was hoarse and she hated the pathetic sound of it. "You can say anything else you like, but please don't say you're sorry."

He remained crouched in front of her, all that intense heat and coiled strength so close, within touching distance. The scent of him made her mouth water, made her dizzy with want, and it was suddenly all too much. She pushed herself to her feet, needing to get away from him.

He looked up. "Where are you going?"

"Like I said, I'm tired. I need to go to bed."

"We haven't finished."

"You might not. But I have." She made as if to go past him, but he was rising out of his crouch in a fluid, graceful movement, the full height of him right front of her, all wide shoulders and broad chest, his powerful arms crossed. A wall of hard muscle blocking her path.

She tipped her head back to meet his gaze, glaring at him. She was tired, angry, and even a bit humiliated, and she just wanted to be alone. Be done with this and with him. "Get out of my way, Gideon."

He didn't move. "I said, we haven't finished."

There were only inches between them and he was so warm, so close. It wasn't fair.

She threw out her hands, wanting to push him away, yet when they landed on the firm plane of his chest, all the strength went out of her arms. The heat of him took her breath away. She looked up, helplessly drawn by that dark gaze. By the desire she couldn't keep inside her any longer.

He stared back and she had no idea what he was thinking, no idea how he could stand there was if nothing touched him when she was burning up.

Afterward, she had no idea why she did it, she only knew that she had to do something.

So she rose up on her toes and kissed him.

Gideon went utterly still.

The touch of her mouth was heat, was fire, and seemed to burn every thought he'd ever had straight out of his head. He couldn't remember the last time he'd been kissed. The last time a woman had reached for him and pressed her lips to his. Oh, there had been plenty of times it had happened, but he simply couldn't remember any of them.

There was only this one moment. Zoe's mouth on his. Sweet and unpracticed, and desperate. And so fucking hot.

She had no business being so fucking hot.

It all came crashing back then, what was happening and who she was. Most especially who she was. His little one. His foster sister. Who was kissing him.

He lifted his hands and took her face between them, pulling her away.

She was flushed, her eyes even bigger than they normally were, her pupils hugely dilated, and he was excruciatingly conscious of her small palms against his chest, her slender hips against his.

"What the hell are you doing?" he demanded, his own voice sounding strange in the deafening silence of the room.

The color in her cheeks deepened into brilliant blocks of red. "I-I'm s-s-sorry," she stammered, looking stricken. "I didn't mean . . . I mean I didn't think—"

"No, you didn't fucking think, did you?" he said roughly, knowing he was being unreasonable, knowing he was frightening her because he could see the fear in her eyes right now. "And you don't fucking listen either. I told you there couldn't be anything between us. I *told* you." He should be treating this the way he'd been doing before she'd kissed him, with calm restraint, and yet that restraint was nowhere to be found. Instead, anger was catching fire inside him, a deep swelling tide of it, and all he could think was how could she do this to him? How could she change things between them like that? Ruin what they had?

She's not ruining things and it's not anger you're feeling. You want her.

No. It couldn't be that. He wasn't a goddamn pervert.

He sucked in a breath, knowing he should let her go, but somehow unable to make his fingers work. They were curled under her jaw and her skin was so soft and so warm. She was trembling.

"I know," she said. "I know, I'm sorry, Gideon. I'm really, really sorry." Tears were welling in her eyes.

It felt like she'd taken up a sharp knife and had stabbed him with it.

"You've got no idea." His fingers tightened on her even though he'd meant to release his hold. "You've got no *goddamn* idea what you're asking for."

She blinked, the tears glittering on the ends of her lashes. "I'm not stupid. I have some idea. I followed you once, to Gino's. And I saw you out back with the waitress."

Jesus. He could barely remember. One of Gino's waitresses . . . That must have been Angel. She'd been into rough sex and so had he, so they'd indulged themselves a couple of times in the alley out behind the bar.

Shock coiled inside him. She'd seen . . . that?

"What do you mean you saw me?" he demanded.

Zoe's mouth was pink from where she'd kissed him, going all pouty and lush. He couldn't stop looking at it. "I saw you push her up against the wall and . . . and s-screw her."

Great. This was getting better and better. Zoe had watched him have Angel hard up against a wall and . . . well, he hadn't been gentle, that was for fucking sure. "Why the hell did you do that?"

"Why do you think?" Her lashes fell. "Just let me go, Gideon. Please."

But he couldn't seem to make himself do it. There was a fire in his blood, burning hot, and whether it was something to do with seeing Novak's men so close to her at the club, with her being so close to danger, or anger at her for changing things, he didn't know.

What he did know was that Zoe wasn't getting the message.

She thought he was someone to look up to, someone to have a crush on, someone to be her hero. She thought he was a man who would make love to her tenderly, lovingly, all that kind of shit.

The silly little virgin had no idea who he really was. If she had she would never have done something so stupid as kiss him.

Clearly he hadn't frightened her enough back in her bedroom, which meant that if he wanted to end this, to bring their relationship back where it should be, he needed to drive the message home now.

"So you watched?" His pulse was suddenly hammering hard in his veins. "Did you get off on it, Zoe? Did you like it?"

The twin spots of red on her cheeks blazed. "If you're going to let me go, then let me the hell go!"

"Did you imagine you were that waitress?" He slid his thumbs along the hot skin of her cheekbones. "Did you wanna be?"

Her lashes lifted in shock, but he saw the flicker in her gaze and he knew what it meant. Of course she'd watched because she'd gotten off on it. And of course she'd imagined herself as that waitress, being pushed up against a wall and having her brains screwed out.

But watching was not the same as doing.

There was only one way to kill that crush of hers and that was to show her she had every reason to be afraid of him. Talking about it hadn't worked. Perhaps showing her would.

He took his hands from her face, only to grip her by her upper arms, walking her backward until he'd pushed her up against the nearest living room wall.

Her mouth dropped open, her pupils dilating even more until there was only a thin rim of gold around the darkness of her eyes. "What are you doing?" Her voice was husky, like the stroke of thick velvet, and he could smell her, innocent lavender and beneath it a deeper, musky, sensual scent. The combination went straight to his head, making him feel almost drunk on it.

"You wanna know what being the waitress was like?" His own voice had become much rougher and thicker too. "I'll show you."

More shock bloomed in her gaze. "But I thought . . . you said . . ."

He ignored her. This would be a hard lesson, but life was full of hard lessons. And clearly Zoe needed a few more. He'd been too easy on her, protected her too well. He didn't want her afraid of him, but fear kept you safe and if she wasn't going to listen to what he had to say, then he had to give her something else to be afraid of. Actions always spoke louder than words.

"When it gets too much for you, tell me when to stop." He didn't hesitate, crossing her narrow wrists in one hand and lifting them above her head, pinning them to the wall and keeping them there.

She gave a soft gasp, her back arching in response, staring at him as if transfixed.

There was a strange roaring in his ears, like he'd taken a punch to the head, blurring his sight and making him feel dizzy. She smelled unbelievably good, the sensual arch of her body making his breath catch.

He took a step forward, closing the space between them, staring down into her eyes as he pushed one thigh between hers.

She made another soft sound, blinking rapidly, and he could feel her pull against his restraining hand. But not very hard. Almost as if she was testing his hold rather than wanting to get away.

He reached down and took her chin in his free hand, gripping her. "Had enough?" The heat of her pussy against his thigh was insanely distracting, and he found himself pushing harder against her.

She trembled, light catching the golden satin of her bra beneath the black lace, making it glimmer in time with the rapid rise and fall of her breathing. Her gaze had gone smoky, focusing on his mouth. "No," she said thickly.

Little idiot. What was she doing? Didn't she know that this was all wrong? Everything about this? So fucking wrong.

In that case, perhaps you should stop.

No, it was too late for that now. She had to learn what pushing the boundaries of their relationship looked like and what he'd require from her. She wouldn't like it, that was for certain, and with any luck, she wouldn't like it enough that she'd never look at him the same way again.

His stomach dropped at the thought, but he refused to think about what that would mean to him. The most important thing was that she stay away from him, and he was going to have to teach her why.

He brushed his thumb along her lower lip and, Christ, it was so soft. He pressed down harder, feeling it give, and her gaze lifted to his, her lips parting. There were embers of heat glittering in her eyes and the fear he'd seen earlier that evening had gone. Brat. He needed to get more serious.

He pushed his thumb into her mouth.

A choked sound escaped her, but she didn't look away. Instead, she closed her lips around his thumb and began to suck, keeping her gaze on his as if he was a challenge she wanted to meet personally.

Holy Christ. The hot pressure of her mouth flipped a switch on inside him, a sharp, electric current coursing straight to his cock.

"Jesus, Zoe." The words escaped in a thick rush and he knew he should pull his hand away. But he didn't. And she didn't stop.

Her tongue licked his skin, then she sucked like she was sucking on a lollipop, tilting her hips and rocking against his thigh.

Clearly she wasn't scared of him in the slightest, and now his jeans were starting to feel way too tight and the feel of her tongue . . . Shit, no. Letting her lick him and rub herself against him like a cat wasn't why he was doing this.

He pulled his thumb away, gliding it over her full red mouth. "Stop," he ordered. "It wasn't my thumb Angel was sucking at Gino's."

"That's not what I saw."

"What? You didn't stick around to see the rest?" He stroked her lower lip again. "Did you get scared, little one?"

"As if." A spark glimmered in her eyes and she took a panting breath. "Show me. Show me what you did."

You shouldn't. This is wrong and you know it.

It was, and yet he couldn't seem to stop slicking his thumb across her mouth, feeling the softness, the cushiony give of her lower lip, watching the smoky look in her eyes.

She wasn't scared like she had been in her bedroom, when he'd told her all the things he'd do to her. She wasn't even shocked.

Obviously, he was going to have to take things up a notch.

Sure, tell yourself you're only doing it to scare her and not because the thought of her sucking your dick makes you so hard it hurts.

No, he couldn't feel that way about her, he couldn't. Yet all the denial in the world didn't change the fact that his dick *was* hard and the thought of putting her on her knees to suck him off made him even harder.

And that if he was any kind of hero to her, if he was any

kind of man, he'd be pulling away, walking straight out of this room, and never going near her again.

But he wasn't that kind of man. He never had been. If she wanted a hero, she was looking in the wrong place.

Gideon let go of her wrists and stepped back. "You wanna see? Then get on your knees."

Chapter 8

Zoe's heartbeat was like the bass line of some hard-core house music, loud and fast and insistent. And it felt like all the air in the room had been sucked out. She couldn't breathe, she almost couldn't stand.

Gideon stood in front of her, all six foot four of him, massive and muscled and putting out so much heat it was like standing next to a furnace. The horrible sympathy was gone from his face, the gentleness that had felt like it was cutting her in two completely vanished.

In its place was only hard intent, black and glittering and hungry.

She'd never been more turned on in her life.

Finally, it was happening. For whatever reason, he was finally seeing her as she'd wanted him to for so *fucking* long. As a woman.

Don't get too excited. This isn't about you.

Yeah, she knew that. He was trying to scare her the way he'd scared her back in her bedroom, only this time it wasn't only words he was using. And hell, maybe she should let herself be scared, save herself the hurt of knowing he wasn't in this for her. But she couldn't bring herself to do it.

She'd wanted him for too many years, and now that it looked like he was actually going to make good on all those fantasies she'd had, she didn't want him to stop. Sure, she *was* scared about it. Scared it wouldn't be like she'd imagined. Scared she'd screw it up. Scared that it would be too intense and she'd be left even hungrier than she was already.

But she wasn't scared enough to stop, not when she was aching as badly as she was now, a deep, relentless throb between her legs. Not with the taste of his skin heavy on her tongue and her mouth burning from where he'd touched it, the skin of her inner thighs sensitized from the denim of his jeans.

Her fingers were tingling, the blood rushing back into them, and she was acutely conscious of every inch of space that separated her body from his. She didn't want that space to be there, wanted to step forward and close it, press the soft, aching parts of her against the hard, hot parts of him.

"Well?" His voice was soft, but the look in his eyes wasn't. "Too much for you?"

It kind of was. She'd never blown a guy before, much less the guy who'd starred in all her fantasies since she was old enough to have them. The guy who'd only five minutes ago told her that there was never going to be anything between them.

So maybe you need to prove him wrong?

Yeah, she really did. And that was the reason she was still standing there, even though she was afraid. The reason she'd opened her mouth and licked his thumb. Why she was going to do exactly what he'd said. Because if this was the only chance she ever got to prove to him that there could be something between them, if only he'd let her show him, then she was going to take it.

He wanted to scare her off? He could certainly try. Sure, she might be a virgin, but she had more spine than to be scared off by the mention of a blow job.

Zoe decided not to answer. Instead, keeping her gaze on his, she did what he asked, sinking shakily to her knees in front of him.

An expression she couldn't quite interpret flickered across his face and then was gone. He was even more intimidating from this angle, towering over her, dark and strong and powerful. His eyes were black, full of hot shadows and more secrets than she could ever hope to unravel.

Her mouth was so dry with desire she didn't think she could speak even if she'd wanted to. A problem when she didn't know what to do now. Did he want her to open his jeans? Or did he want her just to kneel here and wait?

Oh God, she didn't know if she could handle this. She'd thought about this for so long . . . what if she screwed up? What if he didn't like it? What if he was only messing with her and didn't mean any of this?

Fear coiled like a snake in her gut and she had to fight the urge to get up and leave. Because she knew if she did, this would end. It would be over between them once and for all.

"Take my dick out." The words were hard, rough, yet they were the best thing she'd heard all evening. Now she wouldn't have to say anything. All she'd have to do was do as she was told.

She lifted her hands to the button of his jeans, her fingers trembling as she brushed the hard, incredibly hot plane of his abdomen, feeling it tense. She glanced up at him, fumbling with the button, wanting to see his face.

No softness on his rough-hewn features, no tenderness in his black eyes. Only a hard challenge, a dare. He didn't look away as her gaze met his, as she tried to undo his jeans, and he didn't help her either.

Yeah, he was expecting her to pull away. Expecting her to

get scared and run. Well, she wasn't going to be doing that. She was going to show him she could take anything he wanted to give her and more.

The thought settled her and her fingers firmed as she managed to get the button undone. Then she grabbed the tab of his zipper and slowly drew it down. And as she did so, she suddenly became acutely conscious of the fact that he was hard. Very, very hard.

The breath escaped her. This was her doing, wasn't it? Or was it just because she was a woman kneeling in front of him and there was a blow job going to be happening soon?

What the hell does it matter whether it's you or not? You've been wanting this forever. So take it.

She swallowed past the tightness in her throat. Yeah, it didn't matter. What mattered was that now, finally, she was going to get the chance to show him a few things of her own. And hey, the fact that he had a hard-on was already a point in her favor. Meant he saw her as a woman, right?

Carefully Zoe spread open the denim of his jeans. He wore black boxers underneath, the cotton straining to contain his hard cock, and she couldn't resist the need to touch him, trace him through the cotton.

"Stop." The order was low and absolute.

Her hand fell away almost before she'd realized she'd obeyed him.

"No touching. Just do what I told you to do."

A tremor shook her as she slid her hand down inside his boxers, her fingers grazing hot, smooth skin before closing around his dick. He tensed, but said nothing, letting her draw him out.

Her heartbeat was so loud now, she couldn't hear anything else. Here he was, finally in her hand, long and thick, much bigger than she'd thought and she'd given it a lot of thought. Smoother than she'd imagined too, his skin unexpectedly soft.

The scent of him was going straight to her head, engine oil and smoke, and male musk. Everything that spoke of familiarity and safety. Except there was nothing familiar or safe about this, and somehow that made it even more exciting. Even more erotic.

Her fingers tightened around him. She was uncovering all these secrets about him, all these things she never knew, such as what he looked like when he was aroused. What he smelled like. What he tasted like. What he would look like when he came. . . .

She glanced up at him, helplessly drawn, looking into those hard black eyes. Anger glittered there now, a kind of furious hunger that made her chest ache. God, if he was so pissed about this, why didn't he just walk away? Why was he standing there letting her hold his dick?

Her mouth opened to tell him exactly that.

"Did I say you could talk?" he growled roughly. "No, I fucking didn't. If you wanna be that waitress you'd better shut up and open your mouth."

He'd never spoken to her like that before, never with that harsh, demanding edge, and it shocked her. Thrilled her. Made her understand that he wasn't seeing her as a little girl to be protected any longer. That he was seeing her as a woman he wanted to fuck.

The thrill spread out, electric, intense, nervousness and excitement rolling over and over inside her.

She shut up and opened her mouth.

The lines of his face were shadowed, his jaw tight. His eyes deep, velvet darkness. He reached down and with a calm deliberation that had her shaking like a leaf, he drew off her glasses, folding them up and putting them in his back pocket. "Last chance, Zoe." The growl in his voice made her breath catch. "Last chance to stop this."

It's going to change everything if you do this. And it won't ever go back to the way it was before.

Good. She didn't want it to. After all, what's the worst that could happen? He could send her away, or leave himself, and that would suck so hard. But even that would be better than what she had now. Even that would mean she'd be able to move on.

So she said nothing, remained on her knees, kept her mouth open. Giving him his answer without words.

His jaw tightened imperceptibly as if that wasn't the answer he wanted, but he didn't pull away. Instead, he lifted his hands and shoved his fingers deep into her hair, twisting hard, making her gasp.

Then he pushed his cock into her mouth.

She'd often fantasized about this, often thought about it, and she'd thought she was ready for the reality of him. But this was . . . God, she didn't have any words to describe it, not the sheer intensity of the sensation. He was in her mouth, hot and heavy, stretching her lips wide, the salty flavor of him unfamiliar yet not in any way unpleasant.

It was exciting, strange, scary, and thrilling all at the same time. And it was weird how even though the only place he was touching her was her head, she'd never felt so turned on in her life. The throb of her sex was persistent, making her want to slide her hand down to give herself some relief, but she didn't. It wasn't her own hand she wanted.

"Eyes up here." His voice was guttural, and she obeyed, blinking up at him. Without her glasses his face was slightly blurry, but there was no mistaking the burning darkness that were his eyes. "Tell me to stop."

Stupid man. How could she tell him anything when her mouth was full? Not that she was going to tell him that anyway since there was no way she wanted this to stop. No way in hell.

Keeping her gaze on his so he was very clear as to her thoughts on the subject, she shook her head.

He made another guttural sound, and then his fingers tightened on her hair, his hips flexing, pushing his cock in farther, then drawing it slowly back out.

Zoe groaned, the soft sound wrung out of her, and she found she was clutching onto his hard, muscular thighs to brace herself.

He pushed into her mouth again, deeper, and she ran her tongue along the hard length of him, sucking hard. Showing him that she was into this. That she wanted it.

"Tell me to stop, Zoe." The words were rough as gravel, something unsteady in them, something frayed, like he was unraveling at the seams.

She blinked hard, trying to focus on his face, but his features remained stubbornly blurry. Dammit. She wanted to see what she did to him, wanted to see how badly she unraveled him, because it had to be her, hadn't it?

"Zoe . . ." He drew his hips back, pushed them slowly back in. "Little one . . . tell me to stop."

But she shook her head, increasing the suction, her tongue swirling around him, tracing the smooth head and the slit at the top, the salty flavor of him flooding her mouth.

And this time he was the one who groaned, the sound rolling down her spine in a sensuous lick, making her tremble. Yes, God, she loved this. Loved that she was doing this to him. That she was giving him this pleasure and that he was letting her do it.

She wasn't a kid anymore. She wasn't his little foster sister.

She was a woman and she was going to give him the best fucking blow job of his life.

He didn't say it again after that, as if he'd accepted her choice and that thrilled her too. That he respected it and wasn't going to pull away. But he'd clearly also decided that she needed to learn a lesson about that choice, because his fingers tightened even more and he was holding her head very still as his hips began to move faster and faster, fucking her mouth.

Zoe clung on to his thighs, digging her fingers into the rock-hard muscle beneath the denim, letting him take whatever he wanted from her. Reveling in the taste and feel of him in her mouth, listening to his breathing become ragged.

"Good girl," he murmured low and rough. "That's it. Open wider . . . suck me harder . . . fuck, yeah . . ."

She did everything he told her, shaking as he moved harder, faster. As the sounds of his breathing became harsher and the flex of his hips slid out of rhythm.

He was pushing himself hard down the back of her throat and her jaw ached and there were tears in her eyes, but she didn't want him to stop. She didn't want him ever to stop.

She kept her blurred vision on his face, trying to catch the moment when he came undone, her scalp hurting where he was pulling her hair, because he wasn't being gentle and he wasn't being soft. But it was okay, she liked it. She wanted it.

His fingers in her hair twisted hard all of a sudden. "Zoe . . . oh fuck . . . *fuck* . . ."

Then he was thrusting into her mouth, wild and out of control, and the thrill of it was lightning across her skin, knowing she was the one who'd turned him inside out like this.

He groaned when he came, a wordless sound of desperation, and she swallowed him down without hesitation, her own heartbeat loud in her head and her thighs trembling, the ache between them almost impossible to ignore.

He didn't speak as he withdrew from her mouth and eased the painful pressure of his fingers in her hair, and she leaned forward, resting her forehead against the hot skin and hard plane of his abdomen. She wanted a minute to savor this, the thick, salty taste of him in her mouth, the ache in her jaw, the scent of musk and Gideon completely overwhelming all her senses. Because who knew what was going to happen after this?

Things are going to change.

And even though that had been what she'd wanted all along, Zoe felt afraid.

Gideon couldn't believe what he'd done. Couldn't believe he'd actually put Zoe on her knees and then put his cock in her mouth.

His head was ringing, the aftereffects of the orgasm that had practically broken him into pieces moving like tiny electric shocks through his system, and he had the terrible sense that he'd fucked up. Not just in a small way, but in a life-altering way.

He looked down just to make sure of the gravity of the sin he'd committed and sure enough, Zoe was on her knees at his feet. He couldn't see her face, the rough black silk of her hair obscuring it, but he could feel the slight pressure of her resting against his stomach.

Jesus Christ. He'd meant to scare her, show her exactly what she was letting herself in for, force her into pulling away from him and hopefully never coming near him ever again.

Instead, she'd done everything he'd told her to. She'd gotten down on her knees, opened her mouth, and sucked his cock like a dream. Taken everything he'd thrown at her, and he hadn't been gentle and he hadn't gone slow.

And it had been . . . the best fucking blow job he'd ever had.

Holy shit, he was going to hell.

Beneath the shock and the pulsing echoes of his orgasm, he could feel anger starting to turn over heavily in his gut. An anger directed mainly at himself and his lack of control, though he was pissed at her too. For being so determined and stubborn. For wanting to show him whatever the fuck she'd been determined to show him.

"Zoe," he ordered, his voice not quite as hard as it should be. "Look at me."

Slowly she lifted her head and looked up at him, and something in his chest lurched. Her skin was flushed, her eyes glazed, and shit, were those tear tracks glistening on her cheeks?

He went cold. He'd held on to her head extremely tightly, no doubt pulling her hair in the process. Which would have hurt. And toward the end he'd thrust hard in that lovely, lush red mouth of hers. Had that hurt her too?

You fucking asshole.

"Are you okay?" he demanded, suddenly furious with himself. "Did I—"

"No, you didn't hurt me," she interrupted. "And FYI, if you apologize I'm leaving and I'm never coming back."

The ice in his gut began to thaw. Okay, so maybe he hadn't hurt her, but he'd certainly fucking crossed a line all the same. One that he'd never in a million years ever thought he'd cross.

But that wasn't even the worst part of it. What was worse was the fact that even now, as she was kneeling at his feet, looking up at him, his attention kept fixating on her mouth, on the heat of it, on how those soft, velvety lips of hers had felt wrapped around his cock. And he could feel himself getting hard again.

Abruptly he stepped away from her, turning to shove his dick back into his jeans, infuriated that as he did so, his hands were shaking like an old man's. Like a goddamn teenage boy's.

Shit, this was wrong. So *fucking* wrong. What the hell had she done to him? What the hell was the matter with him?

No mystery. You needed an orgasm so she gave you one.

No, Jesus, that wasn't the way it was supposed to go. If those guys back in Anonymous hadn't been Novak's, he could have accepted Tori's invitation. Tori could have given him the blow job and then he wouldn't be so eaten up with fucking guilt.

But you don't want a blow job from Tori. You wanted one from Zoe.

Gideon shoved the thought away, not wanting it in his head. He couldn't be thinking shit like that, he really couldn't. Zoe was . . . Zoe was . . .

Hot. Sexy. Fuckable.

"Gideon."

He didn't want to turn around, didn't want to look at her or her beautiful mouth again. Because he didn't know what he'd do if he did. He'd wanted to give her some reality and he had. Except it was supposed to be her who was running from it, not himself.

Coward.

The voice in his head was snide, but he ignored it, moving toward the door of the living room without turning around.

"Gideon?" There was a note in her voice he didn't want to hear. "Where are you going?" It sounded like bewilderment or confusion. Hurt.

"Out," he answered shortly, ignoring too the tight sensation in his chest.

"No." Definitely hurt this time. "Don't you dare walk out on me. Not after that."

But she didn't understand. He had to get out, had to put some distance between them or else he'd . . .

Push her down onto the couch, pull up her skirt, push your cock deep inside her, fuck her till she screams.

Anger and lust twisted inside him, creating a heavy, flammable mix. All it would take was one spark and he'd go up, and he didn't want to be anywhere near her when that happened.

"Gideon, for fuck's sake!"

He didn't turn, but at the doorway he paused. "If you leave this apartment, I'm gonna lock you in your bedroom for the next week straight. Understand?"

Without waiting for a response, he walked straight out, heading toward the front door of the apartment.

You prick.

Yeah, he was, and maybe this was what he should have been doing all along. Ignoring her completely. That would show her exactly what kind of man he was if nothing else would. That would drive her away. Because after all, she'd always hated it when he ignored her.

Gideon pulled open the front door and slammed it hard behind him, then went downstairs, taking the steps two at a time. He'd had some half thought of going to Gino's, sinking as many bourbons as he could get his hands on, but at the last minute, he veered to the left, making for the door to the garage instead.

Machines, that's what he liked. What he'd always liked. The quiet of the garage where he could sit and fiddle around with an engine for hours on end. Putting bits together or taking them apart, making them fit, making them go. When he'd been a kid, his mother had had an old Ford that he'd used to tinker with. The days where she'd be inside "resting"—aka recovering from one of his father's drunken beatings—he'd go outside, pop the hood, and ignore the feelings of helplessness, of despair that he couldn't protect her. Of loneliness. Leave them all behind him as he focused entirely on the engine. The car didn't even need fixing, it was he who needed fixing. Or maybe even just an escape.

It had been over ten years ago when he'd gotten that last job and finally left the criminal underworld. When he'd taken Zoe and gotten out of Chicago, covering their tracks as best he could. He'd had some money, enough to buy himself a business, and it had seemed natural to get a garage, turn the escape engines had always given him into a reality. Especially when it was going to be permanent.

So he'd headed to Detroit, Motor City itself, and found a shitty neighborhood where no one asked questions and no one looked twice at anyone new. And after a few years, he'd thought he'd done it. That they'd actually gotten away.

But of course, his luck would never hold that long.

Gideon stepped into the garage itself, the familiar smell of engine oil and grease calming something inside him. On the far side of the garage, up on a stand, was the bike he'd been working on. A vintage Harley. Although he loved cars, motorcycles had been his first passion, and he indulged himself whenever he could.

He'd been hoping to restore this one and maybe keep it for himself. Or sell it. Or maybe he'd just keep it to tinker with forever.

Making his way over to the Harley, he stood beside it and folded his arms, trying to hold on to that calm, to settle down into it the way he always did when he was in the garage. Christ, Zee and Levi would laugh themselves sick if they knew what his goddamn emotions were doing right now.

Then they'd fucking kill you for what you did to Zoe.

He let out a breath, trying not to think about that. Reaching out, he ran a hand along the glossy black paintwork of the gas tank. The metal was smooth and cool against his skin.

Not like Zoe. She felt smooth but hot. So very hot . . .

Gideon muttered a curse. Fuck no, he couldn't be thinking about her. He was here to get his head back in the right space, to calm the fuck down. To focus on what was important and that was her safety. That's all that had ever been important to him. She'd been the reason he'd left his past behind him, the reason he was here in Royal going straight, trying to be a good man. And so far, because of her, he'd succeeded. She'd kept him on the right path, and if anything happened to her . . .

Darkness stirred inside him, like a deep sea. Heavy, dense.

Vast. He forced it back down. His darker urges had stayed asleep for years now, and that's how they were going to stay. He wasn't going back to the way he'd been before, a violent thug for whom money was the be-all and end-all, working out his anger at the world by loving his job as an enforcer just a little too much. No, he couldn't afford to go down that path, not again.

What he had to concentrate on was the fact that Zoe was safe at the moment and that's how she was going to stay. He also needed to figure out some kind of plan to deal with Oliver fucking Novak and the threat the bastard presented.

Making a mental note to collect as much intel from his sources as he could on Novak's movements, Gideon stared at the bike another minute. Then he turned and went over to the workshop counter where the bike's exhaust was sitting, all ready to be fitted.

But before he could pick it up, the garage door suddenly banged open and his whole body tensed, a streak of electricity bolting right through him.

Because there was only one person who would have followed him here.

He found he was gripping onto the edge of the workshop counter, his knuckles white, his earlier calm slipping away like oil through a cracked engine casing. "What did I fucking say?" He didn't bother to temper the harsh edge in his tone, nor did he turn around. "I said stay in the apartment or else I'm gonna lock you in there for a whole fucking week."

There was a silence, then the sound of her boots scuffing on the concrete of the garage floor.

He tensed even more because the scent of her was wrapping around him, lavender with a hint of delicious feminine musk, and even though he'd just had one of the best blow jobs of his life, his dick was getting hard again.

"How dare you," Zoe said, her voice unsteady and thick with fury. "How dare you walk out on me like that! How dare you leave me on my knees in the middle of the fucking living room like . . . like you don't even care!"

Oh shit. She wasn't just angry, was she? She was hurt.

Yeah, well, no wonder. She got you off, then you walked away.

He'd had to, though. Didn't she understand that? Didn't she understand how wrong this was?

Gideon turned around.

She was standing not far from him, her hands in fists at her sides, black hair tangled over her shoulders. Golden sparks of rage glittered in her amber eyes, and her delicate features were flushed. And, stupid fuck that he was, his attention drifted immediately to her luscious mouth, tracing the contours of it before going lower, to the quick rise and fall of her chest. To where the gold bra gleamed beneath all that black lace.

Another realization hit him like the blow from an ax, shuddering through him. She was beautiful. A wild, passionate vivid creature, with her small, feline face and her long, slender limbs. Sensual, too, though he'd never really understood how much until now.

God, how had he not seen this? How had he not understood?

Because you've never wanted to see it.

Yeah, maybe he hadn't. Turned out with good reason.

"Why the hell do you think I walked away?" He kept his voice flat, hard. "I walked away *because* I care, Zoe."

"How is leaving me like that caring about me?"

"Leaving you like what?"

The flush coloring her brown skin deepened. "Imagine me getting up in the middle of that blow job and walking away. That should give you a pretty clear idea."

Another strange electric shock jolted through him.

He'd been so caught up in how wrong it all had been, how bad it was to have her on her knees sucking him off, that he hadn't bothered to think about her feelings on the subject. She'd certainly wanted to do it, that had been clear, but he hadn't thought it might go further than that. He hadn't thought she'd actually get off on it.

You fucking idiot. You knew she's wanted you for years. And you took what you wanted from her without returning the favor.

"You don't understand," he said both to her and the voice in his head. "I *had* to walk away. That shouldn't have happened. I shouldn't have done it to you."

A bright flash of hurt crossed her face, and he wished she wasn't so fucking open all the time. Wished she kept something back. Because he hated seeing that look in her eyes and knowing he was the cause. "Did I tell you to stop? Did I tell you I didn't want it? No, I damn well didn't!"

"You should have," he snapped, his own latent anger rising to the surface again. "I told you to."

"Why should I? I wanted it, Gideon. Surely you knew that?"

Of course he knew. "Yeah, but that doesn't make it right."

She blinked at him. "Right? What the hell do you mean by that?"

"I told you, Zoe. Nothing should have happened between us. It's wrong on so many levels I can't even begin to count them all." He folded his arms tight across his chest, forcing himself to hold her gaze and not drift down the slender length of her body. "You're young. You're innocent. You're my fucking foster sister. That's just three. Want me to go on?"

Her mouth flattened. "I don't care that you were once my foster brother. We were only foster siblings for a year anyway. And as for the young and innocent bullshit, well, that's all it is. Bullshit."

"It might be bullshit to you, but it isn't to me." He found

he'd taken a step toward her and he hadn't meant to. "This is wrong. What *I* did was wrong."

"Oh, right, so what I'm feeling for you is wrong too?" Her throat moved in a convulsive swallow. "Is that what you're trying to say?"

"No, that's not what—"

"So you're completely happy with getting a blow job from me, but you don't want to touch me in return?" This time it was she who took another step forward, the pain in her eyes like a knife in his side. "Why not? Do I disgust you? I know I'm not anything like the women you usually go for, but I don't think I'm that ugly."

The knife twisted. Jesus, she couldn't think that, could she?

"It's got nothing to do with whether I find you attractive or not. It's just . . . I've known you since you were six years old. And yeah, okay, I admit, I'm guilty of thinking you're still that little girl." He held her gaze, willing her to understand. "Which makes anything that happens between us pretty fucking wrong in my book."

Her jaw tightened. "What we did up there in the living room didn't feel wrong to me. Wanting you doesn't feel wrong."

"Yeah? Well, it does to me." He knew he was being harsh, knew he was hurting her, but what else could he say? He had to get her out of here and fast.

Abruptly Zoe closed the distance between them, stomping right up to him until she was standing bare inches away, and he had to take a breath. Had to brace himself against that luscious, delicious scent. Against the seductive heat of her body. Against the memory of her beautiful mouth wrapped around his cock.

"If it felt so wrong," she said in a husky, shaky voice, "then why the hell were you so hard? Why the hell did you get me to suck you off?"

Something inside him clenched tight and he had to dig his

fingers into his arms to stop himself from reaching for her, pulling her even closer.

"Because I'm not a good person." His own voice was getting rough. "Because pushing me is a really stupid fucking idea."

She didn't move, didn't look away. "I don't care what kind of person you are. Jesus, Gideon. We crossed a line back there and there's no going back over it. So what's the point being all weird about it now?" There were shadows under her eyes, so damn obvious in the harsh fluorescents of the garage. "You can't . . . give me that and then not touch me. You can't. It's not fair."

The tightness in his chest refused to go away, frustrated anger eating a hole in his gut. Christ, he had to get a handle on these goddamn feelings. He had to get a handle on himself, keep everything under control. Because he couldn't lose it like he'd lost it upstairs. No matter how much she'd wanted it, no matter how badly she wanted something in return, he couldn't give in.

"You can't want me, little one," he said, trying to keep his voice steady. "You can't. I'm not the right man for you. Don't you see? I'm trying to protect both of us."

She looked away, biting her lip and blinking furiously as if to hold back tears.

Holding out is all very noble, but is it worth hurting her?

Oh sure, like that was a good justification. He couldn't take any notice of shit like that because all they were, were excuses. Excuses to put his hands on her, bury his cock in her. Take her like she was his.

But she is yours. She has been all along.

No, that wasn't right. He'd stopped being possessive, stopped all of that crap the moment he'd left Chicago. Sure, he defended his territory and he made sure those he cared about were safe, but he wasn't as territorial as the bosses back home.

He didn't take what he deemed his as if it were his God-given right.

That would have made him no better than his prick of a father.

Zoe wasn't his. And she only wanted him because he was the only man she'd ever had any real contact with. Which made her crush on him understandable in so many ways and yet another reason why he had to stay away from her.

"You should go to bed," he said flatly. "This conversation is over."

She glanced at him and for a second the pain in her eyes was bright and sharp. Then abruptly she reached for his hand and pulled it, making him uncross his arms. "What are you—"

But before he could finish, she brought his hand down and underneath the little leather skirt she was wearing, pushing it between her thighs so the heat of her pussy was right there, burning against his palm.

He went utterly still.

She was so wet, soaking almost, and trembling, her breathing fast and the pulse at the base of her throat racing. Her eyes had darkened from bright gold into a dark, deep amber, and she was looking at him like she was drowning and he was her last chance of rescue. "Please, Gideon." Her voice was a thread of sound. "Just once. Please. And I will n-never ask anything of you ever again."

He shouldn't do this. He should pull his hand away from her, tell her no, that she should go to bed. That she had her own hand if she was that desperate.

But he couldn't seem to do it. The danger to her at the club with Novak's men being so close made him want to keep a tight grip on her, keep her close, and the thing that had pushed him into the situation upstairs had him by the throat again, a deep, hungry kind of possessiveness he didn't want. The thing that whispered to him that she *was* his, no matter what he told himself. That she was right, they'd crossed the line already and there was no going back. That she was a virgin and taking her now would make her his forever, no matter what else happened. . . .

The tightness in his chest relaxed all of a sudden, as if a key had turned inside him, unlocking him.

There was no fighting this. No fighting her. She was so determined, so stubborn. She wanted to keep pushing him? Well then, she was going to need consequences. And not just one spanking and a rough blow job. That was only a small taste of the darkness inside him, a tiny glimpse of the man he was inside.

She needed to see him as he was. As he *really* was.

He stared into her eyes, saw her desperation, her hope and her fear. And he spread his fingers out slowly, curling them so they pressed into the wet fabric of her panties, making her gasp. "No, little one. Not just once. You wanna give yourself to me, then you have to understand something. I'll take everything. Every single fucking thing. Your heart. Your mind. Your body. Your entire fucking soul." He pressed his fingers harder against her pussy, sliding his middle finger a little higher so it brushed over her clit, tearing another gasp from her. "So you better be sure, Zoe. You better be real fucking sure you know what you're asking for."

Chapter 9

Zoe couldn't stop shaking. The pressure of his fingers against her sex felt agonizing, the fierce look in his eyes almost burning her to the ground.

Stupid to have taken his hand like that and put it between her thighs, but she'd been beside herself with rage. At the way he'd left her on her knees in the middle of the living room. Turning and walking away from her as if she'd meant nothing. As if now he'd taken what he wanted from her, she didn't matter anymore.

It wasn't happening; just wasn't.

So once she'd gotten herself together she'd charged downstairs to confront him and at least let him know how pissed she was at him. She hadn't really thought anything through. She was just mad and turned on, and she wanted him to touch her so badly she couldn't think straight.

She didn't know why he kept rejecting her, not when it was clear he wanted her. After all, why had he put his dick in her mouth upstairs? Why had he looked at her like he wanted to eat her alive?

You're selfish to keep pushing him.

Yeah, maybe she was. But he kept giving her mixed messages and it hurt. It just damn well hurt. He should have let her walk away upstairs. He should have let her go to bed, yet he hadn't. He'd put himself in her way and demanded they talk about it.

It wasn't fair.

You're not being fair either.

No, but too bad. She'd crossed the line now and they both knew it.

"Well?" he demanded, curling his fingers a fraction more.

Her heartbeat thundered in her head, so loud it was a wonder she heard anything of what he'd said.

"Your heart. Your mind. Your body. Your entire fucking soul . . ."

He was trying to scare her again, no doubt about it. But surely he must know by now that saying all that wouldn't. Not when he had all of those things already.

"I k-know," she stammered. "Believe me, I know. And I want you to take it. I want you to take everything."

He'd begun to move forward, forcing her back, his hand firmly where she'd put it, his eyes glittering strangely in the harsh garage light.

"No, I don't think you have any idea what you're talking about," he said, low and harsh. "But that's okay. Soon you will."

A small twist of foreboding clenched in her gut.

Do you really understand what you're getting yourself into here? There's so much you don't know about him.

Well, yeah, there *was* a lot she didn't know about him. But that didn't change the fact that she did know *him*. He was protective and strong and understanding. So what if he was possessive? She *liked* him possessive, especially if she was his lover. Anyway, he wouldn't hurt her. He wouldn't do anything she didn't want.

She swallowed, her breathing getting faster and faster. She

wanted to push herself against his hand, make him move his fingers on her. God, just *touch* her, ease the ache somehow. But he kept on walking her backward until cold metal pressed against the backs of her legs.

"Gideon?" Her voice had gone all husky and weird. "W-what are you doing?"

He didn't say anything, taking his hand away from between her thighs, then grabbing her by the hips. She gasped as he lifted her, reflexively holding onto his forearms as he deposited her on the hood of the Chevy he'd been working on. She could feel the muscles flex beneath his skin, hard and strong, lifting her like she weighed nothing. So hot. His strength had always been such a damn turn-on for her.

He let her go, putting his hands flat on the hood on either side of her, leaning on his palms, staring straight into her eyes. The force of his gaze hit her like a wrecking ball smashing through an abandoned building, and she could feel herself caving in, collapsing under the weight of it, breaking apart, crumbling.

He didn't speak and for long moments all she could hear was the sound of her own rapid breathing and the scream of the tension in the air pulling tighter and tighter. His black eyes were inches from hers, the ferocity in them unrelenting, and that dark, musky male scent of his was making her feel dizzy. She had to force herself to stay still, to not wriggle against the cool metal of the car's hood, relieve the stinging heat between her legs.

"You're gonna do exactly what I say," he said after what seemed forever, the fraying edges of his voice whispering over her skin. "No questions, no hesitations. Understand?"

She gave a shaky nod, her throat too tight to speak.

"Lean back on your hands."

Well, that was easy enough. She put her palms on the hood and did as he'd asked, leaning back on them. It put space between them and for some reason that felt more threatening than being close to him.

Threatening, hmmm? You feeling threatened now?

Maybe. But it wasn't a bad feeling, though. It was . . . exciting. Like she was leaving the safety of a familiar haven and taking a step into a much larger, more dangerous world. And that, of course, was bound to feel a bit scary.

Gideon tilted his head, his gaze dropping down her body, slow and leisurely. As if he had all the time in the world to look at her, examine her in detail. It made her pulse race even faster till it was resounding in her ears like hail on an iron roof.

Then he leaned forward, put his hands on her thighs, and slowly slid the hem of her skirt up to her waist. She shivered at the heat of his palms on her skin, sending goose bumps everywhere, at the brush of the leather and then the cool smoothness of the metal under her butt. At the feeling of exposure. Then his hands slid back down to her knees and with casual strength, he pushed them apart.

A soft sound escaped her and she had to fight the instinctive urge to close them again, not that she could have anyway since he was holding them open. And looking. God, he was looking right down there, between her legs.

The shivers increased, the sound of her frantic breathing embarrassingly loud. But she couldn't seem to get it under control. Couldn't get herself under control either. The expression on his face was mesmerizing. She'd never seen it before, at least not directed at her. Ferocious, hungry. Intense. As if she was his sole focus. Oh, he'd looked at her with such attention before, but never like he was a wolf and she was prey.

God, she fucking *loved* it. And she loved, too, that she finally got to see this side of him. It was like he'd given her one of his secrets to keep.

"Keep your legs apart," he ordered, his gaze on her sex. "And don't fucking move them."

He reached between her thighs then and casually pulled aside the crotch of her panties, his fingers brushing her pussy, and another gasp escaped from her, because, holy shit, the sensation was as sharp as an electric shock.

Then with a kind of calm deliberation, he slid two fingers through her slick folds, gliding them through her wet flesh before stopping them on either side of her throbbing clit. She couldn't stop the tremble that shook her entire body or the low moan that escaped her dry throat, a shock of pleasure piercing her.

She wanted to lift her hips, get him to move his hand, get his fingers to rub her, stroke her, anything but sit so close to where she needed to be touched and yet not quite there.

"G-Gideon . . ." His name came out all raw and desperate. "Please . . ."

He ignored her, his gaze down between her thighs, the intensity of his focus making her even hotter. "So wet," he murmured, his fingers moving in a long, slow glide that once again avoided her clit, only squeezing gently on either side of it. "All of this for me?"

He was touching her. Finally, he was touching her right where she'd wanted him to touch her, where she'd fantasized about for so long. And she was so close to coming already the pleasure felt like pain. Yet it wasn't enough, it still wasn't enough. He was making her wait, the bastard.

"Y-y-yes," she stammered, hardly able to speak. "F-for you."

He stroked her again, his fingers sliding easily through her wet flesh, and she couldn't resist the urge to rock her hips, desperate for more pressure, for more touch. But then his hand stopped, and she nearly whimpered with disappointment.

"Did I stay you could move, little one?"

She heaved in a panting breath. "N-no."

"No," he agreed. "I didn't. So keep still." Then he gently pinched her clit as if delivering a warning.

Lightning flashed along each and every nerve ending, and she cried out at the sensation, so intense she couldn't work out whether it was pleasure or pain.

"Good girl." There was a darkness in the words, and a heat that made her tremble even more, like a tree being battered by a hurricane. "You're such a good girl for me." His fingers slid up and down, squeezing her clit, deepening the sensation, and she had to bite her lip hard to do as she was told, to keep still. Because she wanted to show him she could do it. Because even now, even here, like this, his praise made her feel like she was ten feet tall and bulletproof.

He lifted his gaze from between her thighs and stared right at her, looking into her eyes as if he were seeing right inside her. As if he knew exactly what she was thinking, exactly how crazy the touch of his finger was making her.

"Don't think you're getting a reward just yet," he said quietly. "You pushed for this, Zoe, you pushed hard and that means I get to push you hard too." The blackness of his eyes was like midnight. "You're not gonna come until I tell you to. And if you do . . ." He paused. "Well, let's just say I'm gonna be very disappointed."

That strange foreboding twisted tighter. She didn't know how she felt about that, because she'd always hated disappointing him and he knew it.

Of course he knows it. Why do you think he said it?

Bastard. It meant there was only one answer she could give him. "I . . . w-won't, I promise," she said, the words escaping in a breathless rush.

"I wouldn't make promises you can't keep." His stroking fingers stopped. "Especially when I'm in charge." He gave her no warning, pushing one finger inside her, then another, sliding them in deep, keeping his gaze on her as he did so.

Raw pleasure exploded through her, brilliant as summer

lightning, and she cried out, unable to stop the helpless lift of her hips.

The look in his eyes flared. "What did I tell you?"

Her whole body was quaking, her hands pressing down hard onto the metal of the car.

He eased his fingers apart, stretching her, the pleasure burning. "I told you not to move."

"I-I'm s-s-sorry. I didn't m-mean to." Her voice was so hoarse it didn't sound like her own. "I won't d-do it . . . again . . ."

Slowly Gideon drew his fingers out of her and pushed back in, watching her with that intent, absolute focus. "You wanted this, Zoe." The words were soft and rough, full of dark sensuality. "But I don't think you can take it. I don't think you're strong enough." Another thrust of his fingers, forcing her higher, stretching her wider.

She felt like she was slowly coming apart at the seams. "I c-can. I can do it . . . oh God . . . G-Gideon . . ." Her knees were shaking, her thighs quivering. Like a rubber band being pulled slowly yet inexorably back, the tension building inside her higher and higher. She was going to snap. She was going to break.

He leaned forward, one hand beside her thigh, the other between her legs, his fingers buried deep in her pussy. Then, his gaze like black fire, swallowing her whole, he twisted them, curling them up inside her as he pressed his thumb down on her aching clit.

The orgasm burst through her, overwhelming her resistance like a force of nature, unstoppable, inexorable. Her head fell back and she shut her eyes tight, unable to keep the shuddering cry of release inside, disappointment mixing with the explosion of pleasure, because she hadn't managed to last the distance. Hadn't managed to show him that she *was* strong enough for this, for him.

She collapsed back on the hood of the car, flinging an arm across her face, not caring that her knees were spread wide and that he could see everything. Too late for that anyway.

The back of her forearm felt wet and she realized there were tears in her eyes.

Oh great. Why the hell was she crying? And why should she feel so disappointed when she'd just had the most intense orgasm of her life? Yeah, it had been amazing, and sure, he'd given her an order and she'd wanted to obey it, but really, did she have to feel *quite* that disappointed?

It was just sex, wasn't it?

Gideon's hand had fallen away from her, the garage suddenly silent apart from her short, hiccupping breaths.

She didn't want to look at him. Didn't want to see the expression on his face for some reason, and she certainly didn't want him to see the tears that were on hers.

"You didn't do what I told you," he said, rough and husky. "That means you don't get your reward."

She swallowed, her throat tight and aching. "But I t-tried." The words sounded thick and muffled behind her forearm. "You weren't being fair."

Powerful fingers closed around her wrist, her arm dragged away from her face. He was bending over her, looking down into her eyes, his expression unyielding. "I told you I'd be hard on you. I warned you. There's a reason I didn't want you pushing me, Zoe." There was no mercy in his black eyes, only a flame that seared her inside and out. "Nothing about me is gonna be fair. I'm telling you that right now."

"So what does that mean?" she asked shakily.

"You came when I told you not to. That means a punishment."

"Gideon—"

But he didn't wait for her to finish, his hands on her hips, flipping her over so she was facedown on the hood of the car, her feet barely touching the ground.

She sucked in a startled breath, staring down at the glossy black paintwork of the Chevy, every sense she had focused on the man behind her. On his hands as they shoved her skirt up to her waist. On the snap and release of the lacy fabric of her panties as he ripped them up the side. On the intense heat of his palms as he squeezed her ass, his fingers digging into her soft flesh.

She whimpered, unable to help herself, shutting her eyes as the shakes took hold again, her hands flat on the metal beneath her. He squeezed her hard, sending a hot sting of pleasure/pain arcing through her. The aftershocks of her first orgasm were setting off little earthquakes inside her, and when he slid his hands down the backs of her thighs and curled his fingers inward, brushing the folds of her pussy, the sensation made her gasp. Too much. It was too much.

"Gideon, please . . ."

But he ignored her, his fingers pushing between her thighs, stroking her sex again, then sliding in, tearing a groan from her. There was heat up against her, the hard length of his body pressed to the backs of her thighs, to her spine, the weight of his body pushing at her as one large, masculine hand came down on the hood of the car next to hers. "I told you you'd better be sure." His voice was right near her ear, his breath warm against the side of her neck. "I told you I was gonna take everything. That I wouldn't be fair. That I'd push you. You gonna back out on me now?"

The movement of his hand between her thighs was relentless, his fingers sliding in and out, fucking her in a hard, sure rhythm, making her knees tremble. And that foreboding was a twist of cold in her gut. Already this wasn't anything like what she'd fantasized about. Her fantasies of him had all been pretty tame, the basic in-a-bed, missionary-position stuff, with a blow job thrown in for good measure. There hadn't been any orders and a car certainly hadn't been involved.

You imagined him the way you thought he would be. Not how he actually is.

"N-no," she said hoarsely, feeling something inside her drop away. But of course she'd imagined it *that* way because . . . well, she knew him. Didn't she?

The hand next to hers moved, and suddenly she was being pushed facedown onto the metal hood as he gripped the back of her neck. "This time," he said in a low, rough voice. "Don't fucking move."

She shivered, the foreboding turning over and over, joining with the pleasure to create a hot, raw, desperate feeling that scared her. A deep, primal fear that had her mouth going dry and another whimper building in her throat.

Run. Get out now. Save yourself.

Yet she didn't move. Because he'd told her not to and so she wouldn't. Because that was the whole reason he was doing this, to scare her away, and she wasn't damn well going to be scared.

But telling herself that did nothing to quell the fear or the intense, aching pleasure, the two so intermixed she didn't know which was which.

She was almost near to climax again by the time his fingers slid out of her, quivering and gasping, her breath fogging the paint beneath her. All she could do was stand there with her cheek pressed to the metal, trying to keep herself upright, trying desperately not to move.

There came the sound of a zipper being undone and the crinkle of foil. She couldn't stop shaking. Oh Jesus, this was actually going to happen. Gideon was going to take her virginity on the hood of a car, in his goddamn garage.

Again, it wasn't like anything she'd dreamed, but she wasn't going to complain. At least it was actually happening.

She took a harsh, ragged breath as his hand touched her hip and gripped her tight, the blunt head of his cock pushing against the entrance to her body.

No, it wasn't how she'd thought it would go. She'd wanted to look at his face, into his eyes, have his bare skin on hers, not be facedown on the hood of a car while they were both pretty much fully dressed.

He told you not to push him. He gave you a choice. You were the one who thought you could handle it, so fucking handle it.

Zoe screwed her eyes shut tight and tried to fucking handle it, but as he began to push into her, a wail tore from her throat. It hurt, it really did, and he was relentless, pushing deeper, his fingers digging into the flesh of her hips.

"Breathe." The order was a rough growl from behind her.

So she did, opening her mouth and drawing in long, ragged breaths that turned into groans as he lifted her hips, sliding even deeper. Her hands clawed at the metal as the burning pain moved outward, her vision blurred and hazy with sudden tears.

This was nothing like she'd imagined. Nothing at all.

The feel of him inside her was too much, stretching sensitized tissues, the unfamiliarity of it oddly bewildering. She wanted to grab on to something and yet there was nothing to grab on to.

A sobbing sound filled the garage, and she realized with a kind of shock that it was her. That her cheeks were wet and the paint under her cheek slick.

Gideon's fingers dug in and she felt him pull back, sliding out of her, before thrusting back in. Then he did it again. And again. Until the burning pain began to change, the bright edge of it becoming sharp with pleasure.

She didn't understand how that worked. How could pain be pleasure? It didn't make any sense. But there was no denying it, no denying the intensity of it either. The feel of his hard cock inside her, pressing against the walls of her pussy, making her feel so full she didn't think she could stand it. Then the slide of it as he pulled out, the delicious friction as he pushed back in.

The combination of sensations confused her, terrified her, and thrilled her all at the same time.

"Remember what I said." The words were guttural, his voice as hoarse as hers. "You can't come until I tell you. Don't disappoint me again."

Her chest went tight and she opened her mouth to tell him that no way was she going to do that, then his hand slipped around her hip and underneath her, pushing down between her thighs, finding her clit. And he slicked his thumb over and around the hard little bud, stroking her as he thrust deeper, harder.

Zoe groaned, white lights bursting behind her eyes, the pain fracturing apart under the weight of pleasure. She could hear him, the harsh sound of his breathing behind her, feel the blazing heat of his body against hers, inside hers. It wasn't what she wanted. She wanted to see him, touch him, having him touch her, not . . . this.

Yeah, and this is why it's a punishment, idiot. Still think you can handle it?

Something crystallized inside her, determination shifting.

Oh yeah. She could. She would take this from him, show him she was strong enough to do whatever he wanted and give him whatever he asked for.

She would be his good girl. And then, perhaps, he'd actually give *her* what *she* wanted.

So she thought about anything else, about cleaning house and the boringness of having to do the garage accounts. About how much she hated cooking and how dull it was when the rest of them started talking about baseball.

Anything so she didn't focus on the pleasure, raw and intense, building inside her. The push of his cock and the agonizing touch of his thumb on her clit.

Until she was sobbing against the metal of the car, harsh sounds tearing from her throat, her whole body shaking and shaking and shaking. Then his voice, so close to her, his lips brushing her ear. "Come, Zoe. Come now."

And she did, screaming into the silence of the garage, the sound of it echoing off the hard surfaces of the walls, high and ragged and thin as the pleasure broke her apart, shattering her like a glass bottle thrown onto a concrete floor.

She wasn't really conscious of anything much after that. The pace of his thrusts increased as he slammed her against the hood over and over, but she felt weirdly disconnected from her body, as if she was hovering above it, watching from a long way off. She was barely aware when he came, his cry of release harsh and guttural, the raw sound of his breathing loud in her ear.

For long moments they stood there unmoving, her pushed up against the car with him hot and hard and panting at her back. Then he pulled out of her, moving away, and it was all she could do to stay upright. There was no strength in her legs, and she had to push her palms hard against the metal to stay where she was and not slide into a heap on the floor.

The sound of clothing being dealt with came from behind her, and then Gideon's hands were on her too, smoothing down her skirt, covering her up. She felt boneless and heavy, like she'd had a shot of some wicked sedative and now was completely unable to move.

He flipped her over again, and this time she couldn't even be bothered to put her forearm over her face to shield herself from his gaze. She only looked up into his dark eyes, feeling naked and vulnerable, utterly stripped of every defense she had. He didn't say a word, and his expression was completely opaque. But she could read the hard lines of his face well enough. They were merciless, intent. There would be no softening, not even now.

She trembled when he reached for her, but he only lifted her into his arms, and despite that hard expression, he gathered her against his chest gently enough. Without speaking he carried her out of the garage and back up to the apartment. And she thought he might take her into her own room, dump her on the bed, and leave her alone for the night. Part of her was almost hoping for it, because God knew, she could use some time to process what exactly had happened down in the garage.

But he strode right by her bedroom door, continuing on down the hallway, and her whole body clenched tight. No doubt about where he was taking her now. To his bedroom.

It was dark as he stepped inside with her, but he didn't bother with the lights, kicking the door shut behind him instead. The sound echoed through her, heavy with portent, though why she didn't know.

A prison door closing, maybe?

No, that was stupid. Sure, he wanted her to stay in the apartment and she'd been slightly dramatic about having to do that, but this wasn't a prison. He wasn't her jailer. Then again, there were worse places to be a prisoner than Gideon's bedroom.

The room itself was scrupulously clean—unlike hers. There were no clothes on the floor and the bed, pushed up against the wall by the windows, had been neatly made. The dresser, on the opposite side of the room, had no plethora of bottles sitting haphazardly on it, and the bookshelves nearby weren't crowded with knickknacks, and paper and all sorts of other stuff, just his neatly shelved collection of science fiction classics.

He was way tidier than she was and was always a bear when it came to making sure she tidied up after herself.

She blinked as he carried her over to the bed. Crazy, she was crazy. Why the hell was she thinking about his tidiness when she was in his room and he'd obviously brought her here for more of what had gone on down in the garage.

You don't want to think of what he might do.

A tremor shook her. What had happened already had been almost more than she'd been able to handle as it was. Could she really deal with more of the same?

She wanted to go back to her room, slide into her own bed and pull the covers over her head, curl up into a ball, and not think about what she and Gideon had done. Not think about the intense pleasure or the deep foreboding. The scariness of the whole situation.

But she'd decided she was going to prove him wrong. Take his punishment and be his good girl. She couldn't pull out of this yet.

He set her down so she was standing next to the bed and, with calm, deliberate and steady hands, began to pull off her clothes. She let him, shuddering yet again as he got rid of her black, lacy top and the bra underneath it, then tugged down the skirt she wore. It wasn't cold in the room, but goose bumps rose all over her skin anyway as the last item of clothing came off. He didn't look at her, merely sinking to his haunches in front of her and dealing with the laces of her boots, removing them with the same calm deliberation as he'd removed every-thing else.

She'd never been naked in front of anyone before and didn't know what to do with her arms or her hands. Whether to cover herself or fold her arms across her chest, or let them merely hang loose at her sides. Her throat felt dry, her heartbeat begin-ning to race again, uncertainty tightening inside her. There was a dull ache between her legs, and she couldn't tell whether it was pain or rising desire again, though she was going with pain. Because she couldn't want him again so soon, not after the last orgasm. Could she?

Gideon put his hands on the backs of her calves, then ran his palms up her legs in a long, slow caress, stopping just below the curve of her ass. Her breathing began to slide out of control once more, because the feel of those hands on her skin seared like a blowtorch.

Then they dropped away and he came to his feet in a smooth, impossibly graceful movement. She gulped in some air, her lungs starved of oxygen, her heart feeling like it was battering away inside her chest, trying to get out. Light from the street outside leaked into the room around the edges of the curtains, but even so, his face was impossible to read. Merely a collection of vague shadows and deeper darkness, pools of black where his eyes should be.

He's right. You have no idea what you're getting yourself into.

Too late for that now. Too late for regrets or second thoughts. She'd pushed him into this and now she had to deal with the consequences.

He put his hands on her shoulders, turning her very deliberately around, so her back was to him. Then without any warning, he pushed her down onto the bed on her stomach.

The sheets smelled of laundry liquid and Gideon, so familiar it made her want to cry, though she didn't really understand why that would be. Because he wasn't hurting her, at least not in a bad way.

You're out of your depth and you know it.

Yeah, maybe that was it. Maybe that was the problem.

The bed dipped and she felt him behind her again, kneeling astride her, judging from the feel of the rough denim on either side of her thighs. God, he hadn't even taken his clothes off.

"Why am I the one who gets to be naked?" Her voice was a shock in the silence of the room, sounding out of place and wrong.

"Because that's how I want it." There was a pause. "If you can't handle it, you know where the door is."

Zoe gritted her teeth, staring into the darkness in front of her. Damn him. She could handle it and she would.

Another long moment passed.

Then, obviously taking her silence for acquiescence, he touched her, a long, slow stroke down the curve of her spine.

She tensed, her heart jumping, her mouth dry.

He did it again, caressing her like a cat, except this time his hands didn't stop in the small of her back. They carried on over the swell of her buttocks, squeezing. Then he shifted and she shook as his fingers slipped between her cheeks, spreading them apart before squeezing them together again.

Zoe buried her face in the cool cotton of the sheets, her face burning, fighting the urge to jerk away from his touch, to protect herself. She was supposed to be taking this, wasn't she? She was supposed to be letting him do anything he wanted. But this . . .

He spread her again, one thumb pressing against the tight ring of muscle between her buttocks. She stiffened, unable to help herself, biting her lip hard to stop from protesting or crying out, or maybe even just bursting into tears. But he didn't relent, pressing harder until the tip of his thumb pushed inside her, tearing a muffled, choked sound from her.

She shook, her face turned against the sheets, the dull ache between her legs now something more, something intense, that pleasure/pain building again. Gideon pushed harder, deeper, and she gave a little sob, because it was dirty and wrong and nothing like anything she'd fantasized about. Yet she was panting, wanting movement, wanting friction, wanting something to ease that ache.

He reached around her, hooking his arm beneath her hips and tugging her up on her knees so her butt was in the air. Then he slid his free hand between her thighs, his fingers stroking through the slick folds of pussy, finding her clit with unerring accuracy and circling around and around.

All the breath rushed into her lungs, the pleasure as sharp and bright as an electric shock. She tried to pull her hips away from the thumb buried in her ass only to come up against the fingers stroking her clit. Then they slipped into her pussy, deep inside, moving with firm insistence, drawing another inarticulate noise from her.

She panted against the cotton, trying to get a handle on everything she was feeling, but it was too much, way, way too much. All her emotions were tangled and knotted, like a ball of old yarn, and there was no way she could free them. Fear and embarrassment, a dark, dirty craving deep in her soul. Pain and discomfort. Bewilderment and confusion. And pleasure, a blinding, annihilating pleasure that was rapidly becoming the whole of her world.

Her thighs were shaking, her nipples pushing into the mattress beneath her, hard and sensitive and aching. Her hips wanted to move and yet she didn't know where to move them, because there was no escape from the torture. No escape from the brutal pleasure that was slowly tearing her apart.

He said nothing as he played with her, his thumb in her ass and his fingers in her sex, making her writhe and twist and sob against the sheets. And when he finally made her come, she screamed into the mattress, the pleasure detonating inside her like a bomb blast, utterly overwhelming her.

Her ears were ringing and she couldn't move, and when he pulled his hands away from her, she lay on the bed almost stunned. Sounds came from behind her, footsteps and rustles, but she didn't really pay attention.

She felt like she'd been hit over the head with a baseball bat.

Then the bed dipped again, and his hands were on her, lifting her hips, the push of his knee against hers, easing them apart. A helpless groan escaped her, because she couldn't do this again, she really couldn't.

"No," she said in a raw whisper. "I can't. . . ."

"Yeah, you can." His heat against the backs of her thighs and this time without denim, only hot, bare skin. "You will."

Firm fingers on her sex, spreading her open, and his cock sliding into her, stretching her, making her burn. And she cried out because she was sore from last time and from the orgasm that was still sending aftershocks through her. But he didn't stop and he didn't go slow, making her fingers curl tight into the cotton of the sheets.

Yet despite the pain and the discomfort, the fear and the strange disappointment that sat in her gut, despite the fact that she'd come three times already that night, her body woke to aching life again. The pain twisted to become pleasure, the thrust of him inside her an unbearable, intoxicating thrill she couldn't get enough of.

She didn't want to do it again. She couldn't bear the intensity. But it was happening all the same and this time it was different. She could feel his skin against hers, hot and smooth, the powerful muscles of his thighs flexing as he thrust. The movement of his hips was slower, almost leisurely, the slick sounds of flesh sliding into flesh providing an erotic soundtrack.

His hands moved on her, stroking her spine, then shocking her with the hard slap of his palm over one buttock.

Zoe blinked back the prickle of tears fiercely, biting down on her lip and clinging to the pain to hold herself together, to not let herself get torn apart again. But the pleasure rolled over her, crushing her, the sting of his palm against her skin focusing it like a sunbeam through a magnifying glass. It set her on fire, burned her, and she flamed in the night, moaning into the sheets as he thrust harder, deeper. Until she couldn't hold on any longer, couldn't stop herself from breaking like she had downstairs. Only this time she didn't even have the strength to scream, letting out a thin, high thread of sound instead, her body shaking itself apart. Then his fingers found her clit once more and she came to pieces in his hands.

She wasn't aware of anything after that, only of the darkness and the feel of the sheets against her burning skin, and the sound of someone sobbing as if their heart would break.

She didn't know it was her until his arms came around her and she felt the heat of his naked body against hers. Sensitized beyond bearing, she shoved at him, unable to bear the closeness, but he didn't let her go. Instead, he pulled her in tight to his chest, her head turned into his neck, his arms like iron bars at her back.

This was familiar. This she knew. The scent of him, the warmth of his body, the knowledge that she was safe and protected. It eased something inside her and she stopped shoving, pressed her face to his skin and wept for reasons she didn't understand.

Then, despite the fact that her soul felt like it had broken in half and been badly glued back together, her body like she'd run three marathons in a row, the sobs eventually quieted and she fell into a sleep so deep it was like death.

Chapter 10

"What the fuck are these?"

Gideon pushed up the visor of the protective helmet he wore when he was arc welding, and glanced over.

Zee was standing near the Chevy, frowning at something dangling between his fingers. It was black and lacy, and undeniably feminine.

"Underwear, I think you'll find," Tamara said with some amusement from behind him.

"Yeah, but whose underwear?" Zee glanced over to where Gideon stood beside the Harley. "Levi and Rachel have a hot date here over the weekend?"

Jesus. Zoe's panties. They must have fallen under the Chevy and they'd both forgotten all about them. Slowly Gideon put down the welding gun, trying to decide just what the hell he was going to say, because he was pretty sure "*Oh yeah, they're Zoe's. I tore them off her when I fucked her over the hood of the Chevy on Saturday night*" would go down like a lead balloon.

You goddamn hypocrite.

He gritted his teeth. Yeah, he knew that. He knew *exactly* how big a hypocrite he was. The word had been going around and around in his head all fucking weekend. It whispered to him every time he pushed her down on the bed, or up against a wall, or over the kitchen table. Every time he touched her to orgasm or put her down on her knees to suck him.

He was a hypocrite. A total fucking hypocrite.

Yet even now, even right here with his friends just a few feet away, all he could do was stare at Zoe's panties, getting hard at all the memories they set off.

"Gideon?" Zee was looking at him strangely. "You know whose these are?"

He blinked then, pulled himself together, strode over to where Zee stood, and tugged them out of his hand, stuffing them into the pocket of his overalls. "Yeah. They belong to a friend of mine."

Zee's eyebrows rose. "Uh-huh. Which friend—"

"You here for a reason, Zee?" It was a graceless change of subject, but quite frankly, Gideon couldn't be bothered with any niceties. He was already feeling on edge, and what had gone down between him and Zoe over the weekend hadn't made him feel any better.

She'd wanted him, pushed him, and so he'd made the decision to show her exactly what she was letting herself in for. It had been a shock for her, he knew that. Mainly because she saw him only in terms of the big foster brother who'd protected her since she was small and not who he actually was. And that wasn't an easy lover or an easy man. Certainly not easy enough for a sweet little virgin like Zoe.

Guilt turned over inside him like a huge beast turning over in its sleep, heavy and slow.

He'd made her cry that first night, as he knew he would. Yet that had been a deliberate choice. Going easy or slow, being tender and gentle with her would have given her more fuel to stoke the flame she carried for him, and that wasn't what he'd intended.

He needed to show her the reality of what she was asking for because no matter what she said, she really had no idea. Rough and hard and dirty, that's what he was and that's what he liked, and that's what she had to accept. Except when he'd confronted her with it, she hadn't run screaming from him like he thought she would.

Oh, she'd been shocked and scared, no doubt about it. But he'd given her chances over and over again to leave, and she hadn't taken any of them. Not even on Sunday morning when, for the first time since he'd taken her to live with him, he hadn't made her pancakes. Instead, to draw a line under the relationship they now had, he'd pushed her over onto her back and fucked them both into insensibility.

You sick fuck.

Yeah, he was. And he was going straight to hell.

Regret twisted, cutting deep, but he ignored the sharp pain in favor of the dull anger that simmered alongside it. Anger at himself for giving in to her, for letting her push him to this. He should have been stronger, shouldn't have let her get to him so badly, because, Jesus, she was the innocent one here.

You should have been kinder to her. You should have been gentler.

Yeah, he should have. But he hadn't. And he didn't know where that left them, but one thing was certain: They couldn't return to the way things had been before.

"Yeah," Zee said, giving him a narrow look. "We're going to Gino's tonight, meeting up with Levi and Rach to have another look at those plans of Levi's. Thought you were gonna come. Didn't he text you about it?"

Fuck. Levi had and he'd forgotten all about it, immersing himself in engines and grease so he didn't think about the guilt clawing at his insides or the consuming need for Zoe, the strength of which had completely blindsided him.

"Yeah, he did." Gideon pulled off his welding helmet and stalked back over to the workshop counter, dropping it with a clatter. "I'll go take a shower and meet you guys there."

At that moment, Zoe appeared at the top of the stairs that led up to the garage's office, and every muscle in his body closed up tight like a fist.

She wasn't wearing anything different from what she usually wore, black skinny jeans, a pair of dirty blue Chucks, and a tight dark blue tank top, and yet he couldn't take his eyes off her.

The tank top molded to her slender torso, outlining her small, round tits and the graceful indentation of her waist. Her legs looked outrageously long in the black jeans, and he suddenly wanted them around his waist, holding on as he pushed inside her, as he made her scream. Her hair was a black cloud, held back from her face by a couple of barrettes that made her seem acutely young and vulnerable. And sick bastard that he was, he wanted to take out those barrettes, wind her hair around his wrist, and pull hard on it as he took her from behind.

Yeah, he'd own up to it now. He'd name it. He wanted her. He wanted to fuck his little foster sister so badly he could hardly think.

It was wrong, so very, very wrong.

But that's the kind of guy you really are after all.

He couldn't deny it. That kind of bad he'd grown up with and had embraced when he was younger, back when he'd been securing his reputation as the go-to man for muscle in the Chicago criminal underworld. Territorial, possessive, short-tempered. Mean as fuck. He'd been famous for it. Now he could feel those old urges, the ones he'd thought he'd buried for good, all rising back to the surface, turning on Zoe.

She didn't look at him, her gaze firmly directed to Zee and Tamara, and for some reason that annoyed him. She'd been doing that all weekend, staying quiet, not saying a word to him. Not that there had been anything much to say, but still.

"Zoe," Zee said. "You gonna come?"

A crease appeared between her brows. "Come where?"

Zee shot him a puzzled look. "You told her, right?"

Actually he hadn't. He'd had other, more important things on his mind.

"Told me what?" Zoe's gaze shifted to him, her mouth in an annoyed line.

"The others are going to Gino's to discuss those plans," he said, knowing she was going to be pissed about it. "I meant to tell you but . . ." He paused. "We had a busy weekend."

She blushed, heat blooming over her skin, her gaze flickering away from his. "Uh. Right. Yeah. Well, sure. I'm definitely coming. In fact, I'm ready right now." Zoe put a foot out onto the next step down.

"No, you're not." The words were out of his mouth before he could check them.

She froze, and there was a surprised silence as all three of them looked at him.

Jesus. Okay, perhaps he was sounding crazy, especially when the others weren't aware of the other thing he'd almost forgotten about in the haze of sex and hunger that had been going on all weekend: the potential threat to Zoe's life.

This isn't just about Zoe's life.

No, it wasn't. It was about those old feelings again, the ones that whispered to him that she was his. That he had to protect her, keep her here in the apartment so no one could take her from him, no one could hurt her, touch her. No one but him.

"Excuse me?" The edge of outrage in Zoe's voice was clear.

Not that he needed to hear it, not with the gold embers of anger that had started to smolder in her eyes.

He pushed himself away from the workshop counter and headed for the metal stairs that led up to the office. "Gimme a minute, Zee."

"Gideon," Zoe said. "You'd better not be—"

He started up the stairs. "A word in the office, little one."

Her jaw tightened, and for a second it looked like she wasn't going to obey him, but then, letting out an irritated breath, she turned around and stalked up the stairs and into the office.

Following her inside, he kicked the door shut behind them, and it didn't escape his notice that she was standing down the far end of the office, as if she wanted to put as much distance between them as she could.

That, too, annoyed him.

"You can't stop me from going," she said before he could say anything. "This development is something I'm a part of too, and you can't just cut me out."

The enforcer in him wanted to roar that he could do whatever the fuck he wanted and if he didn't want her leaving the apartment then she wouldn't. But he wasn't that man anymore, and he hadn't been for quite some time.

Trying to calm himself the hell down, he said levelly, "Okay, but you're coming with me, understand? I'll just have a shower and—"

"No," Zoe snapped.

He stared at her. "What do you mean no?"

She was shifting from one foot to the other, her arms crossed over her chest, and he wanted to close the distance between them, push her against the wall, pull her arms away and pin them above her head. Hold her there while he slid his hand inside her jeans, stroked her pussy until she was dripping for him, until she made those little choked sounds, those small sobs she always made right before she came.

Shit, if they'd been completely alone, he might have done just that.

"I haven't seen Zee and Tamara for ages," she said, giving him a mutinous look. "And you know what? I could use some time out."

"Time out? What the fuck does that mean?" Like he didn't know. He just wanted her to say it.

Zoe lifted her chin, meeting his gaze. "Time away from you."

"Zoe—"

"No, I don't want to talk about it. I just want to go out with Zee and Tamara and have a night off."

The beast inside him growled, but he decided to let the "night off" bullshit slide and concentrate on the most important thing. "Have you forgotten about those assholes at Anonymous on Saturday night? That Novak is out there and he's looking for you?"

"Of course I haven't forgotten. But God, Gino's is only a couple of blocks up the street and it's not like I'm going out there alone. Zee's with me. He can take care of things if anything goes wrong, you know he can."

It was true. Zee could look after himself, and no doubt if anyone tried to grab Zoe, he'd look after them, too. He hadn't spent years as an underground MMA fighter for nothing.

So you don't really have any reason to say no, do you?

He didn't, and it irritated the shit out of him. Because he wanted to say no. He wanted Zoe to go with him. No one could guard her, protect her like he could. No one.

But refusing this was going to look like a dick move, and that wasn't who he was now. "Okay," he said, even though it killed him. "Go with Zee, then. But if anything happens . . ."

"It won't." She started heading toward the door, and the urge to reach out and grab the back of her neck, hold her there like a kitten caught by its scruff, and kiss her hard, so she knew there was no escaping him, was almost overwhelming.

But he didn't, pushing his hands into the pockets of his overalls instead and following her back out of the office.

Zee and Tamara were waiting for them at the bottom of the stairs, and Gideon didn't like the speculative look the pair of them shared as he and Zoe appeared. What the hell was that? They couldn't know what was going on between Zoe and him, no fucking way.

"I'll come with you guys," Zoe said as she stomped down the stairs.

"Yeah, okay." Zee's silver gaze shifted to Gideon. "Oh, and by the way, you should probably tell Gideon not to bring his girlfriends into the garage."

Zoe stopped dead on the stairs. "What?"

"Pair of panties under the Chevy. Not a good look, man."

Fucking Zee. Gideon had to restrain the urge to punch his friend in the face. They'd never guess those panties were Zoe's of course, but she'd gone quite still all the same, and he could see her hand on the metal rail next to the stairs. Her knuckles were white.

"Yeah, thanks, Zee," Gideon growled. "Now get the fuck out of here. Levi gets antsy if you're late."

The sound of his voice must have jolted Zoe, because abruptly she moved in a jerky fashion, coming the rest of the way down the stairs. "Thanks for the heads-up," she said, her voice only slightly shaky. "Must keep an eye out for rogue underwear."

Once again, Gideon noted Zee narrowing his gaze at Zoe, then flicking a glance at Tamara, who gave a slight shrug.

Right, so they'd seen something was up. Seemed like a good idea to talk to Zoe about how they were going to handle this when it came to their friends. Not that he had any idea how they were going to handle it, but obviously they were going to need to.

Only if you're going to keep screwing her.

Like that was in question. Of course he was going to keep

screwing her. He'd told her he'd take everything and so he had, and he'd keep doing so until he'd killed her crush completely. It was the only way.

After the others had gone, Gideon locked up the garage and went upstairs to the apartment to take a shower and get changed. He felt uneasy and restless, though he couldn't quite put his finger on why. At least until he found a scrap of gold fabric underneath his bed. It was Zoe's bra, the lace coming off one cup from where he'd jerked it off her.

He stared at it and a surge of desire went through him, so strong he had to stand there quietly for a few seconds, his hands in fists, trying to get himself under control. And along with it the acidic bite of regret.

That morning he'd left her sleeping, getting up to go for a run through Royal's quiet pre–six a.m. streets. He'd needed some distance from the incessant pull of desire that had him wanting to wake her up and have her rough and raw all over again, and he'd thought she probably needed the recovery time he hadn't allowed her earlier.

Plus, he'd wanted to check out the streets, see if there was anyone suspicious hanging around. Good thing he had, too, because there had been a car parked down in an alley not far from the garage. A low, black car, too expensive and too new to be anyone's in Royal. It had to be Novak's, he'd lay money on it.

The urge to stalk down that alley and confront whoever was sitting in that car had been strong, but he'd made himself run past without making it obvious he'd seen the car. Hopefully, continuing to let Novak think he didn't know the prick was after Zoe would lull him into a false sense of security, giving Gideon time to make his own plans for taking Novak down.

He'd run a couple of blocks, then stopped to follow up on those texts he'd sent to his contacts earlier about info on Novak. Sadly no one knew anything, which was shitty but not unexpected. Then he'd gone on to finish his run, returning an hour later to find his bed was empty and Zoe in her own room, the door firmly closed.

The possessive beast in him, incensed at being shut out, had demanded he kick her door down, go in, and grab her, because things had changed between them and she had to understand how. There could be no distance from him, not now, not ever. But enough of that aching guilt remained that he'd backed away from the door, letting her have her space.

Didn't do anything for the other ache, though. The burn of desire that had his dick hard for her again not even a solid seven hours since the last time. He didn't understand what was happening to him, why now, after years of not seeing her as anything more than a little sister and friend, he should suddenly be consumed with lust for her.

But whether he understood it or not didn't change the fact that he felt it. Neither did it change his decision to show her the truth of what it would mean to be with him. And with any luck, if she knew what was good for her, she'd eventually tell him to fuck off.

If you even let her.

Gideon shoved that thought out of his head, threw her ruined bra back into her bedroom, and continued getting ready.

Fifteen minutes later he walked the couple of blocks up to Gino's, the closest Royal got to a local bar. He kept a subtle lookout as he went, scanning the streets for any signs of that car or any of sign of Novak's heavies, but there was nothing. A group of young guys across the street, hanging around outside the liquor store, yelled a greeting and he raised a hand in return. There were no new faces there, no one suspicious attaching themselves to the crowd so he didn't stop.

If Saturday night hadn't happened, he might have thought he was being paranoid. That he was falling back into old habits. Bad habits.

Gino's was full of the usual regulars when he finally got there. Joe and Clive, a couple of alcoholics balanced precariously on their barstools and slumped over the bar, already out of it. While Bobby, a Vietnam vet in his sixties, nursed a bourbon and shot the breeze with Gino himself behind the bar.

They all looked toward the door as Gideon came in and he nodded to them, heading down to the table in the back where he and the others often sat.

Sure enough, his friends were already there, seated around the table, their attention on a big piece of paper Levi had unrolled and kept flat with a couple of beer bottles holding down the edges. The development plans for Royal.

Levi was sitting with Rachel in his lap, and she was pointing at something on the plans and smiling, her lovely face lit up. Levi's hand rested possessively on her stomach, his gaze on her strangely tender for a guy who looked like he could snap telephone poles in half with his bare hands.

Gideon paused, taking a moment to watch them before they knew he was there, because it was good to see both Levi and Rachel so happy. God knew, they both fucking deserved it. And then there was Zee and Tamara. Zee had his arm around her, holding her close, her blond hair drifting over his shoulder, and Gideon could hear her laughter mixing with his deeper baritone.

Another couple who deserved every happiness.

They'd all come a long way from the days at the outreach center where he'd found them. The center he'd come to when he and Zoe had first moved to Royal. He'd gone there because of her, because she'd liked it and because he'd needed some kind of absolution. A way of giving back after everything he'd done. So he'd volunteered his time, hanging out and talking to the down-and-out teens, the ones society had forgotten about. Giving them a sympathetic ear or a shoulder to cry on, or advice when they needed it.

But it had been Zee and Levi and Rachel he was closest to. The kids who were most damaged, who'd needed him most, and so he'd been there for them the way he'd been there for Zoe.

His gaze shifted to her, where she sat at one end of the table, looking isolated in comparison to the two couples on either side. Her hands were in her lap, the expression on her face making his chest get tight. What the hell was making her so sad? Was it him? Was it what was happening between them? Because if so that was a good thing. That was what he'd been hoping for.

It should have made him feel better. But for some reason it didn't.

She must have sensed him standing there in the shadows because her head turned abruptly, her big golden eyes meeting his. Color swept through her face, a full-on blush that made his cock get hard and the tension in the air between them pull so tight he could almost taste it.

Shit. They should have stayed home. Or he should have finished up his work early, then taken her upstairs to the apartment and worked out this insanity in bed *before* they went out.

Her eyes darkened, her mouth opening. Like she had the same thought he did and it made her feel the same. And he couldn't look away.

He could feel his hunger begin to rise, sinking claws deep inside him, the sensation new and sharp and painful. God, if he'd have known he was going to feel this way about her, he'd never have confronted her the way he had on Saturday night. He'd never have touched her at all.

"Hey, Gideon." Levi's husky voice was a shock to the system. "Come on, man. Rach's giving everyone the rundown."

Aware suddenly of where he was and the fact that he was staring at Zoe like he was starving and she was something good to eat, he dragged his gaze from hers and forced his mouth up into a smile, walking forward. "Great. Who's bought me a beer?"

"You're late." Rachel frowned, mock stern. "I was going to drink your beer myself."

"Yeah, well, I thought you'd prefer me showered than sweaty after a day of arc welding." He grabbed the back of the only free chair, on the opposite end of the table from Zoe, and pulled it out, sitting down.

"Is that what the kids are calling it these days?" Zee raised one dark brow. "Must remember that."

"Huh." Rachel leaned back against Levi's broad shoulder, her gaze flicking from Zee to Gideon. "I hear innuendo. Is there something you're not telling us, Gideon?"

"That's a fucking big word, Rachel," he replied without heat, keeping his voice level. "You sure you know how to use it?"

"Zee found a pair of lacy black panties on the garage floor," Tamara said before Gideon could change the subject. "And no, before you ask, they weren't mine."

Rachel gave him a wide-eyed stare, understandably so. He didn't take that kind of thing into the garage, never had. Until Zoe. "Any comment, Gideon?"

"No," he said flatly. "It's my fucking garage. My fucking rules."

"You don't normally bring chicks in there though," Levi commented. "She must be special."

Zee snorted. "Yeah, especially if you're doing her on that goddamn Chevy."

Gideon kept the expression on his face entirely neutral, showing nothing at all of the irritation building inside him. "Any particular reason you're all so interested in my love life?" he asked mildly.

"Uh, maybe because you involved yourself in ours?" Rachel gave him a sweet smile. "Deny it if you can."

He couldn't and they all knew it.

"It's payback, man." Zee had a particularly smug look on his face. "Can't count the number of times you told me to 'keep it out of the workshop.' "

They were only having fun; Gideon knew that. And if it hadn't concerned Zoe he'd be joking along with them. But it *did* concern Zoe, and he found he'd lost his sense of humor completely.

Down at the other end of the table, the woman in question was leaning back in her chair, her shoulders hunched, a tight look on her face. Her cheeks were flaming and behind the lenses of her glasses, her eyes had gone very large.

"Just some woman I picked up at Anonymous," he said. "No big deal."

"Aw, come on. That's all we get?" Rachel glanced down the table at Zoe. "Did you see this mysterious woman then?"

Zoe's eyes went wide, taking on a rabbit-in-the-headlights look. "Uh, n-no. Why would I?"

"Well, considering you two were joined at the hip on Saturday, I thought you might have caught a glimpse at least."

Zoe looked down at her hands as if they were the most interesting thing she'd ever seen. "No." Her voice was quiet and husky. "I didn't see anything."

"Hey," Gideon said, keeping a firm hand on the anger straining its leash. "Leave Zoe the fuck out of this, okay? It's got nothing to do with her."

Rachel stared at him in surprise and he realized that actually, his hand wasn't quite as firm as he'd thought. "It's a joke, Gideon. Chill the hell out."

A tense silence fell and he was aware again of Zee's speculative gaze flicking from him and to Zoe, then back again.

He needed to say something, break the silence, get everyone back on track and away from uncomfortable subjects like who he'd apparently fucked on the hood of that Chevy.

Leaning forward, he was about to take control of the conversation, when Zoe suddenly shoved her chair back, got up, and stalked off without a word.

She didn't know what had gotten into her. She just hadn't been able to sit there any longer while the rest of them discussed . . . her, basically. While Gideon talked about her being some random woman he'd brought home from Anonymous.

She knew he was only protecting her, that he was keeping what was happening between them from the rest of their friends. But it still made her feel weird and uncomfortable and . . . there was something hurtful about it as well. They were all joking around, like it was funny, something to tease Gideon with. But it wasn't funny to her. It was real and overwhelming and very intense, and she couldn't bear the thought of anyone laughing about it.

Someone called her name as she turned and walked down toward the back of the bar, but she didn't stop. She wanted quiet and some space to get herself together, so she headed for the bathrooms out back, going down the dark, narrow corridor that led to the ladies'.

Probably a dumb thing to do to go off by herself, especially given the apparent Novak threat. But shit, she wasn't actually going outside. No one would get her here. If the threat was even a thing. Hell, she only had Gideon's word that those guys at Anonymous were Novak's thugs.

You should be taking that a lot more seriously. Gideon is.

No, no. She didn't want to think about that. She had already more than enough on her plate with what was happening between her and Gideon, let alone having to spare thinking time on a potential threat to her life. That was a bridge too far.

Stopping outside the door, she didn't actually go in, leaning back against the wall instead and pushing her hands in the pockets of her jeans.

Chatter from the bar drifted down the corridor, along with

the heavy guitar from some seventies metal band that was playing on the jukebox.

Zoe closed her eyes and took a deep breath.

Gideon hadn't stopped looking at her the entire time. Sitting
across the table from her, relaxed back against the seat with a
beer bottle in his hand, he'd looked like he normally did. Chilled
out. Yet there had been nothing relaxed about the way he'd
stared at her, nothing even remotely chilled out. Those black
eyes of his had burned, and she'd known exactly what he was
thinking about: all those dirty things he'd done to her up in his
bedroom, the things their friends didn't know about.

She shivered, because he wasn't the only one who hadn't
been able to look away. She'd been unable to stop looking at
him as well, all her once-innocent longing, that schoolgirl
crush, changed beyond all recognition.

Because she knew now what it was like to have him touch
her, kiss her. To have his cock inside her. She knew what he
tasted like and what sounds he made when he came. What used
to be imagination was now reality, making a dark kind of
hunger rise up in her, one she'd never experienced before, so intense it scared the shit out of her.

Wanting someone who didn't feel the same was safe. Her
fantasies were vague and while there was no chance they'd be
reciprocated, she could imagine whatever she wanted and it
would all be okay. No one would get hurt. Nothing would
change.

But he'd taken those innocent fantasies of hers, broken them
in half, then stomped on the pieces. Making her realize how
scary it was when that want was returned. When it meant that
the one person she'd always counted on for safety wasn't so
safe anymore. Was, in fact, the reason for her fear.

God, she needed to talk to someone about it, but that was a
problem since the person she usually talked to was the one who

was causing all the drama in the first place. There was Rachel, of course, or even Tamara, yet the thought of actually saying out loud what she and Gideon were doing made her want to curl up into herself with embarrassment.

She also didn't want to face any disapproval, not of her and certainly not of Gideon. Not when she'd been the one to force the situation.

"Zoe."

Her eyes snapped open and she turned her head, her heart sinking all the way down into the soles of her Chucks as she saw the tall, massively built figure standing just in the corridor's entrance.

Gideon.

Why did it have to be him following her?

Oh, come on. You would have been pissed if it had been anyone else.

Okay, sure. She would have been. But his following her meant she was going to have to talk to him and she didn't think she was ready for that. It was bad enough having to deal with the reality that they'd been sleeping together let alone having to talk about it.

"Oh, hey," she said. "I'm just going to the bathroom. I'll be five minutes." Pushing herself away from the wall, she made as if to head into the ladies' room opposite. But he was already coming down the hallway, his long legs closing the distance, coming to put himself between her and the door to the bathroom.

She froze, her heartbeat accelerating.

His dark eyes were sharp, and when he put his hands on the wall on either side of her, leaning on his palms and crowding her with the hot, muscled length of his body, all the breath left her lungs and her skin pricked with heat.

Dammit. She'd hoped sleeping with him would make her

less obsessed, but if anything, it only made her want him more. A scary, very adult kind of desire she was still struggling to process, the one that gloried in all the dirty things he did to her.

"What are you doing?" She made herself meet his hot, black gaze. "I need the bathroom."

He ignored the question. "Why did you walk out? And don't give me that bathroom bullshit."

She didn't know what to tell him when she couldn't even articulate the reasons to herself. "I . . . don't like everyone joking about it."

"Why not? Would you prefer they knew the truth?"

"No. No, I don't want that either." She bit her lip, trying to ignore how close he was standing to her, how the seductive scent of him was wrapping itself around her, reminding her of different things now. Not so much safety and home any longer but other, darker things. Fingers on her skin. His teeth at her neck. His cock inside her . . .

"So what's the issue? Because everyone noticed you leaving. They were asking me what's going on with you."

She shivered, shoving away the erotic images playing themselves over and over in her head. "You know what's going on with me."

His gaze didn't waver. "The fact that we're sleeping together?"

"Of course the fact that we're sleeping together." Her cheeks heated, which was annoying and weird given the amount of times he'd made her come.

"What about it?" He said the words like it was no big deal they were having sex. As if it wasn't anything to get excited about or upset about.

"I just don't like everyone making fun of it. And I don't like . . ." She stopped, realizing suddenly how it was going to sound and what it would reveal. But there wasn't any point not saying it. Gideon would only get it out of her one way or another. "I don't like being just some random woman you picked up in Anonymous."

He frowned, and she wished he would move because she couldn't think with him standing there, crowding her the way he was. "Well, what did you expect me to say? I couldn't tell them the truth, that those panties were yours and I'd ripped them off you."

Zoe shifted on her feet, uncomfortable and angry and trying not to let it get to her. Trying not to let *him* get to her. She didn't know why she felt mad about this, why it felt almost like hurt, but it did all the same. "I know that." She folded her arms tightly, as if she could calm the beat of her heart with the pressure alone.

He was staring at her, his gaze focused and intent, which didn't help. "You didn't want to be treated like a little girl, Zoe. You wanted to be treated as my lover. So this is me treating you as my lover."

Right. So why didn't she feel any better? Why did she still feel upset?

Kicking her heels against the wall, she looked down the hallway toward the bar, as if making sure no one was coming down it. "Well, okay, then."

"Bullshit, it's okay." He leaned in closer, dipping his head so their gazes were on the same level. "Look at me."

Her jaw tightened. She really didn't want to.

"Stop acting like a sulky teenager and look at me."

Dammit. When he used that voice, she found it next to impossible to resist. Turning her head, she met his dark eyes and felt the heat roll over her, inevitable as the dawn breaking. They were the same color as thick, black espresso coffee and had the same kind of kick to them, the kind that buzzed in her veins, made her feel on edge and wired.

"You wanted this, Zoe. You asked for it. I warned you, remember?"

Yeah, the last thing she needed were "I told you so's."

You had no idea, you dumb idiot. And you can't blame him when he tried to tell you no and you didn't listen.

But all the logic in the world did nothing to alleviate the anger and inexplicable hurt that twisted inside her. "So I'm not any different from any woman you pick up?"

Gideon cocked his head to the side, the look in his eyes impenetrable. "What? You wanna be different?"

Yes, of course you do.

Her gut hollowed out. How could she want to be treated the same as any of his lovers and yet want to be different as well? It didn't make any sense.

"I . . . maybe. I don't know."

He kept on looking at her, and she had the impression he was reading her as easily as he'd read the pages of a book. It made her feel exposed in a way she'd never felt before with him. "You wanna be special, little one? Is that what this is about?"

Her throat tightened, a wave of emotion going through her, almost overwhelming her. "Just . . . everything's different, Gideon. We've done all these things, but we haven't talked about anything. We've just . . . you know. I mean, we didn't even have pancakes yesterday." It sounded so ridiculous, like a kid complaining they'd missed out on a treat, and she wished she hadn't said it.

"Of course it's different. You think sex doesn't change things?"

"How would I know? I've never had it before."

He said nothing for a moment, but she could see something glittering in the depths of his eyes. Maybe anger or frustration, she couldn't tell. "We can't go back to the way things were. Not now. I told you that."

Tears pricked the backs of her eyes, because as soon as he said it, she suddenly realized that's exactly what she wanted.

She wanted to have their relationship stay the same, only with sex. She wanted to be his lover, have him treat her like an adult, not a little girl, yet she also wanted to continue to be special to him. To have him be the protective, understanding figure she'd grown up with. The man who had her back no matter what.

But clearly it didn't work that way and she'd been naïve to think it did.

Desperately she swallowed down the hurt. "Why not?"

"Because I can't," he said flatly. "If you want to stay in my bed, this is the way it has to be."

"So, what? We sleep together, but that's it? There's nothing else? We're just strangers?"

Something in his expression flickered. "That's what being my lover is all about, Zoe. All I want from them is sex. Nothing else."

She'd known this. She always had. He never had girlfriends, never had any relationships, only hookups. And this hadn't ever bothered her—in fact, she liked it because she probably would have felt jealous of anyone else. She'd never thought that it would now apply to her, though.

"I don't want to be a stranger to you, Gideon." Her voice had gotten rough-edged. "I thought . . . I wanted more than that."

And yeah, it was definitely anger she saw in his eyes now, it flickered, leapt like a flame. "Fuck's sake. This has all been about what *you* want. What about what *I* want?" His tone was dark, as rough as hers. "I didn't want this. I told you I didn't. But you had to keep fucking pushing."

Her own anger rose, made worse by the fact that he was right. "Oh sure, blame it on me. Okay, I did push, but I didn't force you to put your dick in my mouth. That was all you."

He moved. One minute his hands were on the wall on either side of her head, the next he'd wrapped the fingers of one hand around her throat, her pulse beating hard against his palm. She stilled, breathing fast, trembling and afraid, and yet excited, too. God, she was sick. She loved it when she made him lose his cool.

"It doesn't matter what you want," he said harshly. "You're my lover now, which means I call the shots. And the only thing that should concern you is that your pussy is fucking mine, understand?"

The breath rushed into her lungs. She should hate the possessiveness in his voice, the way it reduced her to merely her sex. Yet a dark part of her loved it. Loved being his. She always had.

Maybe you should accept it. He's right, you can't go back to what you had before, so what's the point wanting what you can't have? Haven't you been doing that long enough already?

The realization hit her like a glass of cold water poured over her head. Because wanting what she couldn't have was *exactly* what she'd been doing for years. Wanting Gideon and yet never having him. Now she had him, like she always wanted, and yet . . . somehow it wasn't what she'd thought. *He* wasn't what she'd thought.

Yet the step had been taken, the line crossed, and they couldn't go back. So she could go on wanting more the way she always had, wishing things were the way they'd once been yet knowing that could never happen, or . . . she accepted what she had now.

You're my lover now. . . .

Yeah, she certainly fucking was. So maybe she should start acting like it. Maybe she should start owning it.

She drew in a breath, feeling calmer and less unsettled, as if she'd walked off the edge of a cliff and now all she had to do was fall. Then she reached up and jerked his hand from her throat, shoving him away hard.

"If you want it, then you'd better come and get it, hadn't you?" she said flatly.

Then she turned on her heel and walked down the corridor without another word.

But not toward the bar.

Zoe walked in the opposite direction, where the door led to the alley outside.

Without pausing, she pulled it open and went through it.

Chapter 11

Gideon clenched his hands into fists, watching Zoe disappear down the corridor, the door to the alleyway slamming shut after her.

He didn't understand why he was so fucking angry.

He'd gotten up to see what was wrong because she'd obviously left the table for a reason and he had a good idea what that reason was: the reality of what was happening between them being slammed home by the comments of the others.

It was his own fault. He should have talked to her earlier and he hadn't. So he'd followed to her to try to calm her the hell down because if she wasn't careful, the others would guess what was up and he didn't need that on his plate as well.

Except he hadn't expected her distress to kick him in the guts like that. There had been hurt in her eyes and he'd fallen back into big brother mode, wanting to help her, do something to make her feel better the way he usually did. Yet he couldn't do that now, not when the thing that was going to make her feel better was the thing that he'd known, as soon as she'd said it, he couldn't give her. It hurt him in some obscure way he hadn't expected, which was stupid. He'd only given her the reality she'd asked for, plus plenty of warnings about what it was going to mean. It wasn't his fault she hadn't been prepared for it.

His dominant, possessive streak growled, telling him to go take what was his. That she couldn't walk away from him and he wasn't going to let her.

So he turned, striding down the corridor after her.

He'd given her distance all day. Time for another lesson on what being his lover meant.

The alleyway outside was narrow and dark, a Dumpster down one end of it. The concrete under his feet was pitted and all his senses went into high alert. This was the place where everything had changed for Levi and Rachel. This was also the place he'd had that waitress up against the wall while Zoe, little Zoe, had watched him.

In fact, there she was, in that same exact place, leaning up against the wall in a darker part of the alley. Her arms were crossed over her chest, her gaze pinned to his, waiting for him. The expression on her face was guarded and stubborn, yet there was a softness to her mouth, the way there always was when she cared deeply about something.

"What the hell do you want from me?" he growled, stalking over to her. "I gave you what you asked for and this is the reality, Zoe. If you don't like it, you know what to do."

The lenses of her glasses flashed in the dim light as she lifted her chin, her head against the brick of the building at her back. "You always treat your lovers like shit then?"

Anger flared inside him. "Of course not. You should know me better than that."

"No, actually, and I think that's the problem, Gideon. I don't know you." She swallowed and he couldn't take his eyes off the movement of her lovely throat. "I thought I did, but I don't."

He prowled closer to her, recklessness growing in his gut,

fueled by anger and the constant craving he couldn't seem to shake. "Did you ever think that there might be a reason for that?"

She didn't move, continuing to watch him as he came nearer. "Then tell me what it is. Isn't that what lovers do? Tell each other stuff?"

"Yeah, not my lovers, baby. They don't need to know anything but how good my cock feels inside them." He stopped in front of her, looking down into her eyes. "And for the record, none of them have ever complained about the way I treated them."

Her chin had gotten a tilt to it that was definitely defiance. "Then consider this your first complaint."

Something kicked hard inside him, the part of him that enjoyed a good fight. The same part that had spanked her. That had taken her hard on the Chevy in his garage. That had thrown her onto his bed and ruthlessly touched her everywhere no matter the shell-shocked look on her face. The beast inside him that was bad and always had been.

He reached out, put his hands on her hips, the warmth of her body seeping into his palms. "What? You wanted more romance? Dinner and fucking roses?" Gripping her, he turned her around so she faced the wall. "Me being all gentlemanly and considerate and asking politely before I stick my dick in you? I'm not that guy, Zoe. He's a fantasy you created. He isn't real." Keeping one hand on her hip, he let the other slide down over her ass, squeezing her.

He ached. Christ, he just fucking ached.

She turned her head, her profile so delicate against the hard brick. "Don't be a coward, Gideon."

He growled, squeezing her ass again, relishing her soft gasp. "What the fuck does that mean?"

"You keep turning me around so you can't see me. Why? You can't look me in the eye while you're fucking me?"

Jesus.

You might think she doesn't know you, but she does. She's not stupid.

No, Zoe was very, very far from being stupid.

He slid his fingers over the curve of her ass and down, pushing between the backs of her thighs to where she was warm and damp, running his thumb over the seam of her jeans, pushing lightly. Her lashes fluttered and she shuddered, taking a sharp breath.

"I might just like fucking you from behind." He pressed his thumb against the denim again, right where her soft little pussy was, pushing. "Ever think of that?"

Her lashes fell completely, lying in lush dark fans on her cheeks. Her mouth had opened, full and pouty. "No," she said. "You don't want to look at me. You want me, but you hate it."

She's right. You do hate it.

He stilled, hearing the undercurrents of hurt and anger in her voice. "Zoe—"

"Thing is, I don't hate wanting you. And you should know that I don't hate what you're doing to me either. In fact . . ." She took a ragged breath. "I like it. I mean, it's not what I thought or expected. But . . . it's exciting. *You're* exciting."

Oh Jesus Christ.

He stared at her profile, his hand between her thighs, feeling all that damp softness and heat, and the possessive thing inside him clawing at him, sharper this time.

"I know it's selfish of me." Her voice had dropped to a whisper. "And I know I pushed you into this. But I just . . . I want to see you. Please?"

It had always been her honesty that got to him. The simple way she opened her heart up and let him look inside. He hadn't ever had anyone who'd trusted him enough to do that, not one single fucking person.

After his mother had been killed, he'd gone from foster home to foster home, and he'd soon learned that being too open was always a recipe for pain. He'd kept himself locked up tight so that no one would ever get in and hurt him, keeping everyone at a distance. Then he'd met Zoe and things had changed. She'd only been six, and yet somehow her honesty reached inside him and unlocked him. He'd found himself opening up to her in a way he hadn't with anyone else for years. Maybe it had been because she was so young. Maybe it was just her.

Whatever it had been, it reached inside him now and held on tight. And he was turning her back to face him before he'd even realized what he was doing.

She looked up at him, her eyes gleaming gold behind the lenses of her glasses, her black hair a dark cloud around her head.

"I'm not the man you think I am, little one," he said hoarsely. "I'm not a hero, and I don't want you putting me on a fucking pedestal."

Her brow creased. "I know you're not. I'm not stupid, Gideon."

"Whatever you think I am, it's worse."

She said nothing for a long moment, and weirdly it made him feel uncertain and unsure. "How much worse?"

"It's better you don't know."

Her hand came out, a palm pressing to his chest, the heat of it burning through the cotton of his T-shirt. "What if I want to?"

No. He wasn't having this conversation with her, not now and certainly not here. Revealing secrets wasn't part of the deal anyway.

Reaching for the hand against his chest, he slipped his fingers around her wrist. Her skin was so warm, the bones beneath so delicate. Breakable. Fragile.

Vulnerable.

He shouldn't be doing this to her, not out here, in a dark,

dirty alley with a Dumpster down one end of it. But she'd come here for a reason and so had he, and it wasn't to talk.

So he gripped her slender wrist tightly and slid her hand all the way down his chest and over the front of his jeans, to where his cock pressed hard against the denim. And he held it there, looking down into her golden eyes. "You're not here to talk, Zoe. And neither am I."

She blinked but didn't pull her hand away. "Okay. But if you're not going to give me anything of yourself, the least you can do is look at me." It sounded like a challenge, but underneath, he could hear a thin, fragile edge. "I don't want to be just another random woman you screw, Gideon."

She's not a random woman you screw, and nothing you do will ever make her into one.

Something twisted in his heart, sharp and cruel as a knife.

Of course she wasn't, yet he was trying to force her into that role all the same. And if he did, if he kept pushing her the way he was doing right now, he would only end up hurting her, perhaps breaking her. Because she wouldn't run from him the way any other woman would. She wouldn't tell him to fuck off.

She was too strong, too stubborn, and sex and the mess that went along with it was brand-new to her. She was too honest for games and too inexperienced to understand how to protect herself. She had no emotional defenses at all.

You should never have touched her.

He shouldn't have, but he had, and it was too late now. Which meant he was going to have to give her this, because the thought of hurting her more than he already had was unbearable.

Unless it's yourself you've been protecting all along.

Stupid fucking thought. How could she hurt him? He was the dangerous one, not her.

But shit, she was such an innocent, and it wouldn't do to

completely destroy her experience of men. He owed it to her to give her something that wasn't merely the anonymous kind of fucking he had been giving her.

"Keep your hand there," he ordered, carefully taking the hem of her tank top in his fists and holding her gaze. Then he pulled his fists apart. Hard. The fabric was thin and it ripped beautifully, the sound of it loud in the alleyway. Almost louder than the sound that escaped her. He didn't stop or hesitate, though, keeping his gaze on hers as he reached for the delicate lace of her bra and jerking that apart too, so the cups fell aside, baring her.

Her eyes were huge and dark, the dim light of the alley shining on the high, round curves of her tits and the flat, shivering plane of her stomach, gilding her perfect skin. She made no move to cover herself, her hand staying exactly where he'd put it, her palm pressed against his already rock-hard dick.

It was a beautiful sight. *She* was a beautiful sight.

He stepped in closer in case there was anyone around, because he didn't want anyone else looking at her. This was for him. This was *all* for him.

Gently he reached for her glasses, taking them off and stowing them in his pocket the way he usually did. Then he took her chin in his hand, tilting her head back against the brick wall behind her.

She stared up at him, her pupils so dilated there was only a thin rim of gold around the edges, like the sun eclipsed by the moon. And the expression in them . . . It twisted the knife in his heart even more, because she had no game face, did Zoe. Everything she felt was all out there for him to read. Fear. Hope. Desire. Trust. As if she were a woman who'd never been hurt.

He held her chin tightly, the fragile bone structure of her jaw beneath his fingers, the softness of her mouth near his thumb.

"You shouldn't look at me like that," he said quietly. "You shouldn't look at any man like that."

Her eyelashes fluttered, long and thick. "Look at them like what?" Her voice had gotten that smoky quality to it, an ember of burning gold glowing deep in her eyes.

"Like you'd give them anything they wanted." He lifted his free hand and cupped one breast, the satiny feel of her skin a glory on his palm.

She took a ragged breath, her breast lifting against his hand in time with it. "I'd give *you* anything you wanted. You know that."

Of course he did. A mistake. She'd learn that soon enough.

He slid his thumb over the hard peak of her nipple, circling, making her shudder. Then he took it between his thumb and forefinger, pinching. Her mouth opened, another gasp escaping her, big golden eyes fixed to his, her fingers on his dick squeezing him through his jeans, an almost involuntary movement. His own desire coiled tight, making him feel feral and even more possessive than he did already.

He leaned down, closer to her, so his mouth was almost brushing hers, feeling her tremble in his grip. "You shouldn't. I will hurt you, little one."

"I don't c-care." She was breathing very fast. "I wouldn't be here if I didn't want whatever you give me."

And you keep telling yourself she's not dangerous.

But she wasn't, and there wasn't anything about that statement that should have made him uncomfortable. Yet . . . the look on her face and the expression in her beautiful eyes hit him like a brick to the back of his head.

She *would* give him anything he wanted. Anything at all.

The dark and hungry thing rose up inside him, that possessive, territorial part of him, desperate to claim what was his. Take it and never let it go.

She's yours in every way there is. . . .

Gideon bent his head and took her mouth, and she opened to him without hesitation, her head tipping back even farther to allow him access. He took that too, kissing her hard and deep as he covered her breast with his hand, squeezing. She made a soft sound, arching against the wall, kissing him back shyly, tentatively, and yet with an unpracticed kind of hunger that had a growl vibrating in his chest, making the feel of her hand so close to his aching cock too fucking much.

He knocked it away, pulling open the button on her jeans and jerking down the zipper. Then he released the hold he had on her jaw and slid his hand over her stomach, pushing beneath the waistband of her panties and farther, through soft, damp curls to the slick flesh between her legs.

She shuddered against him, and he pushed one thigh between hers, his fingers finding her hard clit, stroking her over and over till she was making soft sounds deep in her throat and moving her hips against his hand.

He pinched her nipple again, keeping his mouth on hers, and she quivered, the sounds she was making becoming more frantic. So he did it again, and again, giving her a small fraction of pain because he knew she got off on it, at the same time as he forced his thigh harder between hers. She groaned, her hips lifting as she arched against him, seeking more friction, more sensation.

She was such a greedy little girl for him. A desperate innocent. It made him so hard and so goddamn hungry he could barely think.

He kissed her jaw and down her neck, tasting the salt on her skin, licking it from the hollow of her throat before going farther, to the where he cupped her breast, lifting it to his mouth. He flicked his tongue over her nipple, then sucked hard on it. She gave a soft wail, her hands reaching for him, her fingers sliding into his hair and curling into it, holding on tight. The slight prickle of pain made him even hungrier.

He wanted her coming apart for him, wanted her crying for him. Wanted her to understand that no one else could give her this. No one else could make her feel this way. And he didn't much care why he felt that way, he just did.

Gideon pulled away from her, then dropped to his knees in front of her, not giving a shit about the dirty ground or pretty much anything else. He slipped his fingers into the waistband of her jeans and jerked hard, pulling them down to the tops of her thighs and her panties with them, so that pretty little pussy of hers was bare to him.

Then he gripped her hips and pinned them to the wall behind her, holding her still, and he leaned forward and licked her, one long, slow taste right up the center of her sex.

Her fingers in his hair tightened and she moaned his name, her slender body shuddering. He licked her again, another couple of times, long and leisurely, then he leaned in closer, circling her clit with his tongue, making her jerk in his hold, her breath coming in sobbing gasps.

She tasted so good. Of lazy summer day heat and warm honey, but there was a spicy kick to her too, that threatened his own self-control, that made him want to spread her wide and eat her right up till she was screaming in his arms.

"Gideon . . ." Her voice was all husky, and he loved the sound of his name when she said it like that. "God . . ."

"Give me your hands, little one," he murmured as he tugged her jeans farther down, wanting to taste her deeper. She pulled her fingers out of his hair, letting him take them, not protesting as he slid them down between her thighs. "Hold yourself open for me."

She obeyed him without hesitation, spreading the slick folds of her pussy for him, her fingers trembling in a way that made his cock so hard it was painful. He wanted to kneel there and just look at her, spreading herself open, waiting for him. Shaking for him. Her breath came in raw, hard pants, and she was all smooth skin and wet flesh, gilded in the dim light.

He leaned in, inhaling the salty, musky scent of her arousal. Then he covered that gorgeous pussy with his mouth, pushing his tongue inside her. She bucked against him, crying out, and he went deeper, keeping her pinned in place with his hands on her hips.

"Gideon!" Her hands were on his head now, holding on tight as her knees buckled. "Oh . . . *God . . .*"

He'd wanted to take his time, eat her out long and slow, no matter where they were or that their friends were probably wondering what the hell had happened to them. And he would have done so if he hadn't been so goddamned fucking hard. But he wanted her to come first before he fucked her, so she'd be nice and slick and ready. So he went to work on her pussy, sliding his tongue in and out, using his fingers on her clit, until she was giving little sobs and the only thing holding her upright was his hands on her hips.

Then he put his mouth over her clit and sucked hard, and she screamed, the sound bouncing off the walls of the alley as her body trembled, no doubt making anyone who was nearby wonder just what the hell was going on.

And as much as he wanted to ease her back down before he pushed inside her, he knew he couldn't afford the time. He rose to his feet, keeping his hold on her, moving her along the wall so they were deeper into shadow.

She was half leaning into him, her mouth full and red from his kisses, her tank top hanging in torn pieces, baring those luscious tits with their hard, caramel-colored nipples. Her jeans and panties were down around the tops of her thighs, and he pulled them down even more, suddenly feeling so fucking desperate it was hard to think.

He reached into his back pocket and dug out his wallet, finding a condom and pulling open the packet. Then he unzipped his jeans, getting his dick out and rolling down the latex. Jesus, he couldn't believe it; his hands were shaking as much as hers had been.

Zoe's eyes were closed, her cheeks deeply flushed as she leaned against his chest, and there was something so deeply vulnerable about her right in that moment that his whole chest got tight.

She needed to be picked up and carried home, wrapped in blankets and put to bed. Not screwed hard and fast in an alley behind Gino's of all fucking places.

But he wasn't going to stop. He couldn't.

He eased her back against the wall, positioning himself, the head of his cock pressing against the slick heat of her pussy. She groaned, her hands clutching on to his T-shirt. "Gideon . . ."

"Don't tell me to stop." His voice came out broken and cracked, like wood left to dry out in the hot sun.

Her head lifted and she blinked at him, and he knew she'd heard his desperation, that she could probably see it in his face even without her glasses on.

It made him feel exposed, like he'd betrayed something he shouldn't have.

He made as if to stand back, wanting to spin her around, put her face to the wall, but she clutched tighter onto his T-shirt as if she knew exactly what he was going to do, holding him close.

"I'm not g-going to say stop," she said unsteadily. "I told you I'd take whatever you w-wanted to give."

It was too late to move her, too late to pull away. He could only lean in, pressing her up against the wall, pushing hard and deep into her. She cried out, and he could feel her pussy clench hard on him, the sensation nearly making his eyes roll back in his head.

So fucking good.

He wanted to go slow, make this last, but there was no fucking way in hell that was going to happen. All he could do was hold tight to her hips as he drew back, then pushed in again, sliding deep, going faster, harder. She shuddered, her wide eyes looking up at him, and he found himself looking back at her, falling into her amber gaze, so bright it was like looking into the sun.

She was so beautiful. She always had been.

He leaned in close, put his forearms to the wall on either side of her, surrounding her, hiding her from sight. Because this was just for him. She was just for him.

Zoe didn't take her eyes off him, and soon he'd forgotten why he'd even wanted her to. There was only her delicate face and the hot gold of her gaze, the tight, wet heat of her body, and the soft gasps she made when he thrust into her. The relentless pleasure, coiling tight inside him, threatening to rip him apart.

She wound her fingers tight into his T-shirt, shaking against him, and he angled his thrusts so he hit her clit, grinding into her, making her sob incoherently as her pussy convulsed around his cock.

Then he let himself go, driving deep and hard, shoving her against the wall, his own breathing harsh and rough, until the pleasure became blinding, and the orgasm hit him like a hammer straight to the back of his head.

Chapter 12

Zoe tipped forward, her forehead resting on Gideon's broad chest. He had leaned in toward her, his weight on his braced arms, crowding her against the brick at her back. He was breathing very fast, the heat roaring off him like a hot exhaust pipe, the thunder of his heartbeat in her ear, the air between them full of the scent of clean, male sweat and sex.

She didn't want to move. Everything about the moment was perfect, his heat, his ragged breathing, the feel of him inside her . . . Every damn thing. She didn't care that the brick was rough against her spine or that they were in a public alleyway where anyone could see them. Her entire awareness was centered on the man in front of her and what she'd done to him. Because she *had* done something to him, that much had been obvious. And it made her realize why she'd been quite so upset with him earlier.

He'd been treating her with cool, detached authority all weekend, no matter the passionate things they'd gotten up to in the darkness of his bedroom, and it made her feel like he was holding her at a distance. As if he had all the power and she had none.

But not now. When he'd pushed her up against that wall, surrounded her, she'd seen something catch fire in the darkness of his eyes. And it had been so *fucking* good to watch him, to actually see the pleasure unfurl across his rough, blunt, beautiful features. To see what he looked like when he came.

To know that *she* was the one who'd put that fire there. *She* was the one who'd made him feel all those things. *She* was the one who'd given him all that pleasure.

She'd never been conscious of having any kind of power in her life. In fact, if she'd thought about it, she would have said she really didn't have any power at all. But right now, with Gideon pinning her to the wall and clearly still recovering from the effects of a pretty goddamn powerful orgasm, she felt very powerful indeed.

She closed her eyes, letting herself rest against him, claiming the moment for herself.

Then, far, far too soon, he moved, withdrawing from her. "We need to get back." His voice sounded rough. "The others will be wondering where we got to."

Zoe bit down on a protest because of course he was right, the last thing she wanted was one of the others coming out to look for them. But she only leaned back against the wall, feeling shaky and raw and not really like going anywhere right now.

Gideon dealt with the condom, tucking himself away. Then he turned to her and, very matter-of-factly, he set about adjusting her clothing, pulling her jeans and panties up, tugging the zipper closed. Putting on her glasses.

Maybe she should have been annoyed by the gentleness of his touch, like she was a child needing to be dressed. But she wasn't. Instead, she felt soothed and taken care of.

God, why did they have to go back into the bar? She couldn't bear to face the others and pretend nothing had happened, not after she'd just come entirely to pieces in Gideon's arms. In fact, all she wanted to do now was go home and perhaps spend the rest of the night in his bed.

Gideon let out a breath, his gaze on the two halves of her tank that were sagging open, the remains of her bra along with it. Oh damn. She'd forgotten about that.

Without a word, Gideon gently gathered the fabric in his hands and pulled it tightly over her breasts, tying it in a knot between them. Her midriff was left bare, and it was probably quite obvious that her top had been ripped in half, but still. It was better than the whole world seeing her breasts.

Zoe found her throat getting tight. There was something about watching his big, scarred hands tie the fabric together, covering her, that made her ache. Made her want to get away from him, get some space.

God, she was kind of a mess.

You've been a mess for a while now.

Yeah, and it wasn't getting any better.

His fingers slid along her jaw, tilting her head back, and she looked up at him, his face shadowed in the light of the alleyway. "You okay?"

No.

"Yes." Her voice sounded shell-shocked. "But I think I . . . uh . . . need to go to the bathroom."

"Okay. You go while I tell the others we're leaving."

Her heart came to a slow, aching stop. "We're leaving?"

The expression on his face grew intense, the dark flame in his eyes burning hot. "Oh yeah, we're leaving. I have plans and they don't include sitting around a table in Gino's."

It wasn't hard to guess what those plans were, and it made something in her chest expand. She gave him a grin, unable to help it, feeling ridiculously shy and excited and breathless all at once. "What if I want to stay?"

His mouth curved in response, a slow burn of a smile that

made her heart turn over and slam itself against her ribs. "Too bad. You're coming home with me, no arguments."

She wanted to tease him more, but he bent his head and for one soul-shaking minute there was only his mouth on hers, a fierce, burning kiss that left her breathless and trembling.

"You get to the bathroom," he murmured against her mouth. "Otherwise I'm not gonna want to leave this alley."

She felt a little drunk even though she hadn't had any alcohol whatsoever, and almost dizzy, a sharp pleasure fizzing in her blood.

You're ridiculous.

Yeah, maybe she was. But who cared? She was going home with Gideon, and who knew what would happen after that? Lots of sex with any luck, and then she'd fall asleep in his arms. She was okay with that, more than.

He stepped away from her and turned to the door back into the bar, holding it open for her. She grinned at him, pausing to brush her fingers across his chest as she went past, purely because she couldn't help herself, before stepping into the dim corridor and heading for the bathroom.

There was no one else in there and thank God, especially when she glanced into the mirror. Because she sure as hell didn't recognize the woman looking back. A woman with black hair everywhere and a too big, too swollen mouth. With huge, dark eyes and deeply flushed skin, a ripped tank top pulled tightly over her breasts. A woman who looked like she'd been screwed up against a wall. Which was exactly what she was.

Zoe couldn't stop the smile that turned her mouth, watching as the other woman smiled too. Okay, so she really didn't want the others to see her like this, because the questions they'd ask would be a nightmare. But she had to admit, she looked pretty awesome. Sexy and mysterious and maybe even a bit dangerous.

Perfect for Gideon, right?

A thread of discomfort coiled in her gut, though she didn't quite know why. Dismissing it, she bent and splashed some water onto her hot face before trying to tame her hair so it didn't look like she'd been dragged backward through a hedge. There was nothing to be done about the ripped top, but she tried to fold in the ragged edges so it wasn't quite so obvious.

A couple of minutes later, giving her hair a last smooth-down with her palms, Zoe turned and pulled open the bathroom door.

And stopped dead.

There was a man standing outside and it wasn't Gideon. A man in what looked to be a very expensive and well-made dark suit. He was a stranger to her, obviously not a local, not in that suit, and he didn't smile. There was a tattoo on his neck, three little stars, and she couldn't help feeling she'd seen that tattoo before somewhere. . . .

Unease prickled down Zoe's back, and she glanced down the corridor toward the bar to check if Gideon was there. But the corridor was empty apart from the stranger.

Could it be he only wanted to use the men's bathroom?

"Miss James?" His voice was flat, shattering that idea.

"Uh, yes?" A reflexive response, which was dumb. Now it was too late to pretend she was someone else.

"Could you come with me, please? I have someone who'd like to talk to you."

Oh shit.

Something lurched in Zoe's gut, all of Gideon's dire warnings—the ones she'd pushed firmly to the back of her mind because she didn't want to deal with them—suddenly screaming in her head. Because there was no doubt as to what all this was about. There simply wasn't any other explanation for some random stranger in a suit approaching her.

It had to be Novak. Her father.

Her mouth went bone-dry, and she felt suddenly sick.

"Uh . . . now's n-not a good time." she said, forcing a smile on her face even though she stumbled over the words and her voice was weak and shaky. "I'm here with some friends."

The man changed position, casually blocking the corridor so she couldn't get to the bar. His expression remained utterly blank. "I'm afraid I'm going to have to insist."

Her gut lurched again, reflexive fear clutching tight inside her.

No, that was crazy. Okay, so this guy seemed vaguely threatening, but she'd been wanting to meet her father for a long time now, hadn't she? And sure, Gideon had told her Novak was shady, but he'd never given any reasons to back up those accusations and refused to discuss them when she'd pushed. Maybe it was because he was being way too paranoid and more than a little overprotective.

Swallowing her fear, Zoe lifted her chin. "Did my d-dad send you?" she asked, stumbling embarrassingly over the word.

The man smiled, his blue eyes remaining very cold. "All your questions will be answered if you'd just follow me."

Well, what did she have to lose? Gideon wouldn't be happy with her if she went off with this guy, though, especially if she didn't tell him. Then again, if she did, he'd probably stop her and she'd miss her chance to finally meet her father.

But what if Gideon's right? What if Novak is dangerous?

She'd be on her own, no one knowing where she was. . . .

"Uh . . . how long is this going to take?" she asked, stalling for time.

"Not long." He made a gesture to the door that led to the alleyway. "After you."

Since Gideon had told her who her father was, she'd been subconsciously avoiding the subject. Mostly because of what was happening with Gideon, but there was also some part of her that hadn't wanted to know. That wanted to stay ignorant because it was safe.

But she'd been safe for far too long. Hadn't that been what the whole of the past week was about? Leaving the shelter of innocence and ignorance, and taking a step out into a larger, more dangerous world.

Maybe the time had come to take another step.

Without giving herself a chance to second-guess, Zoe turned and headed back to the alley for the second time that night.

The man followed her as she stepped outside, urging her down the alleyway and onto the narrow street it led to. There was a sleek black car waiting by the curb, an Escalade, she noted almost absently. The man pulled open the door and gestured at her to get in.

A thread of fear wound through her, but she ignored it, getting into the darkness of the car.

The smell of leather seats and a man's aftershave permeated the interior. It wasn't unpleasant, though it didn't make the unsettled feeling in her gut any better.

Another man sat in the backseat. Older, in his sixties probably, with thick white hair. Handsome, too. The aura of money and privilege clung to him like the material of the dark suit he wore clung to his broad shoulders, and there was a kind of old-world glamour to him that reminded her of Hollywood movie stars.

Then he turned more fully toward her and her stomach dropped away.

At first she thought his eyes were dark, but then the light from outside hit his face and she realized they were the exact same color as hers.

So that's where they came from. You got them from him.

A feeling she couldn't quite articulate fluttered in her stomach, something like fear and hope and a strange kind of wonder.

Finally, here he was. Her dad.

How many fantasies had she woven around this man? Around her idea of who he might be. How many times had she imagined what and where he was, and whether he ever thought about her? Whether he even knew he had a daughter? And if he had, why had he never contacted her. . . .

"Hello, Zoe." His voice was deep and rich, a politician's smooth tone. "I'm sure I don't need to introduce myself, do I?"

Her voice wouldn't work, and for some reason the tips of her fingers had gone all cold. Weird. There was no reason to be afraid.

Come on. Pull yourself together. Gideon isn't here, you're on your own.

Yeah, shit. She was. For the first time in . . . well, ever, probably. Because even when her mother had first gone to prison and she'd been shipped off into the foster system, she hadn't been this alone. Gideon had been there. And when he'd aged out and she'd gone to another home, and then another, they'd stayed in touch. She'd written to him, letter after letter, posting them whenever she could to an address he'd given her. He'd written back, and sometimes, the rare, lucky times, he'd visited her.

He'd never not been there for her.

Except for now.

Zoe clasped her hands together, trying to still the nervous shakes. Getting all emotional wasn't going to help.

She stared at the man sitting next to her, trying to reconcile him with the fantasy she'd had in her head for so many years. The one where her father turned out to be a really nice guy who was thrilled to learn he had a daughter, who wanted to get to know her, be involved in her life. Who opened his arms, gathered her in close, and told her everything was going to be okay and that he was sorry for all the years of silence.

But of course, she knew, deep in her heart, that kind of thing only happened in the movies. It wasn't real life. And in fact, she had no idea about who her father might be, because her mother had never talked about him.

The only thing she'd had was a photo she'd found in her mother's jewelry box, not long after Claire had gotten out of prison and Zoe had gone back to live with her. It had been of this man, younger and less polished, but with the same expensive gleam of money and power. Zoe had known as soon as she'd seen the photo that it was her father, but she'd never said anything, too afraid of disturbing her mother's often fragile good moods.

Claire had been a tight-lipped, cold kind of woman, changed by her time in jail, and what with working two jobs just to get by, she didn't have a lot of time to spend with Zoe. A fact she never failed to point out just about every day.

Zoe knew her mother resented her, that her birth had been a mistake. Yet as soon as she'd gotten out of prison, she'd brought Zoe back to live with her without hesitation. It had always seemed weird, that a woman who didn't want her child, should claim her back all the same, but that was another thing Zoe hadn't wanted to think too deeply about. Whatever motivation her mother had, Zoe knew she wasn't going to like it.

"Of course I know you," she said, trying to make her voice sound calm and suspecting it didn't. "You're Oliver Novak." She paused. "You're my father."

His smile wavered slightly, as if he hadn't expected her to be aware of that fact. "You're well informed, I see. How long have you known?"

There was something about him that annoyed her, something she couldn't quite put her finger on. He didn't seem pleased to see her at all, and he made no move to hug her or even shake her hand.

Are you surprised? He might be in shock.

Except he didn't look like he was in shock. He just looked . . . oddly detached.

She glared at him, a small curl of anger sitting in her gut.

"Don't you think I should be the one asking you that question?"

This time his smile remained firmly in place. "A fair point. Though if you're thinking this is going to be some kind of lovely father-daughter reunion, you're sadly mistaken."

Something shriveled up in her chest, but she refused to acknowledge it. Of course she hadn't thought that. Of course she hadn't been that naïve.

She set her jaw, gripping her hands together tighter, concentrating on her anger instead of the bitterness that felt horribly like disappointment. "So why am I here then? That asshole outside told me you wanted to talk to me about something. It better not take long. I have people who will be wondering where I am."

Novak glanced toward the driver's seat. He didn't say anything, but abruptly Zoe felt the car begin to move. And this time, panic flared inside her, Gideon's voice telling her Novak would stop at nothing to "silence" her echoing in her head. Shit, where the hell were they going?

"Relax," Novak said calmly, as if the car wasn't moving and he wasn't taking her God knew where. "We're only going for a little drive and no, it won't take long. I want to present you with a proposition."

Zoe resisted the urge to clutch on to the seat. "What kind of proposition?"

"All in good time." Novak paused, looking at her, the lights from the darkness outside sliding over his handsome face, making his eyes glitter. She almost had the impression that he was as curious about her as she was about him. "You don't look a bit like me, thank Christ," he said after a moment. "Except around the eyes. Just as well you take after your mother."

The shriveled thing in her chest shuddered, though she tried not to take any notice of it. "Lucky me."

"Yes, lucky you." He gave a soft, cold laugh. "I've been searching for you a long time, did you know that?"

"Can't have been looking very hard." She couldn't keep the sarcastic edge from her voice.

A faint smile flickered over his features. "Or maybe you were just hidden very well."

"Hidden?" She frowned at him. "What do you mean by that?"

"Perhaps you should ask Mr. Black."

Gideon? What the hell had he got to do with any of this?

Oh, come on. You've wondered why he refused to give you any reasons for being so certain about Novak.

"I don't—"

"We're not here to talk about him, Zoe. Suffice to say that it took me a long time to track you down, and if it wasn't for Mr. Rush's experiment with that development, I may not have found you at all."

She bit down on her curiosity. She'd ask Gideon about it later. "Okay, so why are you tracking me down?"

"Simple reason. As you may or may not know, I'm running for senator, and the last thing my campaign needs is an illegitimate child popping up and announcing herself to the world."

The shriveled thing in Zoe's chest crumpled into dust, the backs of her eyes prickling. Crazy. She'd thought she'd long ago given up all those fantasies of her dad coming to claim her, to take her away, back to his home where they'd live together as a family. So there was no reason for his flat statement to hit her so hard, no reason at all. Hell, she didn't even know this asshole, and clearly he *was* an asshole. Disappointment was the last thing she should be feeling.

"I wouldn't do that," she said. "I'm not that kind of person."

Novak's smile was cynical. "We're all that kind of person, Zoe. All it takes is a little incentive to bring it out."

"What's the point? Even if I say something, why would anyone believe me?" She didn't quite know why she wanted to justify herself to him, only that it was important he know she'd never even think of doing anything like that. "It would be your word against mine."

He tilted his head, giving her a measured look that she didn't much like. "You know your mother did a paternity test, don't you? She mailed me the results. With demands for money."

Zoe stared at him, shock sliding icy and thick through her veins. "What?" Her voice sounded all faint and strange. "But I . . . I mean, she never said anything about it. She never talked about you at all."

He said nothing for a long moment, studying her with the same golden eyes she saw looking back at her in the mirror every morning. "We were from very different worlds, your mother and I. She used to clean my house." He let out a breath. "It only happened a couple of times. So it was a shock to find out I had a daughter. Even more of a shock to receive the results of a paternity test and demands for money in the mail, ten years after our liaison had ended."

She didn't know why she should be so surprised, given how angry at the world her mother had seemed. She was always complaining about how little money they had and how difficult it was to make ends meet, as if it was Zoe's fault. But now it seemed clear why she'd been so keen to have Zoe back when she'd gotten out of prison. She'd been her mother's ticket to riches.

A hollowness opened up inside her, and she had to fold her hands over her stomach in a vain attempt to ease it.

"She threatened to tell everyone that I'd fathered a child if I didn't give her what she wanted," Novak went on. "And at that time, it was . . . a difficult situation for me." His voice was quiet, and yet there was something vibrating in it that sounded horribly like rage. "I gave her money for a while and then . . ." He trailed off. "I heard she died."

Zoe swallowed and looked down at her hands. About six months after she'd left with Gideon, her mother had died of a drug overdose. A habit she'd picked up in jail and never managed to kick.

Sometimes the guilt of leaving ate away at Zoe like corrosion inside an engine. Making her wonder what would have happened if she hadn't been so lonely, if Gideon hadn't been so convincing about her going with him.

Nothing would have happened. Mom wouldn't have wanted to change and certainly not for you.

"Yes," she said quietly. "She did."

Novak was quiet another long moment. "I'm not sorry about your mother—I'm sure you can understand why. And I'll never be a father to you. But I can offer you something nevertheless. All I ask in return is that you keep my identity a secret." He paused. "And that you leave Detroit. In fact, I want you out of Michigan altogether."

Abruptly it felt like a large fist was squeezing around her heart. "What do you mean you want me out of Michigan?"

"I don't want you in my city, Zoe. I can't have my campaign put at risk, especially when there is so much at stake." He gave her a slight smile. "If I make senator, it's going to mean great things for Detroit, and I'm sure you won't want to do anything that would jeopardize that."

Her throat felt dry and scratchy, that odd kind of hollowness gaping wide inside her. She'd thought a lot of things about the day she'd meet her father, about what he might say, what he might do. She'd just never thought he'd actually tell her to not only get out of his life, but to get out of his city and his entire state as well.

"And what do I get?" she asked, trying to sound cool and with-it, and not like a desperate little girl.

"Just like your mother, aren't you?" Novak's smile took on that cynical edge again. "Don't worry, you'll get something. In fact, it's not just something, it's a lot." His gaze glittered in the light, a businessman at the height of his power, and Zoe knew that this really had nothing to do with her in the slightest. He was negotiating a deal and that was all. "Certain sources have told me that your grades at school were very good indeed. Which must make you interested in going to college, I bet."

She froze. How the *hell* did he know that? "I . . . might be."

"Which colleges are you looking at?"

She didn't want to give anything away, but it seemed pointless to deny it. "I don't know yet."

"You'll be an older student, I suppose. And no doubt you'll be looking for financial assistance."

"I . . . guess."

"I could help you, Zoe. My alma mater is Princeton. I can put in a word for you, get you a place." His mouth curved. "Call it help with your college fund. You'll love it and New Jersey is a fine place to be."

Princeton. Jesus Christ.

The fingers around her heart squeezed tighter.

"And . . . and if I don't want to leave?" She had to force the words out. "If I want to stay here in Detroit?"

His expression didn't change, and maybe that was the worst part. That he kept right on smiling. "Then I'm afraid I'll have to make life extremely difficult for you and your friends. And make no mistake, Zoe. I can do that." Another pause, the glint in his eyes becoming more pronounced. "Especially for Mr. Black."

Everything in her went cold. "Is that . . . a threat?"

He stared at her, his expression non-threatening. Yet she could feel the threat anyway, filling up the interior of the car like a thick, choking fog. "Call it a warning."

"Like you can even touch him," she said in a rush. "Gideon isn't afraid of—"

"Oh, I think Mr. Black is very afraid." Finally, the smile disappeared, leaving a cold, hard expression in its place. "And with good reason. But it's not only Mr. Black who needs to worry. I can make life very difficult for the rest of your friends too. Those development plans Mr. Rush was working on, for example. Permits will need to be obtained, various permissions granted. I'm sure you can see where things could get . . . stalled, shall we say?"

Anger spiked in her gut. Those plans meant a lot to her friends and to her, the kind of development that was sensitive to the neighborhood and the people who lived there. The kind of development that Royal desperately needed.

"You mean you'll stall them," she said before she could stop herself.

"Does it matter who? It's merely incentive for you to think about my offer." He raised a brow. "Unless you want to accept right now?"

Bastard.

Anger and fear twined in her gut. College and leaving Detroit. Leaving her friends. Leaving Gideon.

Leaving her *home.*

"I . . . need to think about it," she forced out.

Novak smiled at her again. "Very well. You have two days."

Gideon tapped his fingers on the tabletop, staring fixedly at the corridor that led to the bathrooms. Where the fuck was Zoe? Did it really take ten minutes to do whatever the hell she was supposed to be doing in there?

The others were bent over the plans, Tamara arguing about something with Zee while Rachel made the odd comment. Levi was sitting back in his chair, obviously leaving them to fight about it among themselves. He had a lock of Rachel's hair curled around one finger, and kept stroking it with his thumb.

Jesus, the guy was besotted.

He'd told the others that he'd gone to check on Zoe and she'd told him she wasn't well. So now he was going to take her home. None of the rest of them had even noticed his and Zoe's absence, nor had they argued—his taking Zoe home when she wasn't well wasn't anything out of the ordinary.

What *was* out of the ordinary was the fact that she hadn't yet come out of the bathroom.

Fuck. What the *hell* was she doing?

Starting to get annoyed now, because that was easier than the other feeling that gripped him, the one that felt a hell of a lot like fear, he shoved his chair back and got up again.

Rachel gave him a glance. "What's up?"

"Zoe's taking a long time in that bathroom." He skirted around the table, heading back toward the corridor again. "Going to check out what the fuck she's doing."

He didn't wait for a response, making a beeline for the women's bathrooms, then pausing outside the door to knock loudly on it and call her name. Only to get silence in return.

The thing he didn't want to call fear turned over inside him, and he was shoving open the door and stepping inside before he could think better of it

But the bathroom was empty.

His blood began to run cold.

Turning, he went out again, going into the men's room just to be sure. But she wasn't there either.

Something was rising inside him, something murderous, a red haze beginning to settle over his vision. He knew this feeling, it had happened before, in the darker days before he'd realized how he had to change and who he had to change into. And even before then, as a young boy staring at the body of his mother, at his father's hands wrapped around her throat.

It was a feeling that whispered to him of violence and rage, and normally he didn't listen to it, kept it locked down tight.

But this was Zoe and tonight no locks were going to be strong enough.

He left the men's bathroom and stalked down the corridor to the door that led to the alley, stepping out into the darkness. Nothing moved out there; it was as silent and empty as it had been when he'd had her up against the wall.

He walked down the alley to the street, looking up and down, trying to spot anything that would give him a clue as to where she'd gone. But there was nothing.

She'd vanished.

The red rage clawed up inside him, making his hands clench into fists, every muscle in his body tensing in readiness to fight.

Novak had taken her, he was sure. There could be no other explanation.

Christ, he'd been stupid. Stupid to let her come to Gino's. Stupid to let her out of his sight. He'd gotten complacent over the years, he'd gotten soft.

Gideon stared into the darkness.

He would find her, even it if meant tearing this city apart. Then he'd light it on fire and watch the whole fucking thing burn.

Taking a long, slow breath, he turned and began to run, heading back to his apartment. The others would probably wonder where the hell he'd gone, but he wasn't going to waste time letting them in on what was going on. He needed to find Zoe and fast, and he was going to do it alone. No point dragging everyone else in on this.

He got home in record time, letting himself into the apartment and heading straight for the bedroom, where he kept a gun in the top drawer of his dresser. Pulling it out, he gave it a reflexive check before sticking it into the waistband of his jeans at the small of his back. Then he took out the burner phone that had his more private contacts on it, scrolling through the list to find the one he wanted, hitting the call button just as the door to the apartment slammed shut.

He froze, every sense on high alert. It could only be one person, right? Quickly he cancelled the call and stepped out of the bedroom, glancing down the hallway.

Zoe was standing with her back to him, carefully doing up the locks on the front door.

Something yawned wide inside him, a desperate kind of relief that mixed with the adrenaline burst of his rage, creating a need that burned in his veins as if his blood were gasoline and someone had taken a match to it.

He was moving down the hallway fast, before he'd even had time to think, making straight for her, because she was whole and apparently uninjured and she was right fucking here. After he'd thought her lost.

She must have heard him coming because she turned around suddenly, her eyes widening, two golden coins glittering in her pale face. "Gideon? Where have you—"

He didn't let her finish, gripping her by her upper arms and pushing her up against the door, caging her there by putting his forearms on either side of her head and leaning in, surrounding her. His heart was battering itself against his ribs like a hungry dog pulling on a leash, and if he didn't touch her right the fuck now, he didn't know what he'd do.

She was breathing very fast, her pulse frantic at the base of her throat, but he didn't say anything. He just needed a moment to assure himself of her safety, of the fact that she was alive and right here with him.

His mother, dead on the kitchen floor as his father had stormed past, not noticing his son by the doorway. Gideon had crept into the room, reached for her hand. It had still been warm and he'd thought . . .

No. That had been years ago and he'd gotten over it. Way over it.

Bending slightly, he rested his forehead against Zoe's, inhaling her scent, feeling the warmth of her slender body against his, trying to stop the gallop of his heart and get himself under control.

"It's okay," she said softly. "I'm here. I'm fine."

He wanted to tell her that of course she was fine, that he hadn't been afraid and enraged and ready to turn the whole city upside down looking for her. But the time for that kind of bullshit had passed.

"Where the fuck did you go?" It came out as a demand, his voice thick with the remains of his rage. "One minute I was waiting for you at Gino's, the next you'd gone."

Her gaze flickered. "I . . . needed a moment to think."

Oh no. Oh *hell* no.

"Don't you *dare* fucking lie to me!" He curled one hand into a fist and slammed it against the door beside her head, making her jump. "Not now, Zoe. Not fucking now." Dimly a voice in his head was telling to calm down, that he was going to scare her, but he couldn't seem to do it. The rage and the relief were overwhelming, almost making him shake. "Was it Novak?" Another demand. "Did he take you? Did he hurt you? Tell me. Tell me, *now.*"

Zoe's face was very pale, her gaze searching his, staring at him as if she'd never seen him before in her life. "Yes, okay, it was him. But no, he didn't hurt me. He only wanted to talk."

Both hands were in fists now, and he was pressing them hard against the wooden surface of the door as if he wanted to smash right through it. Maybe he should. God knew, he had to do something to get himself the fuck under control.

He moved closer, so he was nearly pressed against the length of her body, surrounding her completely as if he could keep the whole world out. Jesus Christ, no one was going to touch her, not ever again. He'd kill anyone who even thought about it.

"And you went with him?" He tried to make the question at least sound more or less civil. "You didn't think you might wanna tell me where you were going?"

Zoe put out her hands, her fingertips against his chest as if she wanted to keep him at a distance. It made the hungry, possessive part of him growl in denial. "A guy was waiting for me outside the bathroom and he wouldn't let me speak to you. I had to go with him or . . . Anyway, he didn't give me much of a choice."

Gideon went very, very still, the red rage starting to descend again. "Novak threatened you?"

"No." Her golden eyes came to his. "He threatened you."

He would kill him. He would get his fucking gun and he'd put a bullet in Novak's brain. End this once and for all. No one threatened what was his, no one.

You fucking idiot. You know where all this leads, don't you?

The voice in his head was an old one, knowing and snide, and once again that painful memory was stark in his head, of his mother on the floor and his father choking her. Gideon had been eight.

So much for restraining orders. No one cared about an exwhore, and if she was murdered by her violent, possessive ex? Yeah, well, no one cared about that either. And as for her kid, the son of a murderer, the son of a prostitute, he could disappear into the foster system and no one would give a shit.

There had been days when he'd felt his father's rage inside of him, a fire that never went out. A dark, wordless anger that had only gotten stronger the more foster families he was cycled through, and when he'd aged out, he'd found the outlet for that anger in the darkness of the criminal underworld.

Until Zoe had become the light that had guided his way out of it.

It's still there, though. It's going to eat you alive.

He could feel it too, burning him from the inside out. That violent urge to lock her away where no one would ever touch her or hurt her. So she would remain safe and his forever.

Gideon struggled to unclench his fists, to lock down all that violent, unstable emotion. But it was almost fucking impossible.

And maybe she knew the knife edge he was walking, or at least sensed it, because her fingertips on his chest firmed and began to move, stroking him gently, as if he was an angry animal that needed soothing.

"I'm fine," she repeated. "It was no big deal, okay?"

Her hands felt good on him, but he was in no way soothed. "It's not okay and it's a pretty fucking big deal, Zoe." He shifted one hand, cupping her jaw, holding it tight, her cheek against his palm. "Tell me what happened. All of it."

Again that flicker in her eyes, that hint of reluctance, as if she didn't want to tell him. But hell no, that wasn't happening. His hand on her tightened, and her eyes widened in response.

Tone it down. Give her some goddamn space. You're scaring her.

Yeah, well, she was going to have to get used it, wasn't she? She was his now and there would be no distance, no fucking space. He'd already made that decision back in the alleyway.

"Gideon—"

"Now, Zoe."

"God, you're a pain in the ass." She flattened her palms on his chest, and somehow the relief and the rage burning in his gut began to change into desire. Into the need to have her naked and under him, with him deep inside her.

That would be happening, definitely. But later. First he needed to know exactly what Novak had said to her.

Why? You afraid he might have let something slip?

Something clenched hard inside him, and he found himself

looking into her eyes, trying to catch any hints of fear or anger. Anything that might give away that Novak had let her know a few salient facts about his past. But the fear there wasn't directed at him, and neither, he suspected, was the anger. Or at least, she was angry only because he was telling her to do something she didn't want to do.

In other words, typical Zoe.

"He knows I'm his daughter," she said quietly. "My mom was apparently blackmailing him with a paternity test she threatened to make public if he didn't send her money."

Should he look surprised? Look like he didn't know that already? He decided against it, keeping his expression neutral. "Keep going."

She looked down at her hands where they were spread on his chest. "He's been trying to find me for a while, basically because he wants me to leave Detroit. In fact, he wants me to get out of Michigan completely." The words were steady, but Gideon heard the catch in her voice. "He said that if I leave, he'll get me into Princeton, pay my tuition fees."

Gideon felt like he'd been punched hard in the gut. Bastard. That fucking bastard. He'd been expecting threats of violence, of hurt, because that was Novak's usual modus operandi. But no, the guy had done something far more persuasive. He'd offered her something she actually wanted.

Something you failed to give her.

He ignored the thought, staring down at her. "And if you don't leave?" he demanded. "Did he say what he'd do if you stayed anyway?"

Zoe's slender throat moved in a convulsive swallow. "That he'd make sure Levi's development plans would stall in red tape."

Of course he had. Novak was a consummate politician, and clearly he'd left behind the good old days where threats were backed up with good old-fashioned fists. Now it was all about the right levers to pull, the right buttons to press, what would give him the right leverage.

Gideon and the others could fight violent threats, but red tape? Nothing could fight bureaucracy.

The muscles in his body tightened. It would be so easy to push himself away from her and call the contact he'd been going to call, leave the apartment, and take action. He could feel the heavy, reassuring weight of the gun at his back, reminding him of the days when everything had been simpler. More violent, but much simpler. Where the only thing that had mattered was the relief driving his fist into some other poor fucker's face had given him.

Just like your old man, huh?

No, *not* like his old man. Maybe once, but not now. Now it wasn't about money or violence, but keeping Zoe safe. Keeping his friends safe. The way he hadn't managed for his mother.

"Gideon." Zoe's voice was insistent, and he realized he'd been standing there, zoning out, lost in thoughts of revenge.

He focused on her. "What?"

The look in her eyes had changed, become worried. "Whatever it is you're thinking of doing, don't."

Jesus, what had she seen? If he wasn't careful, he'd reveal himself to her and she'd see what a beast he was at heart.

Wasn't that the whole point?

It was, but now that the moment of truth was here, he found he didn't want her to know. Not about the extent of the bad shit in his past. Certainly not the past that involved Novak and the job he'd given Gideon. The job that involved getting rid of her mother and her mother's blackmail threats. And he'd been going to go through with it too, until he'd found out whom he'd been sent to kill.

But no, he couldn't tell Zoe that. Not yet. His past was a nightmare, and he wasn't ready for her to know about that particular darkness.

Gideon stared down at her. "And what exactly do you think I'm going to do?"

"I don't know. But you look . . . angry."

"I *am* angry." He leaned in even farther, pressing her back into the door, the soft heat of her body right up against him. "I'm fucking enraged. No one touches you, Zoe. No one threatens you, not if they don't want me to come down on them real hard."

Her hands had gotten trapped between them and she gave a little struggle, trying to get them free. But he didn't make any move to help, the desperate need to have her wrapping itself around his throat and squeezing him tight.

She took a ragged breath. "I know, but this isn't some idiot drug dealer. This is Novak, and he's got money and power. He can do whatever the hell he wants."

"Jesus. You've already said yes, haven't you?"

Color stained her cheeks, a bright spark of anger gleaming in her eyes. "No, of course I didn't. I told him I couldn't give him a decision so he gave me two days to think about it." She gave another wriggle. "Please, Gideon. Give me some space. I can't breathe."

But he only released her jaw and leaned in, his forehead to hers again. "No." His voice didn't even sound like his it was so thick. "You don't get any space, little one. You don't get any distance. Not now. Not ever again. I told you you're mine and I meant it. I'm gonna send a message to Novak, one that'll ensure he'll stay away from you and from Royal completely."

Yeah, he'd been complacent too long. Sitting here in Royal pretending the outside world didn't exist, playing happy families with Zoe and the others. Believing she was safe, that he'd gotten her away, that he'd left Chicago and his past behind. But it was always there, that past. Biding its time, waiting for the perfect moment to fuck him up. And he couldn't lie back and take it, couldn't pretend it wasn't there.

The time had come to stop pretending, to stop thinking he'd gotten away.

The time had come to take action.

She'd gone still, her big golden eyes staring up into his. "What message?"

"That doesn't concern you."

"The hell it doesn't." Her gaze narrowed and he felt her arms slide around his waist, her fingers slipping beneath the hem of his T-shirt at the small of his back.

Gold flared, wild and bright in her eyes. "What the hell, Gideon?"

No prizes for guessing what she'd discovered.

His gun.

Chapter 13

He was dangerous, she'd always known that, or at least sensed it. She just hadn't realized quite how dangerous until now. Until she'd felt cold metal against the tips of her fingers instead of warm skin.

Maybe it should have shocked her that he had a gun slipped into the waistband of his jeans, but it didn't. It was like she'd known it from the moment she'd turned around and seen him stalking down the hallway toward her. A man with rage carved deeply into every line of his face. A man harder and colder and infinitely more dangerous in every conceivable way than the Gideon she knew.

It had felt like the final remnants of a mask had been torn from her eyes.

She'd always wanted to know what was behind his laid-back, chilled-out exterior, and now here it was, right in front of her. Danger. Wild fury. Lethal intent.

Shocking and yet thrilling at the same time, because somehow she found the danger of him unbearably attractive. And then he'd pushed her up against the wall, surrounding her in all that beautiful threat, that intense heat, that wild, masculine fury, and she hadn't been able to move for sheer relief.

So good to be close to him, to feel him standing there between herself and the rest of the world, her armor, her defense. She'd let herself enjoy it for a while, because after her father's cold dismissal of her, Gideon's possessiveness was balm to her lonely soul.

Until she'd realized the extent of his fury, seen the violence in his eyes, and what it might mean. Not for her, but for him.

Gideon pushed himself away before she could get a good grip on the gun, leaving a sudden, cold space where his body had been.

"Don't." His voice was flat. "That's none of your fucking business."

"A gun is none of my business?" She blinked at him. "What the hell were you going to do with it? Shoot Novak?"

The expression on his face had closed down. "I was going to do whatever I had to do to keep you safe."

"So yes, you were going to shoot him."

He said nothing, staring at her, and she had the abrupt, dizzying sense that she was looking into the dark eyes of a total stranger.

"Is that what you're going to do now?" A stupid question. That was exactly what he was going to do now, she could see it in his black gaze.

He didn't reply immediately, reaching around to get the gun out of his waistband, looking it over with the kind of professional ease that suggested he'd handled a gun many, many times before.

Of course he has and you know it. You always have.

Maybe she had. Maybe she'd always suspected that something dark lay at the heart of him. And maybe she should have found that repellent or at the very least disturbing.

But she didn't. It only fascinated her more.

"I have to protect what's mine." Again that cold, hard voice. "That's what it's all about, Zoe. Because no one else fucking will."

Fear sent an icy thread coiling through her, and not for herself. God, if he took that gun and went out in search of Novak, and did what she was afraid he'd do . . .

You'll lose him.

The thread of fear pulled unbearably tight.

"No." She moved forward, putting her hands out to touch him, stop him somehow. "Don't you dare. Novak isn't worth going to jail for."

His mouth curved in a smile that was as far from amused as it was possible to get. "You'd actually think I'd let myself get caught?"

"And you don't know that you won't. Gideon, it's not worth the risk." She took a breath. "Look, I'm fine. I wasn't hurt. And he let me go. Hell, he even dropped me off right outside the apartment."

But Gideon's hard, inky gaze didn't soften one bit. "So he knows where you live."

Well, she hadn't told him so . . . yeah, he did. "He won't hurt me, Gideon." She tried to put all her conviction into it. "I'm his daughter."

"You know nothing about him. Less than nothing." He slipped the gun back into his jeans. "Get out of the way, Zoe. That fucker won't be bothering you again."

"No," she repeated, reaching for him, sliding her hands up the hard wall of his chest and around his neck. She'd never used her sexuality to get what she wanted from a guy before, but hell, at least she had a head start with Gideon. "I'm not going to get out of your way. We were supposed to go home, remember?" She arched into him, pressing her breasts against him. "You wanted us to continue what we started in the alley."

He didn't move, staring down at her, the expression on his

face unchanging, but in the darkness of his eyes something glowed hot. "You think he'll ever let you go free? You think he'll give you money for college and you'll never see him again? Men like that don't forget, Zoe. Especially not when it comes to loose ends."

A chill whispered across her skin. "So you keep saying. And yet you never tell me how you know so much about men like him."

His mouth hardened, his jaw tight. "I just do."

Bullshit. He was holding out on her again.

"Perhaps you should ask Mr. Black. . . ."

Novak's voice whispered in her head, the knowing look on his face replaying itself over and over.

The chill became a lurching doubt. "You know him, don't you? You know Novak?"

There it was, a flicker in his eyes, so fast she almost mightn't have caught it if she hadn't been looking right up at him. He must have known she'd spotted it too, because all of a sudden his arm curled around her waist, pulling her in tight. "Best not to ask too many questions, little one," he murmured. "Especially ones you might not like the answers to."

Curiosity shifted inside her, along with that doubt, both competing for space. Did she really want to push this? Did she really want to know the answers to those questions? A few days ago, yes, she definitely would have, but now . . . God, she wasn't so sure.

The man who'd walked down the hallway toward her, who'd handled that gun like he'd been handling weapons all his life, wasn't the Gideon she knew. He was frightening and dangerous and . . . exciting. But it wasn't the fact that he was dangerous that made her hesitate. Once she knew all about *that* Gideon, would she ever be able to go back to the man who'd represented safety and home for the past thirteen years of her life? Would she ever be able to reconcile the two?

You already know you're never going to be able to go back.

"Why shouldn't I ask questions?" She glanced up at him from beneath her lashes, deliberately provocative. This was a dangerous line of inquiry but hell, it seemed to be distracting him enough that he wasn't heading out that door to do something to Novak. "You know everything about me. Why shouldn't I know about you, too?"

"I already told you, all you need to know is that Novak is sketchy as fuck and he'll do anything to maintain his position." Gideon's attention dropped to her mouth, then moved farther, down her throat to where her breasts were straining against the halves of her ripped tank.

Satisfaction began to glow inside her, along with an echo of the power she'd felt out in the alleyway earlier, where she'd seen the effect she had on him, making him totally lose his cool. She could do the same thing here, distract him from that gun and whatever vengeance he'd decided on. Because one thing was certain: She wasn't going to let him do something stupid, not when he was carrying that gun. God, if he ended up going to jail like Levi, she didn't know what she'd do.

"Hmmm . . . that's pretty bad," she murmured, letting one hand fall to the knot between her breasts and toying with it. "Always a good quality to have in a father, right?"

His gaze suddenly lifted to hers, then focused. "You wanted it to be different, didn't you?"

If you think this is going to be a father-daughter chat, then you're sadly mistaken. . . .

Her gut clenched tight, but she shoved the feelings of disappointment and hurt away. She didn't want to talk about that, not now and not with him. Anyway, this wasn't about her and her daddy issues. This was about Gideon and whether or not he was going out to kill a man. Because it sure looked like that's what he was going to do.

She trailed her hand down his chest, loving the firm wall of muscle as she pressed against him, then going lower, the flex of his abs as she traced the hard ridges beneath the cotton of his shirt. "If you don't want to talk about your past, then I sure as hell am not going to talk about my father." Her fingers moved lower, to the waistband of his jeans. She'd never full-on touched him like this before, not with obvious sexual intent, and to be honest, she was feeling nervous and shaky about it. But he hadn't stopped her, so she made herself go on, spreading her fingers out and then pushing her palm over the denim of his fly. He stilled, and she could feel the gradual hardening of his cock against her hand.

A wild thrill went through her, and she glanced up, wanting to see the effect she had on him. Definitely fire in his eyes now, leaping high. And it made her feel so good, the knowledge that she had this power chasing away her earlier disappointment and hurt. "Two days," she said quietly. "I have two days to make a decision. Which means we have time to plan something that doesn't include . . . that gun."

He said nothing, only kept on looking at her, and she couldn't tell what he was thinking, his black eyes depthless, glittering. Then his phone went off, and he reached into his back pocket and got it out, answering it without taking his eyes off her. "Yeah? No, it's okay. We're both back home. . . . Yeah, she needed to get back home quickly so we just left. . . . Right. I'll call you tomorrow." Gideon pressed a button, disconnecting the call and sticking his phone in his back pocket again. "Levi," he said shortly. "Wanting to know if you were okay since I kind of left in a hurry."

"You didn't want to tell them the truth?" She started to take her hand away from him only for his palm to come down over the back of hers, holding it right where it was.

"No. Now's not the time."

He was hot against her palm, hard, the feel of him making it difficult to concentrate. "They're going to have to know, Gideon. Especially when it concerns Levi's plans."

"You think I don't know that? Tomorrow." The pressure of his hand over hers increased, pressing her palm more firmly against him.

Her breath caught. He was getting even harder, she could feel it. "What about tonight?"

"Tonight? I told you, there's a few lessons Novak needs to learn."

"What lessons?" She was pushing, but hell, she needed to know. "Are you going to kill him, Gideon?" Then, because she wasn't above using emotional blackmail, not about this, she added, "Are you going to kill my dad?"

The expression in his dark eyes shifted. "Zoe . . ."

Beneath the heat slowly building inside her, a current of ice water trickled. "I didn't think you were a killer, Gideon." The words sounded shaky and she shouldn't have said them, shouldn't have named her fear so blatantly, but it was out now. She couldn't take it back.

The look on his face changed yet again, except this time she couldn't read it, the silence heavy with something she didn't understand.

Or no, maybe she did understand. She just didn't want to acknowledge it.

He's done bad things. You've always known he wasn't what he seemed and deep down, you always knew it wasn't going to be good. . . .

Gideon's hand over hers dropped away and he let her go, stepping back. He looked suddenly very, very tired. "Go to bed, Zoe."

She blinked at the suddenness of the change, her stomach lurching. "What? But I thought—"

"No." Lifting a hand, he scrubbed it through his thick, shaggy black hair. "Don't argue. Just do it."

All her good feelings began to seep away, taking the heat with them, leaving her with nothing but that steady trickle of cold. "So that's it? You're just going to shut me out again?"

You know what this means, don't you? It means you're right.

But no, she didn't want to think about that.

You never want to think about it. That's why you're in this situation.

His hand dropped, and he looked at her for one long moment. Then he reached behind himself for the gun and went over to the little table that stood beside the front door, laying the weapon carefully down on the top of it.

He didn't say a word as he turned on his heel, or as he walked down to the hallway to his bedroom and shut the door quietly but firmly behind him.

Leaving her standing alone in the hallway.

Gideon slept badly, waking at four a.m. and lying there for at least an hour trying to get back to sleep. But eventually, his brain spinning and his dick hard enough that he wasn't going to go back to sleep anytime soon, he hauled himself out of bed and put on his running gear, electing for exercise instead of pointlessly replaying the shaky sound of Zoe's words in the hallway the night before.

I didn't think you were a killer, Gideon.

The look on her face, that fear in her voice had hit him in a vulnerable place, a place he'd thought he'd managed to keep well defended. Yet apparently not. As soon as she'd said it, he'd felt it like she'd channeled four million volts through him.

A killer . . .

He'd been the guy Novak had wanted to get rid of her

mother, chosen for his reputation—a reputation he'd cultivated quite carefully—as an underworld heavy-for-hire, the go-to guy for men who wanted their rules enforced quickly and as violently as possible.

It was a career he'd put behind him the moment he'd left Chicago—hell, the moment he'd walked into Zoe's house and realized where his job had taken him, who he'd hurt, and what it would mean if he went through with it.

He'd never actually killed anyone before, still less a woman. Yet even though he hadn't put his gun to Zoe's mother's head or pulled that trigger, the fact that he'd gone to her house fully prepared to do it still made him feel like a murderer.

Turned out that no matter how far you put the past behind you, it always caught up. In the end, there was no running from it. No hiding from it.

No matter how badly you wanted to.

He couldn't touch Zoe after that. Couldn't stand her hand where it was, over his dick, holding him as though she wanted him. There had been fear in her eyes and a kind of dreadful hope, as though she'd wanted him to tell her it wasn't true. That he wasn't what she was obviously terrified of him being.

His feet hit the pavement hard, the thick, heavy summer air a suffocating blanket. There weren't many people around this early in the morning, but he passed Ant and Deke, two old vets who liked playing cards on the sidewalk, already dealing out a hand of poker. They raised a hand in greeting, and he gave them a chin lift in return.

Fuck . . . this place. It had been his escape, his retreat, his safe haven, and he'd come to love it. The dirty sidewalks, the abandoned buildings and cracked windows, the drug addicts and all the rest of its filthy glory.

It was honest, that's what he loved about it. There was no pretense to it. Which made his being here ironic, considering all the pretending he was doing. Pretending he was a good guy. Pretending that what he was doing with Zoe was for her benefit.

Last night he'd walked away from her, not answering her question, but it was as good as an admission all the same and she would have known that. And she hadn't come after him, which told him everything he needed to know.

But that was a good thing. A very good thing. He'd let himself get carried away the night before; he'd lost his cool. First he'd fucked her up against that wall no matter that their friends were just inside, then he'd let Novak kidnap her. Sex was getting in the way and he couldn't have that.

So yeah, it was better she kept away from him. She didn't need a past as dark as his fucking up her life. The main thing he needed to figure out was how to keep Novak off her back and her safe in Royal. Because there was no way in hell he was letting her leave. No way in hell he was going to let Novak get his way. And besides, even if she left, she'd never be safe. She'd always be the mixed-race illegitimate daughter he was trying to hide. A man like him couldn't afford to leave a loose end like Zoe lying around.

Dawn was only just breaking by the time he got back to the apartment, sweaty and thirsty enough to drink all of Lake Erie dry. Going into the kitchen, he got himself a huge glass of water and chugged it back before turning on the faucet for another.

The back of his neck prickled.

He turned, half reaching into the small of his back to where his gun used to be, a reflex he hadn't indulged for years, only to see Zoe standing in the doorway, leaning up against the doorframe.

She wore only a pair of her tiny sleep shorts and another tank top, red this time, that molded to her beautiful tits, making his cock stir and his stomach go tight with want. Her hair was a mass of black curls over her shoulders, her eyes serious and dark behind the lenses of her glasses. There was a crease between her brows and a stubborn cast to her jaw, and he knew what that meant. She wanted to talk to him and she wasn't going to take no for answer.

"I think we need to talk, Gideon." Her voice was very direct and very, very firm. "I need to know what you are."

Ah, fuck.

Come on. You always knew you'd have to tell her one day.

Slowly he turned, leaning back against the sink and folding his arms. "You know what I am."

But she shook her head slowly. "No, I don't. I think you only let me see what you want me to see. Not what you really are. Not *who* you really are."

"Zoe . . ."

"What? You know what I am. What you see is what you get with me. I've kept no secrets from you, Gideon. None. Don't you think that maybe you should give me some of yours?"

"Not especially."

She didn't even blink this time. "So my virginity is worth nothing then?"

The goddamned little brat.

He shifted against the sink at his back. "I didn't know that was something I had to pay for."

"No, you just took it."

A flash of anger went through him. "You *gave* it to me, Zoe. Don't pretend otherwise."

"Oh, I know I did." Her gaze was unwavering. "But you didn't have to take it. So don't *you* pretend otherwise."

Dammit. She might be naïve, but she'd been learning a few things, obviously. "Then you should have been clearer you wanted something in return," he said, which was a dick thing to say, but hell, he had to protect her from the truth somehow, didn't he?

Do you really need to protect her? Or is it yourself you're protecting?

The thought twisted uncomfortably inside his gut, the fine edges of that truth feeling like they were gouging holes in him.

No, that was bullshit; he wasn't protecting himself. Hell, if she wanted to know, he'd tell her. Maybe it *was* time after all. Time he stopped pretending the past didn't exist. Pretending he was only a mechanic in Royal just trying to get by, with a little foster sister he'd do anything to protect.

Maybe it was time he started being as honest as the neighborhood he'd claimed for himself.

The crease between her brows had deepened, a faint glitter in her eyes. A beam of morning sunlight coming through the windows had fallen over her face, revealing the deep shadows beneath her eyes. Okay, so, she hadn't slept either.

Somehow that didn't make him feel any better.

"Is it so wrong to want something of you?" she asked. "Especially after last night."

"Why especially?"

"Why do you think? You were going to kill him, weren't you, Gideon? Tell me that wasn't why you decided to bring along a gun. In fact, now that I think about it, why do you have a gun anyway?"

He'd been so full of rage the night before that quite frankly, what he'd been going to do to Novak hadn't exactly been clear. Killing a man, however, was a pretty blunt way to end to things, and though he was a blunt kind of a guy, shooting a senatorial candidate hadn't featured highly in his plans.

But he'd still thought about it. Certainly, he'd been going to inform him that staying the fuck away from Zoe might be a good idea, especially if he valued his health.

"No," he said slowly. "I wasn't going to kill him. I was going to convince him that staying away from you and from Royal might be beneficial to him."

She stared at him, her gaze narrowing. "And the gun?"

"I've had it for years."

"That's not answering my question."

"Okay, so the gun was incentive."

"You've used one before, haven't you?"

He let out a long, silent breath and held her gaze. "Yes. Many times."

"Oh." She went pale at that, but didn't look away from him. "So, apart from last night, when was the last time you used one?"

"Thirteen years ago."

Her throat moved and she shifted against the doorframe. "Why?"

"Why did I use a gun?"

"Yeah."

"Because I was sent to kill someone."

Slowly the color leeched out of her cheeks, the circles beneath her eyes becoming even more pronounced. He shouldn't tell her any more. Then again, she'd wanted the truth.

"Who were you sent to kill, Gideon?" To her credit she said it without one single shake in her voice, even though she knew as well as he did what had happened thirteen years ago.

"I was sent to kill your mom, Zoe." He said it without hesitation, because he was committed now, there was no going back.

Her eyes went wide, her mouth opening in shock. "M-my mom?"

"You wanted to know what I was? Well, back in Chicago, I used to be an enforcer for hire. The criminal underworld always needed guys to do their dirty work for them, make threats, beat the shit out of people, and threaten those who were . . . inconvenient. I was one of those guys." It was easy to say, way easier than he'd thought. Yet the words fell into the silence of the kitchen, heavy as river boulders, smashing right through the cheerful domestic reality of the life he'd built in Royal. Shattering it completely.

"You were a . . . hit man?" Zoe sounded shaken, her voice a whisper.

"No. I stopped short of actually killing anyone. But I came close."

Her arms had dropped to her sides and the look on her face . . . Shock. Horror. He kept his gaze on her because glancing away would have been a pussy thing to do and he wasn't a pussy.

"But . . . Mom . . . I don't understand."

Carefully Gideon put his glass back down on the counter. "She was blackmailing Novak and a guy like him . . . well, you don't do that to a guy like him. He used to employ my services from time to time, and so he knew who to come to when he had a problem he wanted to get rid of. Your mom was the problem and I was the solution." He paused, because if nothing else, she needed to understand this. "Novak didn't give me her name, just an address and instructions to take out the person who lived there. I thought the address was familiar, but it didn't hit me until I pulled up outside and realized it was your house." Horror was stark on her face, but he was on this road now and so he'd tell her everything. "That's why I was there that night, Zoe. And that's why I told you I'd get you away. The danger was real. The danger was me."

"But you didn't—"

"No. I couldn't. Not your mom."

Her face had gone whiter than snow. "What would have happened if you hadn't known me?" There was a crack in her voice now, all her shock and fear bleeding out. "Would you have killed her?" A pause. "Would you have killed me?"

It was a valid question, and yet still it cut him, sharp as a scalpel, peeling him open. "No," he said, fighting against the doubt within himself that perhaps he might have. "I wouldn't. I didn't touch kids or women."

"And yet you were there to kill Mom!"

"Like I said, he didn't give me a name. Jesus, do you really think I would take out someone like her?"

"I don't know!" Something was glittering in her eyes. It looked like tears. "A couple of days ago, I would never have thought that, but now?"

The scalpel turned inward, sliding in between his ribs. He didn't resist it. Fuck, he deserved the pain. "Yeah, okay, that's fair enough. I'm not gonna offer you excuses. That was my life after I aged out of the system, because it was either that, stealing cars, or dealing meth. I wanted out, Zoe. I wanted to get away, and the only way I could do that was with money." He held her golden gaze. "And those guys paid me fuckloads of money."

A tear slid down her cheek, but he made no move toward her, staying right where he was. He had a feeling it wasn't him she wanted comfort from, not anymore.

"So you thought beating people up was a great way to get money?"

"I had no education. I had no prospects. You know what happened to my mom. You know my fucking father was in jail for murdering her. I was the son of a whore, brought up in the foster system, and I had fucking nothing but my fists and a whole lotta rage. So yeah, I thought it was a great way for me to get some money and give society the finger at the same time."

She made no move to wipe the tears away, and he felt each one like acid dripping slowly over his soul. "So why did you come for me? Why did you end up in Royal?" She pushed herself away from the doorframe, taking a step toward him, her hands in fists at her sides. "Why the *fuck* am I even here?"

Yeah, she was pissed, as he knew she would be. As she fucking *should* be. And he didn't know whether they'd ever be able to recover from this. Sex was one thing; all the things he hadn't told her were quite another.

The scalpel twisted in his heart, but he ignored it, wanting to give her the only thing he could. "You're here because you're the one who got me out." He kept his voice steady. "Because you're the one who showed me that there was more to life than fucking anger. The way you came down the stairs to me that night . . ." He stopped, his chest going tight, remembering the shock that had gripped him as he'd walked inside her mom's house, thinking no, it couldn't be. It couldn't be Zoe. And then as he'd stepped through the door, she'd been at the top of the stairs and her eyes had lit up, her face glowing. She'd raced down to him, flinging herself into his arms, and he'd just stood there in shock, realizing who it was that Novak had wanted him to kill. He hadn't known why right then, because knowing wasn't his job, that had only come later. But in that moment he'd understood why the job for Novak had been the last one. It was because of her. Because of Zoe.

"Your mom was my last job," he said, lowering his palms to the counter and putting the heels of his hands on the edge, his fingers curling underneath to hold on to something. "I was gonna get out after that. I told myself I had enough money, that I didn't need that shit anymore. Then I got to your house and you came down the stairs, straight into my arms. You held on to me, like I wasn't a bad person and you weren't afraid. You were so pleased to see me and believe me, Zoe, people were *never* pleased to see me." He gripped the edges of the counter tighter. "I knew I wasn't gonna do it then, but I knew if I didn't, Novak was gonna come after your mother and he was probably gonna come after you, too. And I couldn't let that happen. So I took you away, took you to Royal, where you'd be safe."

"But . . . he didn't come after Mom, did he? She died of an overdose six months later."

"An overdose caused by a bad batch of heroin supplied to her by one of Novak's dealers. A contact in Chicago told me."

She said nothing for a long time, just stared at him, tear tracks gleaming on her cheeks, and for once he had no idea at all what she was thinking. "Why didn't you tell me?" Her voice was hoarse. "Why did you keep that from me all this time?"

"Because I didn't want you to be afraid. I didn't want you walking around fucking scared all the time." He stopped, because that wasn't the whole truth either. "I didn't want you to be afraid . . . of me."

She took a little breath, her lashes long and black and glittering with tears. Then she blinked fiercely a couple of times and began to walk toward him, never taking her gaze from his. There was an intense expression on her face, one that he found unsettling, and he wanted to hold up his hand to make her stop, make her keep her distance in some way.

Christ. That he, of all people, should find one young woman to be so much of a threat. He should never have said it. Should never have opened his big mouth.

He pushed himself away from the counter, to leave or maybe do something else, he didn't know what. But by then it was too late to get out, because she'd stopped right in front of him, her gaze direct and so open he could barely meet it. She smelled good and he wanted to touch her, put his hands out to her. But he didn't. The way she was looking at him cut him off at the knees.

Zoe reached up and took his face between her hands, holding him with a surprisingly strong grip. "I have *never* been afraid of you." Her golden eyes burned. "Not like that. And I never will."

His heart shuddered inside his chest and he raised his hands, wrapping his fingers around her slender wrists. But for some reason he didn't pull them away, even though it felt as if the touch of her hands was searing him straight through. "You know what I am now. You can't tell me you're not afraid."

"I'm not."

"Liar. You've been terrified of me the whole of this past week."

Her gaze didn't waver, the soft pressure of her palms somehow keeping him exactly where he was, even though everything in him wanted to pull away. "Of course I was afraid. But that's because I wanted you. Because I didn't want you to tell me no. Because I didn't know what to expect. Because everything you did was so overwhelming and intense and . . . so good, Gideon. *That's* what scared me." There was a golden spark in her eyes, but this time it wasn't anger. "You scared me because of the way I feel about you."

His fingers tightened. "Stop, Zoe."

"No, I won't stop." She took in a ragged breath and beneath his fingertips he felt the race of her pulse. "You terrify me because I care about you so much. Because I want you. Because I don't want to leave you. I want to belong to you and yeah, that scares me shitless."

He gripped her wrists, a wave of intense possessiveness swamping him, dark and heady. Sure, there was fear in her eyes, he could see that. But something else, something more . . . desperate.

That she cared about him wasn't news. But this? This was different. He could see it in her eyes, bright and glittering in the morning sun.

She loves you.

"Zoe," he said, his voice harsh. "You can't—"

She shifted her hand, placed a finger across his mouth, silencing him. "I can. But it's okay. You don't have to say anything."

He stared back at her, staying silent, something inside him dropping away. He should be putting her away from him, telling her to keep her distance. Telling her she couldn't love a man like him, not now, not ever. He wasn't for her and he never had been.

But after what he'd said, after everything he'd revealed, she was still here. Standing in front of him. Looking at him like nothing had changed.

He found he couldn't move a muscle.

After a moment, Zoe took her finger away, rose up on her toes, and covered his mouth with hers.

And he was lost.

Chapter 14

His mouth was so warm, opening almost immediately, and she shuddered as his tongue touched hers. Her hands slipped away from his face, her fingers sliding down the powerful column of his neck to rest at the base of his throat, feeling the strong, steady beat of his pulse. His skin felt so good and he smelled of clean, male sweat and just . . . Gideon.

Her heart felt too full, too tender, as if her ribs were pressing against it.

After a night of no sleep, of tossing and turning and aching, she'd decided enough was enough. She wanted answers and she was going to get them whether he wanted to give them or not.

Then she'd come into the kitchen and there he'd been, leaning back against the counter, tall and dark and gleaming with sweat from his run. The tank he was wearing was sticking to the contours of his chest and abs, the dark branches of the cherry blossom tattoo that covered his torso extending out from underneath the cotton.

God, how she'd wanted him.

Then he'd finally told her all those things. About his past. About the job he'd been given, the job he'd refused to do in the end.

Because of her.

I didn't want you to be afraid of me. . . .

Yeah, she'd been angry he hadn't told her, so angry. But those simple words and the look in his eyes had cut through that anger like a hot knife through cold butter. Because it had been *he* who'd looked afraid in that moment.

It had made her chest get so tight she could hardly breathe.

He was a man who kept himself isolated, who protected her and all the others, yet held himself apart, making sure no one knew him, not really. And now she knew why. He was protecting her from himself. From his past.

It came to her then, like the ray of that bright morning sun shining into the kitchen, she was seeing him for the first time. Not the adored older brother figure or the hot older guy she had a crush on. Or even Gideon, the protective friend.

But a man, flawed and beautiful and troubled. A man who'd watched his father murder his mother, who'd gone from foster family to foster family. Who'd grown up lonely and isolated and angry.

A man who'd created his own little family and who looked out for everyone else, yet had no one he himself could turn to.

A man who needed a partner, a friend, a lover.

A man who needs you.

Yes, he did. She could be that for him if he'd let her. And it was the weirdest thing. It was like she saw her own behavior in a new light too. No wonder he'd been treating her like a naughty kid. How could he do anything else when she was treating him like an overbearing authority figure? If she really wanted him to treat her as a woman, as a partner, she needed to start acting like one.

So she'd moved straight to him, without hesitation or shyness or embarrassment, telling him exactly what was in her heart. Well, maybe not quite everything. She'd faltered at the last minute, seeing the denial in his eyes. But that was okay, she'd get to that later. Right now the only thing she wanted was to give him back a little something of everything he'd given her. Because that's what a partner did, right? It was a two-way street, give-and-take, stuff like that.

Zoe opened her mouth wider, and it was she who deepened the kiss, who began to explore him, slowly, deliberately, keeping her hands where they were at the base of his throat. Leaning into him so all that hard, packed muscle was up against her, all that wild heat.

He was still and she could feel the tension in his posture, almost like he was holding himself back. Yet his mouth was hot and he let her explore him, responding lazily, unhurriedly. It felt so good. The kiss sweet, with a carnal edge that had her trembling.

But that was okay. She wasn't going to wait to be told what to do like a good girl, not this time. She wasn't poor little virgin Zoe, sighing after a man she couldn't have, helpless with desire and want and that other, bigger emotion that squeezed her heart so tight and refused to let go.

She was a woman who was in love with this man—yes, love, that's what it was—and who wanted to show him he wasn't alone. Who wanted to give something of herself to him in the only way he would accept.

So she slid her hands down that magnificent chest of his, over the hard corrugations of his abs, slipping under his tank to the hot skin beneath. Sliding down farther, under his running shorts and boxers, to curl around the rapidly hardening length of his cock. Then she bit his lower lip. Hard.

He gave a growl deep in his throat, and suddenly one hand

was in her hair, his fingers buried deep in her curls, tugging her head back, his tongue sliding deeper into her mouth, while the other slid over her butt, pulling her hips hard against his.

He was taking control again, the kiss becoming hotter, more demanding, more desperate. Yet she didn't want him to have all the power this time, to be the one taking whatever he had to give. She wanted to be the one giving for a change. So she resisted, tightening her hand around his cock at the same time as she pulled against the hand in her hair, kissing him back, just as hot, just as hungry. She nipped him again, sliding her hand down the length of his shaft, then back up again.

"Fuck . . . Zoe . . ." His voice was raw, guttural, and she loved the desperate edge to it.

She loved him. She always had.

"Anything," she whispered against his hungry mouth. "You can have anything you want from me. Take it, Gideon."

He made another rough sound, and then she was being walked backward to the kitchen table against the wall. He reached forward, not taking his mouth from hers, sweeping everything on the table's surface to the floor. Newspapers and mail went flying, a cup smashed, apples from the fruit bowl rolled everywhere, but she didn't care. In fact, she loved that, too, because all those other times he'd been in control. And now he wasn't. He was wild and desperate, that veneer of the chilled-out guy he liked to present to the world completely stripped from him. Leaving the dark heart of him bare.

She loved that best of all. No one knew this part of him. No one but her.

He lifted her on top of the table, kissing her hungrily, as if he couldn't get enough, and she slid her free hand into soft thickness of his hair, holding on tight, kissing him back with the same desperation as he was kissing her, squeezing his cock harder.

He groaned, roughly jerking her sleep shorts down her legs and off, pushing her thighs wide. She let go of his hair, reaching to push down his own shorts as he pulled her to the edge of the table, the hot, bare skin of his hips brushing against her inner thighs.

She shivered as his teeth closed on her bottom lip the way she'd nipped his. "Gideon . . ." His name was a prayer, ending on a harsh gasp as his hand slipped between her legs, his fingers finding her clit and stroking, making her shudder.

"Christ . . ." he whispered. "We need a condom."

But she didn't want him leaving, didn't want to break the connection they had right in this instant. A shared desperation. A shared hunger. Where right now, they were equals.

"I don't care." Her heart raced, her pulse loud in her head. "You need me. So take me."

He cursed, low and harsh under his breath. And then he was shoving his running shorts down and pulling her even closer to the edge of the table, the blunt head of his cock pushing against her. Then he thrust, sliding deep inside her.

Her breath escaped in a rush, feeling the subtle burn as her pussy stretched around him, followed by the sweet ache of pleasure, and for a moment she just closed her eyes, glorying in it. In the feeling of him inside her, surrounding her.

Then he drew his hips back and thrust again, and she opened them, meeting the shadowed darkness of his, losing herself in all that black, velvet heat. She couldn't look away, consumed by the fire that burned in both of them as he moved inside her, harder, deeper.

She curled her legs around his lean waist, drawing him in and holding him close, the rhythm intensifying.

"Zoe . . ." The rough whisper was a caress all on its own, an edge of tenderness to it that wrapped around her heart. "Little one . . ." The look in his eyes was mesmerizing. Almost as if he felt the same way about her as she did about him.

Not that it mattered. Right now she didn't care if he did or not. The only thing that did matter was the vastness inside her, the ebb and flow of it, as if she were an ocean and he were the moon, pulling at the tide.

She touched his face, the sharp edge of his carved cheekbones, the straight line of his nose. The strong shape of his jaw, roughened with morning stubble. Hard, male, and so achingly beautiful.

He said nothing, the expression on his face so stern and yet the look in his eyes . . . so hot. Burning as he pulled out of her, then thrust back in, harder, faster.

She began to shake, because it was so good, so intense, the edge coming for her and she rushing to meet it. Sliding her arms around his neck, wanting to be as close to him as she could get, she turned her face into his throat, the hot feel of his skin and the scent of him surrounding her.

Then his hand was cupping the back of her head, cradling her, and he was moving even deeper, even faster, the harsh sound of his ragged breaths in her ear. And there was a pressure on her clit, his finger circling and stroking, so that she shuddered and screwed her eyes shut tight, her mouth opening as the orgasm crashed over her with all the suddenness and intensity of a summer storm.

She couldn't stop trembling as the pleasure rocketed through her, sparking every nerve ending, clinging to him as if gravity had suddenly ceased to exist and he was the only thing keeping her anchored.

His movements became wilder, out of rhythm, his hold on her abruptly tight, and then he groaned, his big body shuddering as the pleasure came for him, too.

She didn't move for a long moment afterward, simply holding him and being held in return, and she couldn't say how many minutes passed before he shifted, withdrawing from her. But he didn't pull completely away, gathering her close without a word and lifting her into his arms.

He took her to the bathroom, setting her down and turning on the shower. Then he stripped them both and pulled her into the narrow stall, picking up a washcloth and beginning to slowly wash her. She let him, loving the feeling of his touch and the tenderness in it, before taking the cloth from him and returning the favor. His body was so big and strong, massively muscled and yet with a certain grace to it. Wide shoulders, hard chest, lean hips, the water following all the fascinating dips and hollows, while she followed the water first with her hands and then with her tongue. She traced every inch of the cherry blossom tattoo that wrapped around his torso, while he stroked her hair, and then she fell to her knees in front of him, wanting to touch and trace something else.

He let her, his black gaze on her as she ran her tongue down the length of his hardening cock, taking it into her mouth and sucking him in deep. He kept a hold of her hair in one hand while with the other he stroked her face, watching as she worshipped him with her mouth, the water falling down all around them.

It felt good. It felt right. Like this was the point they'd both been edging toward their entire lives.

She never wanted it to end.

When the shower finally ran cold and they got out, he dried her off and carried her back to his bedroom, laying her down over the white sheets and spreading her legs again, finding a condom this time before sliding inside her, taking her long and slow, as if he had all the time in the world. Making her scream at the end, her nails leaving marks on his back as the orgasm broke her apart, and then he put her back together again with gentle strokes of his hand up and down her spine.

More time passed, though how much she didn't know.

Gideon rolled onto his back, and she put her head on his chest, enjoying the feel of his fingers idly playing with her hair. The branches of the cherry tree were dark against his bronze skin, the blossoms bright. She touched one with her finger as a deep, companionable silence gathered around them.

Such a beautiful tattoo and yet a strange one for a hard man like him.

"This is for your mom, isn't it?" She kept her voice quiet, not wanting to break the atmosphere. He'd told her a few things about his childhood, but not enough. Not nearly enough.

"Yeah. She had the same one in about the same place."

"You don't talk about her much."

"And you know why."

She did. Because of his father and the way his mother had died. "Bad memories, I get it. So . . . is that why you, uh, did the things you did?"

He sighed. "Like I told you. My school record sucked. I mean, I was barely there anyway and ended up not graduating from high school because the local kingpin needed bouncers for a party he was giving. I needed the cash and it seemed like easy money." Gideon paused. "I was good at it too and when the guy needed muscle for another operation, he asked me if I was still interested in working for cash. It kind of snowballed from there."

Zoe had a feeling looking directly at him would make him clam up, so she kept her gaze on the blossom near his left pec, a feminine shape that should have looked ridiculous on the hard, masculine shape of him and yet somehow didn't. "Why, though? I get you were poor and had nothing, but there were other options. There always are."

He was silent for a while, so she concentrated on his chest, tracing the outline of the flower with her finger, enjoying the feeling of his hot, bare skin up against the length of her body. "I was angry," he said at last. "I was so fucking angry. That prick killed Mom and I had nothing." His fingers stilled in her hair. "He took her away, leaving me with nothing at all and . . . I wanted something. I thought that something was money so I could get the things I never had as a kid, so that's what I worked toward. Getting money any way I could."

Her heart tightened in her chest as she remembered the young man who'd used to come visit her sometimes, wherever she was living. They usually met at the park. He'd be sitting on a bench, and whenever she arrived, he'd look up and smile at her. A huge grin that lit up her entire world.

Except . . . sometimes it didn't reach his eyes.

Perhaps even back then she'd known something wasn't quite right with Gideon Black. That he had a core of darkness she couldn't reach. A darkness she'd recoiled from.

Well, she wasn't recoiling from it now. "So how exactly did you get it?" She traced the stem of the blossom where it met the branch, following the branch down to the side of his abdomen, his muscles tightening as she touched him.

Another silence.

"I don't want you to know." His voice was soft, but that darkness was threaded all the way through it. "It's not something anyone should know about me."

This time, she looked up, meeting his gaze in the dimness of the room. "Nothing will change the way I see you, Gideon. Nothing." Because it wouldn't. It would be terrible, yes, but he'd been someone different then, a different man with a different life, and he wasn't that man anymore. She knew it like she knew the beat of his heart beneath her hand and the warmth of his smile whenever he looked at her. Like she knew the feeling in her heart was love, whether she wanted it to be or not.

He took a breath. "That's not why—"

"Isn't it?" She stared at him and she realized with a start that she wasn't afraid anymore. As if accepting the fact that she was in love with him had gotten rid of any lingering fear, which was weird. Maybe it was because she had nothing left to lose. He had her heart, he could crush it in his hands or cherish it, and there was something oddly liberating in the thought.

Gideon's dark eyes held hers for a second, then a subtle, almost imperceptible smile curved his mouth. "You're dangerous, little one. Did you know that?"

"Yeah, of course I'm dangerous. You don't want to mess with me." She folded her hands on his chest and rested her chin on them. "Now spit it out. I can punish you pretty good if I want to."

That subtle curve to his mouth faded, his fingers playing with her hair. "I'm not a good man, Zoe."

"And you're not the best judge of that, clearly."

He coiled a strand of hair around one finger, rubbing it with his thumb. "Why do you want to know all that shit? It was a long time ago."

"I want to know because you don't want to tell me. Because it may have happened a long time ago, but it still obviously matters to you." She paused. "Because you're afraid."

The look in his eyes flickered, his finger pulling her curl tight. She didn't flinch, keeping her gaze on his.

"I can't let you go, Zoe," he said suddenly, fiercely. "If I tell you these things, everything about my past, and you decide you want to leave, I *will* stop you. Understand? You're mine now and I keep what's mine."

A shiver went through her, shaking her down to her soul. "Good," she said, with the same intensity. "Because I don't want to be anyone else's but yours. Now quit stalling and tell me."

So he did, and it wasn't pretty, as she knew it wouldn't be. And when he'd finished, she said nothing, because there wasn't really anything to say. Instead, she slid on top of him, covering him with her body. Then she covered his mouth with hers.

It wasn't forgiveness; that wasn't hers to give. But she could give him acceptance, and it seemed to be enough.

For now.

Gideon woke with a start to the sounds of someone hammering on the front door of the apartment. Zoe was lying on top of him, her hair all over his chest, the gentle, soft weight of her a delicious temptation, making his cock harden like it hadn't been inside her a number of times already that morning.

He turned his head, checking the time, vaguely surprised to see it was eleven a.m. Shit, he should have opened up the garage hours ago.

The knocking came again, even louder and more insistent than before.

Cursing, he shifted Zoe carefully off him, not wanting to wake her, and rolled out of bed, pausing to pull on a pair of jeans, then slipping out into the hallway.

Whoever it was gave another hammer on the door as Gideon approached, and he scowled, undoing the locks, then pulling the door open.

Levi stood on the other side of it, one blue eye and one dark one widening as he took in Gideon, half dressed, standing on the threshold. "What the fuck?" he said in surprise. "You look like you've only just gotten up."

Gideon leaned one forearm against the doorframe, irritated. "I have. What the hell do you want?"

"Some guy's been calling me because he wants to pick up his bike from the garage and he can't because it's somehow not open." Levi raised a brow, the ring in it glinting. "Which is weird because you never not have the garage open. I thought you might have died in your sleep or something."

"Obviously I didn't, otherwise I wouldn't be here standing talking to you."

"Yeah, I get that." Levi abruptly frowned. "Are those what I think they are?"

Gideon glanced in the direction of Levi's gaze, down at his left shoulder. Red lines stood out on his skin, scratches from Zoe's nails. Shit.

"No wonder you slept in," Levi went on, sounding amused. "Tough night?"

Gideon lifted his head and gazed back at the other man.

There were a number of different ways to play this. He could pretend there was someone else in his bed, some other woman he'd screwed to within an inch of both their lives. Or he could deny all knowledge that he'd been sleeping alone all night.

Or he could tell Levi exactly what had gone on with Zoe.

Almost as soon as the thought occurred to him, he knew what he was going to do. He'd told Zoe everything back there in his room, all the shitty things he'd done, all the black, evil acts he'd committed because he'd been young and stupid and full of rage. And she hadn't pulled away from him, hadn't run from the room in horror. No, she'd climbed on top of him, giving him the warmth of her body as if he wasn't bad all the way through, kissing him as if he deserved it.

He hadn't lied when he'd told her she was his now, that she couldn't ask him to tell her everything and expect him to let her go as if none of it meant anything. She'd accepted him, which made her his.

He wasn't letting her go, not ever. Which meant he needed to tell the others exactly how it was going to be from now on, whether they liked it or approved of it or not.

"Yeah," he said slowly. "I guess you could say that."

"Who's the lucky girl?" Levi grinned. "Anyone we know?"

Gideon held the other man's gaze steadily. "Zoe."

There was a silence.

Levi gave him a puzzled look, his brow creasing. Then it cleared, and he laughed. "Prick. I actually believed you there for a second."

Gideon said nothing.

The other man's laugh gradually wound down, the amusement fading, and a slow dawning shock rolled slowly over his handsome face. "You *are* kidding, aren't you?"

"No."

Levi blinked, staring at him, and then, as realization sank in, something else flared in his strange, uneven gaze. Fury. "What the actual *fuck*, Gideon?"

Gideon pushed his arm away from the doorframe, straightening up. He was prepared for a fight, and shit, Levi had every right to be angry with him. God knew that if it had been Levi who'd been screwing around with Zoe, Gideon would have wanted to kill him. Certainly, he'd have beaten him half to death at least.

Unfortunately, it wasn't like he'd been quiet about the love lives of his friends either. He'd had opinions, some of which had been unpopular, and he guessed that made him a hypocrite. But it would have been more hypocritical to not say a word, to hide what they were doing like it was some kind of guilty secret. Zoe was his and the whole world needed to know it.

"Zoe and I are together," he said flatly.

Dark rage flooded over Levi's face. "You *fucking* bastard! What the hell do you think you're—"

"Stop, Levi!" The voice was unexpected and feminine, and before Gideon could react, Zoe was there, putting herself between him and Levi.

She was dressed in nothing but one of his T-shirts, her hair a wild, untamed cloud of black ringlets, and she didn't have her glasses on either, making her look very small, and very, very young. She threw out a hand at Levi, and the effect was rather like a twig trying to stop two massive boulders from crashing together.

Fuck, she must have come up behind him without making a sound.

Levi's furious gaze transferred to her, looking her up and down, obviously taking in the fact that she was wearing barely anything.

Possessiveness roared inside Gideon, and he'd looped an arm around her waist, dragging her back against him before he'd fully realized what he was doing. Fucking idiot that he was. Levi was no threat, not to Zoe.

Levi's expression darkened even further. "Would somebody tell me what the hell is going on here?"

"What it looks like," Gideon said, holding the other man's gaze. "Zoe's mine."

Her hands had come down on his forearm where it stretched across her stomach, resting there lightly. A soothing kind of touch. Yet he didn't feel soothed. He felt feral, an echo of the feeling that had filled him last night when she'd disappeared. Like he wanted to do violence to anyone who would take her from him.

"It was me." Zoe's voice was clear and steady. "I was the one who initiated it. You know how much I wanted this, Levi. The others know too. Well, it turned out that Gideon wanted it like I did, okay?"

"The *fuck* he did!" Levi's hands had curled into fists. "He's your fucking foster brother! He's older than you, you're a virgin—"

"I'm twenty-five," she interrupted. "I'm not a child. And I'm not a virgin anymore. I can make my own choices."

"Can you?" Levi's uneven gaze flicked to Gideon. "Well, I guess that makes it easy when your only choice is him."

There was something sharp and painful in Levi's voice that slid through Gideon like a sliver of glass under a fingernail. A truth he didn't want to think about.

Of course she's in love with you. You were there right from the start, in her life, dominating it. Levi's right, she's never had a choice.

"What's that supposed to mean?" she demanded hotly.

"Think about it, Zoe. How can you be sure when he's the only fucking man you've ever had any contact with?"

"Oh, bullshit," she said, her voice unexpectedly cold. "Don't talk to me like I don't know what I want. Anyway, you're a fine one to lecture me and Gideon when you're the one who spent eight years in jail."

The words hung in the air, sharp with anger, burning with a fierce kind of defiance.

Jesus Christ, she really wasn't holding back, was she?

Levi's expression closed up, and Gideon found he was holding her even tighter as her slender body almost vibrated with anger.

"Yeah, you know what?" The look on Levi's face was like stone. "You're right. I can't say a fucking word." His gaze flicked back to Gideon. "But it's wrong. It's just fucking wrong and I won't be the only one who thinks so."

There was nothing Gideon could say, so he didn't say anything, not when part of him knew Levi was right. That it *was* wrong. That he was a hypocrite. That Zoe had never had any real choice about this.

He still wasn't letting her go, though.

After Levi had gone and Gideon had shut the door, he turned to find her standing in the hallway with her arms folded, a fierce look on her face. "I know, I shouldn't have said that. But I . . . just couldn't help it. It looked like he was going to hit you."

"Actually, I'm kinda relieved you're being a brat to someone other than me." He moved over to her, reached out, and pulled her close. "But . . . maybe you should have let him hit me. It might have made him feel better."

Her hands came to rest on his chest, her head tilting back. He'd said it to make her smile, but she wasn't smiling and that fierce look hadn't softened one bit. "He's not right, Gideon. You know that, don't you?"

Damn her. How did she manage to hook into his doubts the way she did? "He *is* right about one thing. I've been in your life since you were six years old. You've never had a chance to get to know any other guys apart from me."

She scowled. "Oh, not you, too. That's just so much bull-shit. I didn't fall in love with either Zee or Levi, did I?"

Fall in love . . .

He stared down at her, watching the color bloom in her cheeks, a red, rolling wave of it. But there was no doubt, not a flicker of it. In fact, if anything, she looked even more defiant. "Come on, like you didn't know."

His chest tightened painfully, that sliver of glass sliding deeper, and he wanted to tell her she shouldn't say things like that, shouldn't feel things like that, especially not for him. Because how could she say she loved him? She barely even knew what love was.

You can't keep her. You can't.

His hands tightened on her hips, the warmth of her easing the tightness, masking the doubt. "You shouldn't, little one. You really shouldn't."

Her color deepened. "Yeah, well, too late now."

"I can't—"

"No, don't." Her hands slid up his chest and around her

neck, her body arching into his. "We've had this conversation. I don't need you to say anything in return. Just . . . kiss me."

So he did, ignoring the reservations that sat in his gut, slowly eating away at him from the inside. Carrying her back to the bedroom and losing himself in her for a while longer.

While he still could.

Chapter 15

He knew they'd come eventually and sure enough, he'd just finished receiving some intel from one of his contacts during an afternoon break when Levi, Zee, and Rachel came into the garage. It wasn't the right time, not when he had Novak to deal with, but maybe the sooner they got this over and done with the better. He needed to tell them about Novak, too, especially when it was going to put at risk the plans they all had worked so hard to get up off the ground.

Zoe was up in the apartment sleeping, hopefully. He'd given her the day off, which was totally him being an indulgent boss, but hey, she'd kind of earned it. It also made him a dirty bastard for even thinking about it in those terms. Then again, that's exactly what he was. A dirty bastard.

He put his phone in the pocket of his overalls and leaned back against the workbench that ran along the rear wall of the garage, watching as his friends approached, all of them looking as if they wanted to kill him.

Fair enough, too. He would if he were them.

"I guess this is about Zoe," he said into the tense silence, not making it a question.

Rachel stopped not far away from him and folded her arms. "What do you think?"

"Yeah, well, spare me the lecture. Levi already delivered it this morning."

Levi had come up next to her, Zee on the other side, the three of them standing there staring at him like a jury staring at an accused murderer.

"Whose decision was it?" Zee asked in his rough, gritty voice. "Jesus Christ, she's your—"

"You think I don't know who she is? She's my—former—foster sister, yeah, I know. And it was her decision."

"And what?" Rachel was scowling. "You didn't say no?"

What could he say to that? Only the truth. "No. I didn't."

"Perhaps you should have." Levi thrust his hands into the pockets of his jeans. "Fuck, she's so much younger than you are. She's looked up to you her entire life. She's a kid and you know it."

Gideon stared at him. "Just because the last time you saw her she was a teenager does not make her a kid now. She's only a year younger than Rachel."

Levi glowered, unable to refute that particular fact, while Rachel and Zee looked uncomfortable—as well they should.

"Stop underestimating her," he said, his tone hard. "Yeah, she seems young, but that doesn't make her an idiot. Or unable to make her own decisions."

"She's young because you kept her that way." There was no denying the accusation in Rachel's voice. "Whether you meant to or not, that's the way it's turned out. She's an innocent, Gideon. And you, taking advantage—"

"Don't say it." Anger twisted inside him, the edges of it all the sharper for knowing, deep down, that she was right. "I didn't take anything from her that she didn't want to give."

"Really?" Her dark eyes were uncomfortably direct. "So if you'd let her go to college like she'd wanted, let her get a job outside of Royal. Let her have some kind of experience of the world, this would still have happened?"

He shifted against the workbench, the edge of it digging into his back, the dark possessive anger twisting away inside him, wanting to tell her she was wrong. That of course it would still have happened. But underneath that, the sliver of glass, the doubt, lay embedded in his soul.

He *had* stopped her from going to college and from getting a job outside of Royal, but that was because he hadn't wanted to draw attention to her. To make sure she stayed hidden from Novak.

Are you sure it's just because of him?

Gideon ignored the thought, folding his arms tightly. "She made those decisions, not me." Which was only half true. "Anyway, I'll be fucked if I listen to you giving me shit about this. Zoe knows her own mind, I didn't force her into anything at all."

"Right," Levi said. "So it's fine to give me shit about Rachel, but we can't call you out when it comes to Zoe?"

Gideon met his gaze. "Yeah, I gave you shit. But who was it sitting in your fucking apartment telling you to man up and go get her when you thought it was all over?"

Levi's glower deepened, his jaw tightening. But again, the guy said nothing because he had no comeback to that. Sure, Gideon had given him crap about him and Rachel, but he'd also given him advice when it looked like Levi wasn't going to pull his head out of his ass and admit he was in love with her.

Another tense silence fell, broken by the clang of the door at the garage entrance opening, then shutting behind Tamara's slender figure. She looked to be in full-on corporate mode, in a pencil skirt, nice blouse, and heels, her blond hair in a neat bun. "I wondered where everyone was," she said, coming toward them. "Zee wouldn't answer his phone. . . ." She trailed off, obviously sensing the tension in the air. "What's up?"

"Everyone's pissed Zoe and I got together," Gideon answered, because he'd be fucked if he let any of the others explain it for him.

Tamara broke into a radiant smile. "Wow, well, that's awesome." Then she glanced at the others and her smile faded as she took in the stony looks on their faces. "It's not awesome?"

"Think about it, baby," Zee said, wandering over to her and putting an arm around her waist. "Zoe's kind of sheltered, and Gideon's her foster brother. He's way older than her. It's wrong however you look at it."

Tamara frowned. "I still don't get why."

"Tamara, seriously?" Rachel was staring at her.

But Tamara ignored her, stepping away from Zee and looking at each of them. "No, I don't get it. Zoe's a grown woman, she can choose for herself. And as to wrong . . . well, lots of people still think Zee and I are wrong too."

Gideon hadn't expected support from any of them, not about this, and Tamara's words eased a tension he hadn't known was there. But not the doubt, that was still there. A doubt he didn't want to acknowledge.

"That's different," Zee muttered. "Zoe's different."

"How?" Tamara stared at him. "Lots of people told me I didn't know what I was doing when I got involved with you, that I didn't know my own mind. Some of them still do. Hell, I'm not much older than Zoe myself."

Levi murmured something inaudible, and Rachel kept right on scowling, but none of them argued with Tamara.

Of course they didn't know the truth, the root of the doubt

that sat in Gideon's gut. That yes, he'd made sure Zoe stayed sheltered and safe, and at his side. He'd made sure she didn't go out on dates or go to college or do anything a normal twenty-something woman would do. He'd kept her right here with him. To protect her.

It wasn't for her. It was for you. Because she's yours and you didn't want to let her go. . . .

"Enough of this shit," he growled, not wanting to talk about it anymore. "There's something else about Zoe you all should know."

"Really?" Rachel gave him a belligerent look. "You sleeping with Zoe is 'this shit'? And no, I don't think it's enough. I think I want to know exactly what the fuck you're doing with her."

It took effort to keep his grip on his temper, but he managed it. "This is more important, Rachel, believe me. It concerns the development plans we have for Royal."

Another silence fell.

"What about them?" Levi's tone held a dark edge, which was kind of understandable seeing as how the plans were his baby.

Gideon met his gaze. This was another thing they were going to give him shit about and that was *all* on him. He'd made the decision to keep Zoe's parentage secret, and he was okay with that because, quite frankly, it wasn't anyone else's business. Certainly the last thing he'd needed was either Zee or Levi going off on Novak and drawing attention. No, he'd made the right decision there at least.

Did you really, though? Or was that another thing you kept secret so no one could interfere?

He shoved the thought away. "Novak's a problem," he said shortly. "And the reasons are complicated."

"How complicated?" Levi took a step toward him, obviously sensing that whatever it was that Gideon had to say, he wasn't going to like it.

Gideon let out a breath, shifting against the workbench again. "There's a reason Zoe and me left Chicago, and it had to do with the people I used to work for."

"Who?" Zee's question was sharp.

"Just in case you can't guess, Novak was one of them."

"Jesus," Rachel murmured. 'You used to work for Novak?"

"And not photocopying election pamphlets, right?" Levi said, his gaze narrowing. "Do we want to know what kind of work you're talking about?"

"No," Gideon replied shortly. "Though you can probably guess."

Something shifted in Levi's expression. "I knew it. Politicians, man. They're all the fucking same. All into the same shady shit to get as much power as they can."

Zee gave Gideon a look that was very clearly assessing. "That kind of work, huh?"

Gideon stared steadily back at him. Out of all of them, Zee was the most likely to understand the kind of jobs he'd undertaken, mainly because Zee's old man used to be one of Detroit's godfathers of crime. "Yeah, that kind of work," he said. No point in denying it.

The other man snorted. "I knew it. What's with all the mechanic bullshit then?"

"It's not bullshit. You really think I wanted to stay in that line of work anymore? With Zoe here?"

Rachel muttered what sounded like a curse. "I think you'd better tell us what really went down with you and Zoe, Gideon. You must have aged out of the system way before she did, so what the hell were you doing? And how come you were able to somehow take a girl away from whatever family she was with and bring her here?"

Here was the difficult bit, the bit he didn't want to tell anyone. But he had to now; keeping it from them wasn't an option.

He stared at them all, giving each of them, the kids he'd banded together all those years ago, one long look. Then he said, "Novak was being blackmailed by a woman who said she'd had his child. If she didn't get her payment, she was gonna go to the press. She had the proof and everything, it was legit. So Novak employed me to . . . take care of it."

Rachel's eyes widened. "Jesus."

The look on her face made his chest hurt, but he didn't look away. "It was a long time ago and I'm not the same man I was back then."

"And you're wondering why we're so protective of Zoe?"

They're not wrong. You've always known that.

"And I killed someone," Levi said unexpectedly, looking at Rachel, his voice a little rough. "Are you going to judge me, too?"

Rachel gave him a stricken glance, dropping her arms and moving over to him. "You know I didn't mean that."

Gideon watched them a moment. He hadn't expected Levi's sudden support, but he didn't make the mistake of thinking it was all forgiven, not when he hadn't even gotten to his point yet.

"Novak gave me the address I had to go to," he went on, "and it was kind of familiar. But it wasn't until I got there that I realized why." He paused, making sure he had their attention. "It was Zoe's house. And the woman I had to deal with was Zoe's mom."

The silence was deafening, the others staring at him with varying degrees of shock on their faces.

"You mean," Tamara said tentatively, "that Zoe is Novak's daughter?"

"Yes." He kept the word short and clipped. "That's why I took her away. That's why we left Chicago and came here. Her mom didn't give a shit about her except for the paternity test that kept the money rolling in, and I couldn't leave her to be just another loose end fucking Novak wanted 'dealt with.' "

"Holy shit," Rachel muttered. "Why didn't you tell us?"

"Because the less people who knew, the better it was for Zoe. I didn't want Novak discovering where she'd gone. I didn't want any attention drawn to her. I wanted her to disappear."

Levi said nothing, his gaze narrowed. Zee had reached out for Tamara, pulling her close as if he wanted to protect her, but he was looking at Gideon, too, dark, winged brows plunging down. "What happened to her mom? You do the hit?"

"No," Gideon said flatly. "I found I had a line and killing was it. Novak supplied her with bad drugs not long after we left and she died of an overdose."

"And Zoe was quite happy to go with you?" Rachel persisted and, given her background, that was unsurprising.

"Yeah, like I said, her mother didn't care much what happened to her. She went to jail when Zoe was really young and didn't come out again until Zoe was around eleven. She didn't want her kid."

"That's terrible," Tamara said softly. "Poor Zoe."

"Does she know?" Levi's deep voice almost cut across her. "Zoe, I mean? About Novak?"

"She does now."

"Shit," Zee said suddenly. "Novak's here, though. Does that mean—"

"He knows she's here," Gideon interrupted. "And last night the prick took her."

"What?" Levi carefully pushed Rachel away and took a step toward Gideon, a murderous look on his face. "What the fuck do you mean he took her?"

Gideon crossed the distance between them, coming to stand right in front of the younger man, holding his gaze. "He intercepted her in the bathrooms at Gino's. Took her for a ride in his car. He didn't hurt her, but he gave her an ultimatum."

There was darkness in Levi's gaze, the kind of darkness Gideon recognized. Levi had brought Novak here with those development plans of his, it was true, but it wasn't his fault and he had to know that. "Novak was already keeping a lookout for her, Levi," he said quietly. "He would have found her eventually."

Levi didn't bother to deny it. "If I hadn't wanted his fucking money, he wouldn't have been here."

"No, I told you that he was already looking. He must have heard rumors or had a contact scouting for her. There's no other reason a guy like him would have been interested in a small development in Royal."

Levi's jaw tightened. "What ultimatum did he give her?"

Gideon rolled his shoulders, trying to ease the subtle tension that had crept in between his shoulder blades. "He told her he'd give her money for college, get her a place in Princeton, the whole deal. And in return she has to leave Detroit. Leave Michigan completely."

Zee's expression was hard, his silver eyes glittering. "For how long?"

"For good."

"Jesus." Zee grimaced. "And if she doesn't?"

Gideon looked at him. "If she doesn't, then he'll stall the development plans for Royal indefinitely."

Another silence, shocked and tense.

"No," Levi suddenly exploded, his voice rough. "*Fuck,* no."

"No to what?" Zee asked sharply. "To the development or Zoe leaving?"

Levi turned furiously to the other man. "Are you kidding? To fucking *all* of it!"

"Levi." Rachel's tone was soft, her hand coming to rest on his arm. "It's okay. We're not going to let this stand." She flicked her dark gaze to Gideon. "Are we?"

But that was the problem, wasn't it? There were no good answers, at least not ones that wouldn't send them to jail.

"I was going to take care of it myself," he said, trying to keep his own voice calm. "But Zoe didn't want me to."

"Right, and I can imagine what 'taking care of it' would have entailed," Rachel said, her fingers moving absently on Levi's arm in a soothing motion that Gideon found somehow mesmerizing for some inexplicable reason.

Or maybe not so inexplicable. His own forearm tingled from the touch of Zoe's fingers, where they'd rested earlier that morning when Levi had come to the door.

Christ, he wished she was here, even though it was just as well that she wasn't. He wanted her hands on him. Wanted to feel the gentle movement of her fingers on his skin, easing the tightness inside him.

"Yeah, can't see anything wrong with that," Levi growled.

"Sure you can't," Rachel murmured. "You must really like jail."

"What options do we have?" Zee demanded, ignoring Levi's snort at Rachel's comment. "I mean, sure, I'm with you guys about doing that fucker in, but we wanna keep this on the right side of the law."

"Yes, we most certainly do." Tamara was frowning. "There must be some way we can get Zoe out of this, some way we can make life difficult for Novak?"

Levi's intense, uneven gaze met Gideon's. "It has to be permanent, doesn't it? If he's as dangerous as you say, he's not going to want anything to harm his chances at a senatorial position, and whether Zoe's in Michigan or not, she's a threat to him."

Gideon said nothing. The facts spoke for themselves.

"He'd really hurt his daughter?" Tamara asked doubtfully. "I mean, he didn't harm her, he just told her to get out of Detroit."

Gideon flashed her a glance. "He wanted her mother dead,

Tamara, and he was willing to employ me to get rid of her. So you tell me."

She paled. "Okay then. Point taken."

"Fucker," Zee muttered, tugging Tamara closer. "If he's that ambitious, why did he bother with an ultimatum at all?"

"He can't afford for people to disappear, not right now," Gideon said, fighting the intense, primal urge that had him wanting to grab his gun, go after the guy right now, end it before any harm came to Zoe, no matter what she thought about it. "And Zoe's not someone who can disappear without a trace, not these days. Not when she has us."

"You got that right," Levi said. "Which means she's not leaving here either, not because that asshole said so."

"What about the plans?" Rachel tipped her head back to look up at him.

"What about them? Let Novak bury them in red tape. We'll fucking build them anyway."

"Yeah," Gideon growled. "Then we'll be ordered to tear everything down because we don't have a goddamn permit. Do you really want that, Levi?"

Anger sparked in his friend's eyes. "Then we just won't fucking build them at all."

Rachel sighed, reaching up to cup his jaw. "Do you really think Zoe would want that to happen? Besides, I don't think not building them is the answer. If she refused Novak's ultimatum, that still leaves her as a threat he's going to want to take care of."

Zee cursed, letting go of Tamara and pacing restlessly over to the far wall and back again, a great cat trapped in a cage. "Then where the hell do we go from here? If we can't touch Novak and he's gunning for Zoe, then what the fuck can we do to stop him?"

It was the one question Gideon had been dealing with the

entire morning, turning it over and over in his head like he did sometimes when there was an engine that was giving him trouble. Looking for a solution, looking for a fix. Examining the way things fit together and how to make it so everything would run smoothly again.

It had come to him just before the others had arrived, how he could fix it, because *he* had to be the one who fixed it. Zoe was his responsibility and she always had been.

It wasn't a solution any of them were going to like, though given their response to him and Zoe getting together, maybe they wouldn't find it too objectionable after all.

Zoe wouldn't like it, that he did know. Then again, she wasn't going to get a choice.

"There's one way," he said into the tense silence.

Zee stopped pacing. "What?"

"I go to the police. Tell them all about Novak."

Rachel's brow creased. "But . . . do you have proof?"

"Oh yeah, I've got proof." He had lots of it, digital info he'd taken with him when he'd left Chicago, kept for a rainy day. E-mails and financial details, records of payments, plus a few things he'd managed to glean from his contacts. "The shit I did for him . . . Safe to say I've got enough to make sure Novak goes away for a very long time."

"Does he know that?" Tamara asked, her gaze shrewd.

"He probably suspects. But I was a minor minion in the scheme of things, and after I left Chicago, I kept myself on the down-low." He paused, remembering what Zoe had told him about her interview with Novak. "Now though . . . He might be worried."

"God, shouldn't you be concerned about your safety too?" Tamara asked, looking worried.

"Maybe. But I have a network of people who give me info when I need it, and they'll let me know if Novak makes a move on me."

"He'll have the same kind of network, Gideon," Levi pointed out. "He'll know if you make a move on him too."

Gideon met the other man's gaze. "He might. But he won't be able to do anything to me if he's in prison."

"Shit," Zee said roughly. "Why haven't you done it sooner then?"

"Because if I had, that would have left Zoe all alone." Gideon let out a slow breath. "Taking down Novak means I go down too."

Chapter 16

Zoe stared at her computer screen, at the page she had open and bookmarked on her computer. The home page for Princeton University. On her desk, beside the computer, was the folder with all the information she'd printed out years ago. Information on her colleges of choice, classes and scholarships and all sorts of other things, along with various application forms, some of which she'd even started to fill in. That was until Gideon had told her no.

She hadn't pushed him at the time, had let it go even though she'd been pissed off about it. Telling herself there was no point arguing with him because she wouldn't win anyway. But there was a deeper reason, of course. She hadn't wanted to leave him.

She didn't want to leave him now.

Zoe glared at the computer screen, then closed the page, shoving herself away from her desk.

Except leaving was exactly what she was contemplating. Novak—she couldn't bear to think of him as "Dad"—hadn't left her any choice.

There was always Gideon's answer in the shape of that gun,

but she wasn't going to let him do that. He didn't need any more sins on a soul already badly damaged by his past.

Zoe pushed her hair back from her face and grabbed her keys from the top of her dresser, shoving them into her jeans pocket. She'd only woken up half an hour ago, and even though Gideon had given her the day off, she wanted to get back down to the garage, see if he'd managed to figure anything out about what to do with Novak. Then there was the reaction from the others to handle, because after watching Levi go off at Gideon, there was bound to be some kind of reaction.

She didn't want to leave Gideon on his own to deal with it, not when they all seemed to view her like a kid who couldn't make her own decisions. She had to show them that she'd made her choice years ago, that it wasn't simply some teenage crush. That it was real.

"Well, I guess that makes it easy when your only choice is him."

She scowled as she went out into the hallway, Levi's voice echoing in her head. What the hell would he know about it? She'd had contact with plenty of men, him and Zee for example, and she hadn't fallen head over heels for them. Not like she had for Gideon.

They didn't look after you like Gideon did. And all you wanted was someone to want you, someone to look after you.

Zoe set her jaw, striding down the hallway to the front door of the apartment. Okay, so she had a few daddy issues to work out—who didn't? But she would have fallen for Gideon regardless. The past had nothing to do with it.

She tugged open the door and went down the stairs, heading for the garage. Voices echoed as she neared the entrance, Zee's gritty tones audible as she got closer.

God, so the others were already there, and from the sounds of it, they were pretty pissed.

Her throat closed, her chest suddenly feeling tight and sore.

She hated it when they all argued, and knowing they were all arguing about her only made it worse.

She stopped in front of the garage door, reluctant to go in. Which was stupid. She was supposed to be acting as Gideon's partner now, not a scared little mouse crouching outside the door.

"Shit," she heard Zee say in his rough, gritty voice. "Why haven't you done it sooner then?"

"Because if I had, that would have left Zoe all alone." That was Gideon's deep tones. "Taking down Novak means I go down too."

She froze.

"Why?" Rachel's voice.

"Because all that proof? It implicates me, too. I've got records of payments, e-mails, shit like that. They'll charge me, Rach, make no mistake."

Zoe put her hands lightly on the door, her heart crumpling up inside her chest. He must have told them about her, about how Novak was her father. And now he was talking going to the police. Oh God, was that the only answer he could come up with?

"Maybe that's the best decision then." Levi, sounding hard, cold. "And you don't have to worry about Zoe. She'll be safe with us." The implication was loud and clear: She wasn't safe with Gideon.

Zoe leaned against the door, blinking hard. No. No, that wasn't right. The stupid idiots. Did they really think he was someone who'd taken advantage of her? That he'd manipulated her into his bed?

Anger flooded through her and she wanted to storm in there the way she had in front of Levi earlier, tell them exactly what was happening. That she was in love with Gideon and he was—

He's what? In love with you?

Her hand spread out on the door, her chest aching. It didn't matter that he didn't feel that way. It really didn't. The only thing that mattered was that she loved him, that's what counted. They should know that, they should *all* know that.

So what would storming in there do? Gideon could defend himself, he didn't need her. And doing that would be acting exactly the way she'd been acting with Gideon all along, like a kid being told no and reacting angrily.

They wouldn't believe her. They'd tell her what Levi had, that she didn't have the experience to make her own choices.

"What the fuck, Levi?" Zee said flatly. "That's cold, man."

"Better for Zoe," Levi responded, his own voice just as flat. "Don't you think?"

Anger sat in her gut, acidic and unsettling. Fuck them. No one knew what was good for her, but her.

Yet she didn't push open the door; instead, she found herself backing away slowly, a cold realization settling down through her.

She couldn't let Gideon go to the police, even if it was to take down Novak. And she didn't want the others looking at Gideon like he was some kind of filthy child molester either. Which meant there was only one way to fix this.

She had to man up. She had to do what she'd always been afraid of doing.

She had to leave Gideon.

The cold spread out inside her, ice water in her veins, but she ignored it, turning to go back up the stairs and let herself back into the apartment.

In her bedroom she found the number Novak had given her, then she dialed it, a secretary answering briskly.

"I'd like to speak to Mr. Novak," she said, trying to keep her voice firm and businesslike. "Tell him it's Zoe James calling."

The secretary put her through without a word, and soon the smooth tones of her father echoed down the line.

"Hello, Zoe. That was quick. I assume you've made a decision then?"

"Yes." Her heartbeat was racing, but at least she sounded cool and in control. "I'd like to accept your offer. I'll leave Detroit. But I'll want payment and confirmation of a place at Princeton before I go."

"Well of course." There was no hesitation, like he already knew that was the decision she'd made. "It's already arranged. The money's in a special account right now, and if you give me your cell number, I'll text you the details."

She felt cold, shaky. "What about the college stuff?"

"I'll call my contact tonight. It should be all set up by tomorrow." A slight pause. "When can you leave Detroit?"

She stared across her bedroom to the opposite wall, where her dresser mirror was, the edges of it covered with photographs she liked and had stuck there. Photographs of Gideon and her, and the others. Her little makeshift family.

"I can leave whenever you like," she said, her voice unsteady.

"Excellent. The sooner the better I think. I'll send a car for you, organize flights up to New Jersey. If you can be ready—"

"I don't want a car, and I don't want you to arrange flights," she interrupted, the backs of her eyes prickling. "All I want is the college placement and the money to pay for it. Anything else I'll do myself."

There was a silence. Then he said, "Fair enough. But I'll need proof you're out of Detroit."

"I'll text you with it." She gripped her phone hard. "Wait, I've decided I want something else."

"I don't think you're in any position—"

"You leave my family, you leave Gideon and all the others alone. And the plans for the Royal development are to go through without any fuss." She took a ragged breath. "If they don't, if you hurt any of them in any way, I'll go to the media."

Novak gave a soft, cold laugh. "Ah, you're a chip off the old block, aren't you? But of course, Zoe. I scratch your back, you scratch mine, right?"

"Eat shit and die," she said calmly, and hit the disconnect button.

Then she threw the phone down on her bed.

It was done now, and it was better this way. This was her decision, her choice. To protect Royal and the small group of people she called her family.

To protect the man who'd spent so many years protecting her.

Because that's what you did when you loved someone, wasn't it? Not storming about and demanding to be treated like an adult, shouting that you knew your own mind and could make your own choices.

Instead, you calmly went out and did what needed to be done to protect those you cared about. That's what Gideon had done for her all those years, after all.

It was time she returned the favor.

Gideon was about ready to strangle someone. Zoe still hadn't turned up, and after he'd spent an hour or so arguing with the others, no decision had been reached about Novak either.

Mainly, though, he found he was missing Zoe, which was ridiculous considering she was only just upstairs and he'd only been down here a couple of hours.

"I don't want you going to jail," Rachel was saying, glaring at him. "That's not going to happen."

"Damn straight," Zee growled, pacing behind her. "There has to be some other answer."

Idiots. They'd been howling for his blood earlier over Zoe, and now they were all pissed because he was going to turn himself in.

"I don't know that there is any other answer," he said patiently.

"What about an anonymous tip-off?" Zee asked, pausing his pacing a moment. "Could that work?"

"No. I wouldn't put it past Novak to figure out where it came from and then start hunting the person responsible, i.e., me. Which could put us all at risk, and I'm not doing that."

Zee cursed, pushing his hands in his pockets and continuing to pace.

"How long a sentence are you looking at?" This from Tamara, who was standing near Rachel, a worried look on her face.

He hadn't wanted to think about that, but looked like he was going to have to. "Not sure. Fifteen to life, maybe. Though I'd probably get some time knocked off depending on the info I manage to get them on Novak." In reality he had no idea, but best to look at a worst-case scenario.

Tamara paled. "Gideon, you can't do that."

"You sure as hell can't." Rachel too had gone white. "We need you here. Royal needs you."

His heart twisted at the look on her face, the same look he could see echoed on Tamara's and Zee's and yes, even on Levi's. But there wasn't another answer. The alternative was Zoe permanently under threat from Novak, and that wasn't going to happen either.

He might go away for a long time, but at least she'd be safe. And the others would be free and clear to make Royal into the kind of neighborhood it should always have been.

"I know you do," he said steadily. "But Zoe is in danger, and there's nothing I wouldn't do to keep her safe. So if this is what I gotta do, then that's what I gotta do. Besides, apart from anything else, I've done some bad stuff in the past. Maybe it's time I paid for that."

Rachel grimaced. "But that was years ago. You're not doing that stuff now."

"Does it matter how long ago it was? I've broken a lotta laws, Rach. Levi did the time for what he did. I'm not exempt just because I had a few good years."

Levi remained silent, standing off to the side with his arms folded across his massive chest, blond brows lowered.

Rachel made an impatient sound, then turned to Levi and the others. "Come on, guys. We're not seriously going to let him do this, are we?"

"It's not up to us," Levi said shortly. "It's up to Gideon."

"Oh bullshit, Levi. Don't let—"

"It's okay, Rach." Gideon walked forward and put a hand on her shoulder. He didn't want them arguing among themselves, not about this. "Levi's right. It's my decision, not yours."

She turned her head, looking up at him, distress in her dark eyes. "We can't let you go down for this, Gideon. It's not . . . right."

"This is bullshit," Zee said all of a sudden. "I've got some old contacts. Dad's gone down, but I can call some people. We could do something that wouldn't lead back to us. I bet Levi's got a few favors he could call in too, right?"

Levi glanced at him. "Yeah," he said slowly. "I might."

"Then let's fucking do it." Zee turned on his heel, beginning to head toward the garage's exit.

"Zee," Gideon forced himself to say. "Stop. That's not what Zoe wants."

The other man turned, still walking backward. "Just let me make the calls, see what we can do. Come on, Tamara. I need you."

Tamara gave Gideon a worried look, then she followed after her lover, her heels making tapping sounds on the concrete.

Levi rolled his shoulders, dropped his arms, then he too began to turn toward the exit.

"Not you," Gideon said sharply. "You don't wanna break parole."

Levi's glance was dark and intense and determined. "You make your decision, I'll make mine." He put out a hand toward Rachel, who took it. Then she glanced back at Gideon as she followed Levi out.

"You've done what you can for us," she said quietly. "Let us do something for you."

Gideon stood there for a long time after the others had gone, staring at the door they'd disappeared through.

Zee was right, it *was* bullshit. His friends shouldn't have to put themselves at risk for him.

And they weren't going to.

He'd let them make the calls, let them at least explore other options. But he knew they wouldn't find any. Just like he already knew what he was going to do. They wouldn't be happy with him, but they'd have to suck it up.

They were too important. Zoe was too important. And as for him, well, maybe it was time for him to pay for the things he'd done. He'd been avoiding it long enough, after all.

Gideon left the garage, heading upstairs to the apartment and letting himself in. It was quiet so he tried not to make a sound as he went down the hall to his bedroom in case Zoe was still asleep. But when he looked inside, the bed was empty.

Okay, so she was up. Good. They needed to talk.

Turning, he went back along the hall to the living room, pausing outside her room in case she was there, but that was empty too.

He found her in the living room, sitting on the couch, a bulging duffel bag on the cushions beside her. She looked up as he came in, a smile bright as sunlight crossing her face, and then gone just as quickly, leaving a set kind of expression that made something in his gut clench tight.

Slowly, she got to her feet. She was wearing what she usually wore, nothing different about that. A red T-shirt and blue skinny jeans, her faded blue Chucks on her feet. Except this time she was holding her leather jacket in her hand, the one he'd gotten her for her eighteenth birthday and that she never let out of her sight.

He didn't know where the foreboding that gripped him had come from, but it was there all the same, a winding thread of ice that had him tensing up as if expecting an attack.

"What's going on?" He glanced at the bag on the couch. "You going somewhere?"

Her face was pale, but the determined look on her face was infinitely familiar. She'd made a decision about something, and he had a horrible feeling it wasn't one he was going to like.

"I heard you, Gideon," she said quietly. "I heard you all talking downstairs."

He stilled. "Talking about what?"

Her golden eyes were unblinking. "About Novak. About what you're going to do."

"Zoe," he began.

"I don't want you to go to the police," she said before he could get anything else out. "I don't want you going to jail for me."

He met her gaze, held it. "That's not up to you."

"I don't care. You're not going to jail."

"No. You're my responsibility, Zoe, you always—"

"Novak is *my* father," she interrupted with clear, calm certainty. "Which makes this *my* decision. I'm his target and once I'm gone, he won't be aiming at Royal anymore."

Anger began to burn inside him, though at who or what, he didn't quite understand. "If he's in jail, he won't be able to fucking aim at anyone."

"Except you'll be there too. Which defeats the purpose, don't you think?"

"No, I don't fucking think." He took a step toward her. "This is the only way, Zoe. That deal he gave you? The money and college placement? It's bullshit. While you're alive, you're a threat to him, and he's not the kind of man who leaves loose ends lying around."

Her expression didn't change. "I know that. I called him to say I accepted his ultimatum. He'll be expecting me to head to New Jersey, but I'm not going there. I'm going . . . somewhere else, where he won't be able to find me."

Gideon's pulse slowed right down and nearly stopped. "What do you mean somewhere else?"

"He wanted me to leave Michigan. So I will. I'll just . . . I won't go to New Jersey."

He stared at her, small and slender, with her bag at her side and her leather jacket in her hand. Little Zoe who'd never been anywhere but Chicago and Detroit in her entire life . . . "Where the hell are you going then? You have no money. You have—"

"Novak put money in some special accounts for me. I have money."

But he was already shaking his head. "No. Just no. You're not leaving, Zoe. You're staying right here."

There was an achingly sad expression in her beautiful eyes that made his heart feel suddenly thin and fragile as glass. "I can't and you know it. Staying will put the others at risk, and I'm not having you go to jail for my sake."

"You think I give a shit about jail?" He began to stalk toward her. "I couldn't give a fuck."

"I know you don't," she said quietly. "But I do. You've already wasted years of your life looking after me, and I don't want you to waste anymore."

"It's not a fucking waste—"

"No, Gideon. I've made my decision. The others, they're my family, and I love them. I want to protect them. And I love you. I love you so much. . . ." Her voice cracked and she stopped, her throat moving as she swallowed, while he halted, standing there like a fucking idiot, suddenly unable to move. "Dammit, I should have just gone," she went on. "I should have just left. But I thought that would be cowardly and I wanted . . . I wanted to say good-bye."

There was a roaring in his ears, her words sounding like they were coming from far away. Stupid. It wasn't like he didn't know any of these things; it wasn't as if they were new. He knew she loved him, he'd always known that, and hearing her say it out loud didn't make anything different.

Yet he couldn't move.

The angry, possessive thing inside him was roaring at him, furious with denial. Shouting at him to go over to where she stood, take her in his arms, cover that gorgeous mouth of hers, stop all this bullshit about leaving, about protecting him, about how his life had been wasted.

Because what did that matter? His life had been a bust right from the beginning, right from the moment his father had wrapped his fingers around his mother's throat and choked her. That violent, jealous prick, taking and taking and taking, until finally he'd taken her life.

All while Gideon had watched, terrified and not understanding what was happening until it was too late. Too late to save her.

He'd spent years not wanting to be too late to save Zoe, and so far he hadn't been. He'd kept her safe and that was what counted. Who cared about the rest of his life?

And as to love . . . well, he knew how that went. Love was selfish and violent and it killed. He wanted no part of it.

So, what? You could ignore her choice. Stop her from leaving. Keep her with you forever. But how does that make you different from your old man? You're holding on to her, taking everything from her, choking her . . .

Something was closing around his spun-glass heart. A fine pressure. And he could feel himself cracking, little fractures spidering everywhere.

He knew himself too well. Knew that dark part of him, the one that was hungry for her, that wanted to keep her whether she wanted to stay or not. He should never have let it out, Jesus. Never.

She was looking at him now, a gleam of pain in her eyes, along with what he thought was a fragile kind of hope, one she probably didn't even realize was there.

She was waiting for something.

Of course she is. She wants you to tell her you love her.

His hands closed into fists.

If he gave her those words, she'd stay, he knew it as surely as he knew Royal Road in all its dirty, gritty glory. She would stay and he'd go to jail and then she'd be left alone. She would be trapped here, waiting for him, because of course she'd wait. While life passed her by and all the opportunities she should have had were gone.

No. He couldn't do it. Couldn't say it. Because what did "I love you" mean anyway? Nothing. It only meant violence and pain and death.

Far better to keep silent and let her go. Let her believe that leaving would save him when in fact, it was leaving that would save her. She needed to go out into the world without him. Finally get to have the life she should have always had, make the choices she needed to make and for herself, not him.

She needed to have friends. Have lovers. She needed to experience everything life had to offer, not be forever stuck in Royal with a possessive mechanic with violence in his past.

As for him, well, he'd go to the DA's office anyway. No matter what she thought about vanishing, he couldn't leave that to chance. Novak was going down, and if that involved a jail term for him as well, then he'd take it. He'd do anything to keep her safe.

"I guess this is good-bye then," he said, unable to keep the rough sound from his voice.

Something flashed over her face, a fleeting trace of shock, of agony, and then it was gone.

The fractures in his heart deepened, the possessive hungry thing straining at the bars of the cage he'd put around it. But he wouldn't give in. This was the first of the choices she needed to make, and he was going to let her make them. He wouldn't try to stop her or change her mind.

"So . . ." she said softly, her voice husky. "That's it? Just . . . good-bye?"

His jaw ached, every muscle he had coiled tight. "You wanted to go, Zoe. So go. I won't stop you."

She blinked, the light catching on the tears in her black lashes, glittering like tiny diamonds, and her gorgeous mouth flattened as if she wanted to say something else and had caught herself just in time. Then she took a breath, the expression on her face closing up, a lone tear escaping out the corner of her eye and sliding down her cheek.

He felt like the biggest prick to walk the earth, and he was sure the sound of the cracks in his heart getting worse were loud in the silence.

But she only swallowed and gave a little nod. "Okay then," she said. "That's how it's going to be." Her hand gripped the strap of the duffel bag and she hooked it over her shoulder, her gaze meeting his, then flicking away. "Good-bye, Gideon." She started toward the door, only to pause when she drew level with him. "Thanks. For everything." She didn't look at him.

He had to ask. "Are you gonna come back?"

"I don't know." She paused. "Do you want me to?"

Yes. Stay with me. Never leave.

Gideon said nothing.

She gave a shake of her head, then moved past him, and he had to dig his nails fiercely into his palms to stop himself from reaching for her, from lifting her into his arms, taking her into his bedroom, tying her to the fucking bed. Never letting her leave his side again.

Her footsteps grew fainter as she went down the hall and he stared across the room, out the window that faced the street, looking at nothing, not trusting himself to even move. Not until she'd gone.

The apartment door closed, and he made himself count to one hundred, very, very slowly.

It was only when silence had blanketed the apartment, the deep, empty silence of absence, that he let himself move. Going over to the sideboard where he kept his liquor. There was a half-empty bottle of bourbon standing on it, the glass cool against his palm as he picked it up by the neck.

Then he flung it against the wall with all his strength.

It smashed into a million pieces.

Just like his heart.

Zoe couldn't see as she walked down the sidewalk, but that had more to do with the fact that her glasses had fogged up and her eyes were full of tears, rather than her shitty eyesight. Her chest hurt too, like someone had punched her hard right over her heart. No, scratch the *had punched her* part. They were still punching her, over and over, like they wanted to break her ribs.

Every part of her wanted to turn around and go back, race up the stairs, fling herself into Gideon's arms, and tell him she wasn't leaving after all. That all she wanted was to stay here in Royal, with him.

Yet she didn't. She kept on walking.

He hadn't said the words that deep down she'd wanted to

hear, the words she'd told herself didn't matter, the words that the lost, lonely part of her had wanted to hear her whole life.

But no one had ever said them to her. Not her mother. Not her father.

Not Gideon.

If he'd said them, she would have stayed and nothing would have made her leave him. But he hadn't and so now, here she was, walking down the sidewalk away from him. Away from Royal. Away from the only place that had ever felt like home.

She blinked fiercely, wiping away the tears with shaking fingers, swallowing them back.

She really had no idea where she was going to go, but it wasn't to Princeton, that was for sure. She'd go somewhere else. Somewhere where no one knew her—which wasn't difficult since everyone who knew her was right here in Royal.

The streets were full of lunchtime traffic, the sun beginning to get hot, the air sticky and humid. A crowd of teenagers passed her, laughing and shouting to one another.

She gripped her bag tighter, a great, gaping emptiness opening up inside her. It was familiar, that emptiness. She'd felt it a lot when she'd been young, shipped around to different foster homes, another unwanted, unloved kid. The emptiness had stayed even when her mother had come back and Zoe had gone back to live with her, eating a big hole in the middle of heart.

The only time she didn't feel it was when she was with Gideon.

Her jaw tightened.

Okay, so it hurt. And okay, she felt like she was dying inside. But she was doing what she had to do to protect the people she loved. She had to take some comfort in that. Anyway, she'd survived this long without hearing those words, she could keep on surviving. Even if it meant an empty life without Gideon in it.

Zoe lifted her chin, blinked away the tears, and stuck out her hand as a cab began to approach. It slowed, then pulled over to the curb. She tugged open the door and climbed inside, shutting it behind her.

The others were going to be pissed she hadn't said good-bye, but that was too bad. Saying good-bye to Gideon had used up her meager store of courage. She had nothing left.

"Where to, sweet thing?" The taxi driver, an old guy who looked eighty if he was a day, gave her an inquiring look in the rearview mirror.

"The airport," Zoe said.

As they drove out of Royal, she didn't look back.

Chapter 17

A week later, in a crummy bar off the Strip in LA, Zoe looked up at the TV screen above the bar to see her father's face plastered all over the national news.

The guy who was trying to chat her up faded into the background as she stared in shock at the TV. Oliver Novak, prominent businessman and senatorial candidate, had been arrested on suspicion of various crimes from extortion to tax evasion to attempted murder, or so the talking head on the screen said. Then there was a clip of her father being escorted out of his Grosse Pointe mansion by two officers, his hands in cuffs behind his back, his expression stony.

Zoe went cold, knowing exactly what must have happened. Gideon had ignored her and gone to the police anyway.

The stupid, stupid asshole.

The guy next to her was still talking, but she'd long since ceased to listen, hauling her phone out of her pocket and looking down at the screen. There were no texts. Shit.

Opening a new text message to Rachel, she typed in a quick question, hesitating only a moment before hitting send.

She'd only made contact with the others once since she'd taken the first plane out of Detroit. It had gone to Atlanta, but she hadn't stayed there, taking yet another flight bound for LA. She'd stepped out of the terminal at LAX and into the baking heat of a Californian summer, so bright she had to blink back tears. Yeah, it had definitely been the sun, not the homesickness.

Waiting for a bus, she'd switched her phone off flight mode, and predictably it started vibrating like crazy from all the missed calls and voice mails and texts.

She'd ignored them all, unable to deal with them, in the end settling on sending one text to Rachel. *I'm sorry I didn't say good-bye. Tell the others I'm okay. I'll let you know if anything changes.*

Rachel had sent her a reply, a demand to be told what was going on and where Zoe was, but she'd ignored that, too.

She couldn't face them. Just couldn't. If she was going to live her life without the others in it, then she had to put them behind her. It was the only way she could cope.

For a whole week she'd done exactly that, spending her time exploring the city, filling up the emptiness inside her with sightseeing, spending at least one whole day at Disneyland, the next on the beach at Santa Monica, looking at the sea for the first time in her life.

It hurt, sitting on the sand alone, staring at the blue ocean in front of her. Because there should have been someone next to her, holding her hand. There should have been someone to slide his arm around her and hold her close. There should have been a warm chest to lay her head against so she could listen to the beat of his heart and surround herself with the familiar scent of engine oil and leather and smoke.

But there wasn't.

Her decision. Her choice. And it fucking sucked.

The guy chatting her up now was supposed to be her Gideon cure, but she suddenly didn't give a shit about him, her whole awareness centered on the phone sitting on the bar next to her.

Eventually it vibrated back, and she snatched it up, looking down to read Rachel's reply.

Gideon went to the police. He worked out some kind of deal, which means he doesn't have to do time. Where the hell are you and when the fuck are you coming home?

For a second she stared down at the text glowing on the screen, her heart racing, her hands shaking with relief. Then, hard on the heels of the relief came the anger.

Jesus Christ, what was his deal? She'd told him he didn't have to do that. Her leaving had been supposed to save him and he'd gone ahead and handed himself in anyway.

Which kind of means you left for nothing.

Yeah, it really did, didn't it? Her agonized choice. The ripping feeling in her chest as she'd walked away from him. The empty hollowness inside her that had been there ever since she'd left Detroit.

All for nothing.

He'd been going to do it all along, and yet he'd only put up a token protest when she'd told him she was leaving. Hadn't argued when she'd said she was doing it to save him. He'd let her believe that what she was doing was the right thing for all of them.

That had been the thing she'd clung to over the past week, the only thing that had made it bearable. Knowing that by leaving, she'd helped the others. She'd saved Gideon. But now . . .

Now what? Don't make this all about you and your choices. What about him? He was prepared to go to prison for you, while all you had to do was sit on the beach for a week. . . .

She swallowed, staring at the screen in front of her, at Rachel's text blurring in front of her eyes.

Shit. He'd done so many things for her. He'd come back to

her over and over again when she'd been a child, his visits the one bright thing in the world she had to look forward to, and he'd never not come when he'd said he would. He'd never not turned up. Even when she'd gone back to live with her mother, even when he was so much older than her, those visits had continued. He'd remained her friend, the one person she could count on, the one person she knew would listen to her. He'd given her hugs when she'd been small and afraid. His had been the ear she'd poured her troubles into when she'd had problems at school. He'd given her wordless comfort when things with her mother had gotten bad.

He'd been there for her.

Then he'd finally taken her away, to Detroit. Spending thirteen years of his life keeping her hidden and safe . . .

She felt like someone had kicked her hard in the stomach, all the breath suddenly going out of her.

He didn't have to take her with him when he'd left Chicago. He had money, he had prospects, no matter what he thought. The world had been his oyster, and yet he'd given all of that up to protect a lonely young girl.

Now he'd done it again. Risking jail time to make sure the man who'd threatened her was taken out of the picture for good.

Her eyes burned, Rachel's text blurring completely. Who was worth that kind of sacrifice? Certainly she wasn't.

"Hey, are you okay?" The guy next to her sounded concerned. "You had some bad news or something?"

Unable to look at him, she shook her head. "No, I just . . . I just have to go. I'm sorry." She slipped off the barstool, heading straight for the exit without turning around.

Outside the night was thick with heat and neon, the gritty streets reminding her of Royal for some reason, even though they were completely different. The sidewalk was packed with people all out for a night on the Strip, the street full of cars.

Zoe joined the stream of human traffic, not knowing where she was going, only knowing that she had to move, had to fill her lungs with air or else she was going to suffocate.

She'd walked away from him, so full of the importance of her sacrifice for him and for the others, all the while secretly hoping he'd tell her to stay. That he'd say the words she'd wanted to hear from him for so long. But he hadn't said anything; he'd just let her go. Then he'd turned around and made his own sacrifice. Without a word. As if the possibility of at least fifteen years in jail didn't matter to him in the slightest.

She wrapped her arms around her middle, a large boulder sitting dead center on her chest.

He'd let her walk away from him and she had. She hadn't bothered to ask him why, when he'd been so possessive earlier. She'd been too sore, too hurt, concentrating on the fact that he hadn't given her what she wanted.

She stopped in the middle of the sidewalk, oblivious to the curses from other people as they dodged to avoid her.

Shit. So for all her realizations about how she needed to grow up, how she needed to treat him as a partner, a man, and not demand stuff from him like a child, in the end, that's exactly what she'd done.

Why? What the hell was wrong with her?

Zoe gripped herself tighter, forcing herself to move on, to keep walking.

She had to do something, had to give him something back for everything he'd done for her. Something real this time, without wanting anything for herself. Except she didn't know what that could be. The only thing she had to give him was her love, and that could never be enough, not to make up for what he'd given her. What he'd sacrificed for her.

She was, after all, only a girl who nobody wanted. A girl who had nothing to offer anyone except herself, and that certainly had never been enough.

Oh, come on. He came back to you, time and time again. He gave up years of his life for you. Do you think he'd do that for anyone?

Her heart began to speed up, thumping loudly in her head.

She had no answer to that, yet she couldn't deny the facts. He *had* come back to her. Over and over. And she'd never stopped to think about why that was. Why a teenager years older than she was would want to spend time with a child. Why a man would want to spend time with a teenage girl.

Oh sure, there were creepy reasons, but Gideon wasn't that sort of guy and he never had been. He was her friend, that was all. And yet . . .

Maybe she did do something for him. Maybe she helped him in some way. Maybe . . . whatever she had to offer *would* be enough.

Does it matter if it is?

Slowly this time, Zoe came to a stop, staring sightlessly at the crowds of people flowing around her like the water of a stream flows around a rock.

No. It didn't matter.

She didn't matter.

The only thing that did was Gideon.

He had come back to her, always.

Maybe it was time she came back to him.

"Hey, seven o'clock tonight. Gino's. Remember?" The sound of Rachel's footsteps rang as she came down the metal stairs from the office.

Gideon didn't look up from the engine sitting on the workbench. "Yeah, yeah. I remember."

Rachel had been filling in for him since Zoe had gone, and although he was thankful for her help, he hadn't so much enjoyed the worried glances she kept shooting in his direction whenever she thought he wasn't looking.

Even the endless questioning in the tiny room at the police station hadn't been as bad. Or the shouting he'd had to put up with from the others when they'd realized what he'd done the day after Zoe had left.

Yeah, they'd been pissed, as they'd had every right to be. Though luckily the DA had offered him a deal—all the info he had on Novak, plus anything on a few other guys the police had been after. Being an informant didn't exactly lead to a long life expectancy, but it was better than life in prison. And he'd been given anonymity by the police, plus organizing a few things on his own with various contacts of his. If anyone came after him, they'd be in for a nasty surprise.

No, it was his friends who were more likely to kill him, and when he'd told them what he'd done, he'd almost been sorry he hadn't taken a jail term. Especially when Levi had almost thrown a swing at him.

Of course it wasn't only about what he'd done in terms of Novak.

It was also about Zoe.

They all missed her acutely, and he knew that Levi and Zee at least blamed him for the way she'd taken off. That was okay with him. They could hate him for that. But he didn't regret it.

She was off seeing the world, and that was as it should be.

"You okay?" Rachel had stopped near the bench, and he could feel the back of his neck prickling under her anxious gaze.

"I'm fine," he said shortly, even though he wasn't fine. Not at all.

There was a hole inside him, the hole that had always been there, ever since he'd been a little boy coming in from school one day to find his mother dead. A hole that afterward he'd kept filled with hate and with anger. Until Zoe. Who'd smiled at him the first time he'd met her and all the other times since.

Who'd flung out her arms to him without hesitation whenever he'd visited.

Who'd made him feel good.

Who'd filled the hole inside him with laughter.

Who was now gone.

So no. He wasn't fucking fine.

"Sure?" Rachel persisted.

The wrench he was using slipped, his fingers banging painfully against the hard metal of the engine's casing. He cursed. Fucking thing.

"Hey," Rachel said, "look, I've been meaning to tell you, but Zoe—"

"Don't." The word was flat and cold, but he couldn't make it sound any different. "Just don't, Rach. I don't wanna know." And he didn't. The mere sound of her name opened that hole inside him wider, and he couldn't let it get any bigger than it was already. Because if it did . . . Jesus, he didn't know what he'd do.

She gave a soft sigh. "Okay. I hear you. Just . . . We're here for you, Gideon. You know that."

Finally, he lifted his head and met her worried gaze. He couldn't give her the smile he knew she wanted, but at least he could show her he appreciated the sentiment. "I do know. And I'll be okay. I promise."

She looked like she was going to say something else, but then, thank Christ, she only lifted a shoulder and stepped away. "Great. Well, I'll see you tonight. The final plans look amazing and Levi's really excited to show everyone."

He wished he could feel more excited about them himself, but he didn't. He couldn't even pretend. So he only nodded before looking back down at the shitty little engine he was trying to fix and waiting until her footsteps died away and the door clanged shut. And he was finally alone.

Then he picked up the wrench and threw it violently against the wall.

But of course that didn't make any difference.

Fuck's sake. Get a handle on your shit. Throwing things at walls doesn't help.

No, it didn't. When he felt like this, the only thing that helped was Zoe. That was why he'd always been circling back to her for nearly half his life, coming back to her again and again, because she filled the hole, eased the pain. Showing him a better way. She was always there, always waiting for him.

Except this time she was the one who'd gone and he was the one waiting, and he didn't know how to deal with it. He didn't know how to wait. Didn't know what he should do with the void in the center of his life.

A Zoe-shaped void.

She'd been his constant for so long that now that she was gone, he didn't know how to *be*. Christ, he was a fool.

He pushed himself away from the workbench, deciding to give up for the day. Cleanup took him half an hour, and then he was locking the garage behind him and heading upstairs to the apartment.

It hit him again as he stepped inside, the silence. The absence that he hadn't been able to get used to. Which was fucking stupid, because he wasn't a lovesick teenager and he hadn't lost anyone. Zoe was only gone.

Maybe it was empty-nest syndrome or something.

Chucking his keys down on the table beside the door, he went down the hallway, heading to the bathroom and a shower. He was tired and sweaty and dirty, and the last thing he wanted was to go out to Gino's and discuss the plans, but considering he was helping Levi out with the finances behind this, he really had to.

Stripping off his clothes and dumping them in the laundry

hamper, he then moved to turn on the shower. Not bothering to wait until the water had heated, he got in, hoping the cold spray would wake him up.

He was sick of feeling tired.

It wasn't until he'd gotten out and was toweling himself dry that he heard the door of the apartment close. He stilled, his heartbeat slowing.

Who the fuck was that? No one had keys, and if someone had broken down his door, he was pretty sure they would have made way more noise than that.

Quickly he dropped the towel, pulled on his jeans, and went to the bathroom door, mentally going through the list of weaponry he had stashed around the house. The gun in his dresser was the closest since that was right next door.

There was no sound from outside, so he pulled the door open a crack. Nothing down the hallway. He opened it wider, but there was no movement in either direction, and no sound coming from anywhere.

Maybe he'd imagined it?

Then there came a thump from the living room, like something heavy being dropped, and okay, so he hadn't imagined it. Someone else was in the apartment. Someone who'd gotten in with keys.

His heart suddenly came to a roaring stop and he couldn't breathe.

No, it wasn't her. It couldn't be her.

A figure stepped into the hallway, looking in his direction. Small, slender. Black curls cascading down her back. Delicate face with little round glasses perched on the end of her nose. Black T-shirt and the jeans with holes in the knees, scuffed Converses . . .

Zoe.

His gut lurched, something inside him falling away. "What

the *fuck* are you doing here?" he demanded, his voice sounded rusty, all sticky and rough like an engine desperately in need of oil.

Slowly she began to come toward him, but he threw up a hand and she stopped like he'd struck her.

"No," he said, unable to help himself. "No. You can't. I let you go. You were supposed to fucking *leave*. You weren't supposed to come *back!*" He hadn't meant to shout, but it echoed down the hallway all the same, far, far too loud.

Zoe stared at him as the echoes died away, her golden eyes liquid and so, so beautiful. So warm. Full of sunlight and laughter and joy.

Then she kept walking. Like he hadn't said anything.

"Zoe," he said again, because if she got close to him he didn't know what he might do. "Don't you fucking dare."

"You always came back to me," she said in the soft, husky voice he heard sometimes in his dreams at nights. "Why can't I come back to you?"

"Because you can't. You were supposed to leave. You were supposed to make your own choices, go and have a fucking life!"

"I am making a choice." She came closer. "And my choice is you."

"*Stop.*" His hand was out in front of him, as if he could hold her off. "You need to make a different one." He sounded desperate, but he couldn't help it. "You need to make a different choice."

Her chin came up in that way he knew so well. "Why?"

"Jesus, do I really need to give you all the reasons? I can't give you what you want."

The look on her face softened. "I know that," she said quietly. "I know you can't. And I'm okay with that. I just . . . thought you should know that I'm back. That if you ever need me, I'll be around." Her slender throat moved. "You were always there for me, so . . . now I'm here for you."

He blinked, the unexpectedness of it hitting like a punch to the gut. "I don't understand."

"I know what you did for me, Gideon. I saw it on the news. And not only for me, but for the others, too. But that's you all over, isn't it? You're always doing things for other people." Her voice had gotten croaky. "You're always doing things for me. You put your whole life on hold for me and then, like that wasn't enough, you went and risked a jail term just to put my stupid father in prison." She took a little breath. "So I thought it was about time I did something for you."

He stood there staring at her, his skin damp from the shower, drops of water dripping down his back from his half-dried hair, unable to make sense of what she was saying. "You and I are not a business deal," he said flatly. "And you don't owe me a goddamn thing."

"I didn't mean it like that." She held his gaze, the look in her eyes direct. "This isn't about payback. I couldn't pay you back for what you've done for me anyway, not if I lived to be a hundred. This is about the fact that you're important to me and I care about you." She stopped, her cheeks flushing. "And before you say it, no, I don't expect you to say anything. I don't expect anything from you at all. I just . . . I don't have anything to give you but me. It's not much, it's not enough for everything you've done, but still. I'm here. Like you were always there for me."

He didn't know what to say. It was like his brain had gone blank.

"Well." She put her hands in the pockets of her jeans, shifting awkwardly on her feet. "I should probably take off. I thought I might go stay with Rach and Levi, but maybe they're not going to be all that happy with me suddenly turning up on their doorstep out of the blue. Especially when I just left—"

"Zoe." Her name came out hoarse, and he didn't know why he'd said it.

She lifted her chin. "What?"

"Why did you come back?"

"I just told you."

"No. The real reason." He didn't know why he was asking that either. It was almost like he wanted to hear something from her. Something that would fill this aching hole in the middle of his heart.

Her eyes gleamed, bright and liquid. "I came back because I'm a selfish bitch," she said suddenly. "I've been wanting and wanting and wanting all kinds of things from you. Things I had no right to ask for. And when you said no, I've been acting like a little kid, throwing a tantrum when I didn't get what I wanted." Her mouth tightened. "I came back to tell you that I'm sorry. I shouldn't have asked for what you didn't want to give. I shouldn't have pushed you like I did. And I shouldn't have thrown everything you've done for me away like that."

He'd taken a step toward her before he'd even realized what he was doing, because the look on her face made him ache. It was stripped bare, raw and honest, and he could see she was holding back tears.

"I thought by walking away I was saving you," she went on. "But I wasn't. I walked away because you wouldn't give me what I wanted. And that's not something I'm proud of."

She was so close to him and now he could smell the scent of her, lavender and Zoe. It wouldn't take much to reach out and touch her.

"I know what you wanted," he said, holding her gaze, trying to keep his hands at his sides and not reach out for her. "But I couldn't say those words. I knew you'd stay if I did, and I didn't want you to."

There was molten gold in her eyes. "Why not?"

"Because keeping you here is all I've been doing the past

thirteen years. I've been telling myself it was all about making sure you were safe, but it wasn't. It was for me. I couldn't bear the thought of letting you go."

"But I—"

"No, listen. My dad, fuck, all he did was take. Then he took my mother's life. I don't want to be like him. I don't want to be that selfish."

Her eyes widened. "What? But . . . you're not anything like him. You're the most unselfish man I've ever met in my life."

"No, I took from you, Zoe. I kept you here by my side for years. I didn't let you go to college, get a job, get a boyfriend. And I made sure as shit I was the only man in your life." He sucked in a breath. "Then you offered yourself to me and I fucking took that, too. You *loved* me, Zoe, and I didn't care. I was going to keep you anyway, because I'm that kind of man. I'm possessive and mean and I will do harm to anyone who takes what's mine."

"But—"

"Let me finish." His pulse sounded loud in his head, and he couldn't stop looking at her face. Couldn't seem to keep his hands right where they were at his sides. They kept lifting toward her as if he were dying and she were his one chance of heaven. "I was wrong to take you. I was wrong to accept, because you had no fucking idea what kind of man I was, and that's all on me. I didn't tell you. So that's why I let you walk away." He clenched his hands into fists. "I had no right to you. I've been the only man in your life since you were six years old, and you deserve a life without me in it. Space to make your own choices. To find a man you love by choice, not by default."

Tears spilled down her cheeks, and it took everything he had not to reach for her and wipe them away, pull her into his arms. He ached for her everywhere, but he couldn't give in to it. Sure, she'd come back, but that didn't mean he could take her. That didn't mean she was his.

"I never loved you by default." Her voice was thick with tears. "I loved you because you were there for me. Every. Single. Time. You were the *only* one I could ever count on. The one I could tell everything to. You were my friend. You treated me like I was a person, not just some fucking kid who nobody wanted. *That's* why I loved you, you stupid idiot."

He didn't know why that was so difficult to hear or so difficult to believe. Because sure, he'd been there for her, but there was a reason for that. "You know why I kept coming back to you? It wasn't for you, Zoe. It was for me. Because I was losing pieces of my soul with every job that I did. And every time I saw you . . . God, you gave them back to me."

She lifted a hand, swiping at her tears, leaving shiny marks all over her cheeks. "I don't know how. I was just a stupid kid."

"You were never just a stupid kid." Somehow he'd gotten even closer, which was wrong and so dangerous and yet he couldn't seem to help himself. "You were always so pleased to see me. You were never afraid of me, always smiled and held out your arms. I felt . . . like I was a good person with you."

She gave another swipe at her cheeks. "You are a good person, Gideon. You always were."

"But that was for me. Don't you see?" Because she didn't, not really, and no wonder. It was only now that he could see it himself. "It was *all* for me. I wanted to feel good about myself, that's why I couldn't let you go."

"So you built your life around keeping me safe just so you could feel good about yourself?" There was an edge in her voice now. "Does that sound as stupid to you as it does to me?"

He stared at her, willing her to understand. "It's not stupid. It's the truth. That's why I have to let you go. I can't keep on taking from you, little one. I can't keep taking from you to make myself feel better. I just can't."

For a long moment she said nothing. Then, unexpectedly, she gave him a watery grin. "It's okay," she said raggedly. "I

understand. Like I said, I'm not going to ask you for anything."
She turned around. "I'll just get my bag."

What the fuck are you doing?

Gideon ignored the voice in his head, watching as Zoe turned
and walked back to the living room, disappearing through the
door a second before coming back, her duffel bag over her
shoulder.

Are you really going to let her walk away?

He had to. He wasn't going to keep taking from her, keep
her trapped in this narrow version of the life he thought was
right for her. She deserved bigger. She deserved better.

She deserved love.

He went motionless, frozen as she walked past him in the
direction of the door, something clenching so hard around his
chest he couldn't breathe.

Her footsteps retreated down the hallway the way they had
a week ago, but this time he turned to watch her, unable to help
himself.

She'd paused by the front door, looking back at him. Small
and slender and fragile. Yet strong, so strong. Coming back for
him, giving herself to him without wanting anything in return.
Apologizing to him for something that needed no apology.
Bright and beautiful and innocent, yet so smart, too, the way
she had been all her life.

"Bye, Gideon. I'll be around." Her hand dropped to the
handle.

*She made a choice. She chose you. And you're throwing it
back in her face.*

But he was doing what was best for her, wasn't he?

No. You're doing what's best for you.

The pressure around his chest was agonizing and it came to
him then, short and sharp like a bullet from a gun, that of course
this was for him. He'd been holding her at a distance, not to
protect her, but to protect himself.

Because love hurt. It was shouting and violence, fists thrown at night in drunken rages. It was tears of pain and humiliation. It was his mother, her life choked out of her by his father's fists.

But it was also Zoe. And she'd made her choice. She'd come back to him.

Every time in the past, she'd welcomed him. She'd never turned him away. She'd always been there for him then.

He needed to be there for her now.

"Zoe," he said raggedly. "Wait."

Her hand stilled on the handle. "What?"

"Don't go." He met her liquid amber gaze. "Please."

She blinked. Rapidly. "I . . . What do you mean."

"I want you to stay."

"Um. I'm not sure—"

"I want you to stay with me. In my bed. In my life." His voice went all rough and harsh-sounding. "In my heart."

She stared at him. "Why?"

"You know why, little one." Those words had never meant anything to him before. But they did now. Those words meant her, and so he said them without any trouble at all. "I love you."

Her face crumpled, and all of a sudden her bag was dropping on the ground and she was walking down the hallway, coming toward him like she had done so many times in the past.

And like he always did, he opened his arms to her.

And she ran into them.

Zoe buried her head against his chest and cried. Which was dumb, but she couldn't help it. Then his arms came around her, holding her close, and she cried harder, which again, didn't make any sense, because she was happy and relieved and so many other emotions she couldn't untangle them all.

He let her weep like an idiot for how long she didn't know, then his hands were in her hair, tipping her head back, and he was kissing her like he was suffocating and she was the air he needed to breathe.

She had been holding herself back for so long, ever since she'd gotten back to Detroit. Trying to be strong, trying to be adult about all of this. But the journey had been a killer, and she'd been so tired, and when she'd let herself back into the apartment and he'd been standing there in the hallway, wearing only jeans, his bronze skin gleaming and wet from a shower, her heart had inflated like a balloon, swelling up almost to bursting.

There was nothing she'd wanted more in that moment than him.

But she'd been good. She'd told him everything that was in her heart, and then she'd stood back, not asking for anything in return even though she wanted everything. She'd been prepared to let him go.

She hadn't thought he would change his mind.

But he had.

Now she was kissing him back, desperate, not wanting to think, not wanting to talk, not wanting anything but him. He was all around her, hot skin and hard-packed muscle, smelling of the soap and shampoo he'd used, and the familiarity of it made her want to dissolve into tears all over again.

He didn't let her. Instead, he lifted her in his arms and carried her into the bedroom, stripping all her clothes off her before doing the same to himself. Then he took her down onto the bed, touching her, kissing her, stroking her as if she was something precious, something to be cherished.

She tried to return the favor, but his hands turned hard on her, shaking as they pressed her thighs apart, and when he pushed inside her, his whole body shuddered, her name a whisper against her neck.

Zoe closed her legs around his waist, wrapping her arms

around him, holding him as he began to move, deep and slow, then gripping him tighter as the pleasure coiled between them. Then he moved faster, harder, and the pleasure became a hot burn, a sweetness that moved through her like wildfire, and she turned her face into the hollow of his throat, inhaling him.

He began to gather her up, his arms beneath her, lifting her so she was held tight against him, moving deeper still so the pleasure was all she could feel.

She burned there, a small, glowing ember, before igniting into flame as the orgasm exploded through her, shaking and trembling in his arms. And he held her tighter still as it took him, too, the pair of them blazing in the dimness of the room.

Afterward, she lay against him as the weight of a week's worth of sleepless nights finally caught up with her.

She closed her eyes. Just for a second.

When she opened them again, the sun was full on her face, a warm, heavy weight across her chest. Somewhere someone's phone was ringing.

She frowned at the ceiling, for a moment disoriented. Then the weight on her chest shifted, coiling around her, and everything fell into place.

Gideon.

"Good morning, little one." His voice was in her ear, the intoxicating heat of his body pressed all along her spine. "I've been waiting for you to wake up." His fingers spread out on her stomach, easing her back, and she could feel his cock, hard and hot against her butt.

She grinned and turned over, a bubble of pure happiness expanding in her throat. His hair hung over his black eyes, his jaw unshaven, and he looked dark and dangerous, and holy hell, so freaking gorgeous. She touched his jaw, loving the feeling of his morning beard against her palm. "Is that your phone? Shouldn't you get it?"

He smiled, making her heart turn over. "It's probably Rachel

SIN FOR ME / 293

wondering where the hell I am. I was supposed to meet them at Gino's last night."

"Then I guess we should be glad they're not battering down the door by now."

"After you fell asleep last night, I sent them a text telling them I wouldn't be there."

She flushed, a vague memory of rolling over and closing her eyes for a second coming back to her. "Oh."

"You must have been tired." He slid his hand over her hip, stroking her, making her want to purr like a cat. "Where did you come from?"

"LA. I mean, with about twenty stops between LA and here."

His eyes widened. "You went to LA?"

"Yeah." She sighed, running her fingers down the strong column of his neck, loving the feeling of his skin beneath hers. "I wanted to get as far away from Detroit as I could."

He frowned. "You were okay?"

"Well, obviously." She stroked his shoulder. "I went to Disneyland. Beverly Hills. Saw the sea. Got chatted up by some guy."

His frown deepened. "Am I gonna have to kill him?"

She grinned. "You know, if anyone else said that, I would have thought they'd be joking."

"I'm not joking."

Zoe laughed. "I know. But don't worry. I wasn't interested. I'm not interested in anyone but you."

"Better not be." The hand on her side slid over her butt, cupping her, then squeezing slightly, a gentle pressure that made her shiver with delight.

"The others are going to hate this, aren't they?" she asked, trailing her fingers over his chest. "My being with you."

His grim expression eased. "They'll get used to it. After all, nothing's gonna change as far as they're concerned."

"Well, that's true."

There was a comfortable silence for a long time.

Then Gideon said quietly, "I meant it, you know."

"Meant what?"

"That I love you. You're my soul. You always have been."

Zoe put her hand on his chest, right above his heart. The emptiness inside her had gone, filled up with something else. Something bright. And maybe something a little dark, too. Because that was Gideon, the dark and the light.

"And you're mine," she said simply.

His hand covered hers, and for a moment they lay there not speaking, the truth between them in all its wonderful, terrible glory.

Then his mouth curved. "You know what day it is today?"

She blinked at him. "Um. It's Sunday."

"Yeah. And you know what we do on Sundays, don't you?"

Oh. Her chest got tight. "P-pancakes?" she stuttered like the fool she was.

His smile was very special and only for her. "Pancakes."

Finally. She was home.

Epilogue

"You know they're going to be pissed I didn't say good-bye," Zoe said, taking the bike helmet he held out to her. "Again."

Gideon grinned, adjusting his own helmet. "They'll cope. Anyway, I didn't think you needed Rach flapping around making sure you were gonna be okay."

She rolled her eyes and he laughed. Rachel had only just found out she was pregnant and was currently acting crazy, not that Levi was any better. Both of them had been very concerned about Zoe leaving for college, and it didn't make any difference that Gideon was taking her to Ann Arbor and making sure she was settled. They'd still been acting like a couple of overprotective parents. Which is kind of what they were.

"You'll give them my love, won't you?" Zoe asked after a moment, putting on her helmet and doing up the strap. "And to Zee and Tamara?"

"Yeah, of course." He brushed her hands away, making sure the strap was secure. Her eyes had gone very large and there was a certain amount of anxiousness in them. "Hey," he murmured, wanting to reassure her. "It's not like you're gonna be in Greenland or anything. It's only Ann Arbor."

She'd been accepted into the University of Michigan a couple of months earlier, and though she'd been ecstatic at the time, Gideon knew that the reality of leaving Royal wouldn't set in until the time to leave had actually arrived.

Which it had.

"I know. I'm . . . nervous. And I kind of don't want to leave."

"And I don't want you to go. But you need to. We discussed this, remember?"

Leaving for college had been Zoe's decision, and he'd been okay with it. Well, not okay, because fundamentally he didn't want her to ever leave him again. But one thing they were both clear on: She needed to get out of Royal, experience life, occupy that brain of hers with more than office spreadsheets.

"I'm going to miss you," she whispered croakily.

He cupped her vivid little face in his hands, knowing he was going to have to tell her the surprise he'd been hoping to save until they'd gotten to their destination, because he couldn't bear to see her upset. "You don't have to miss me, little one."

She frowned. "What? Why not?"

"I was saving it as a surprise, but I hate seeing you cry." He stroked her jawline gently. "I got us a place near the college. Gonna let the apartment here while we're away."

Zoe blinked, looking puzzled. "But you told me I was going to be in a dorm and have roommates and . . . stuff."

"Do you want roommates and stuff? I don't wanna deprive you of a genuine college experience."

For a second she stared at him, the crease between her brows not budging. Then she asked, "What about the garage?"

"It's not far up the freeway. And I don't mind the commute." He stroked her bottom lip. "But I'm serious, if you don't want me hanging around and cramping your style—"

He never got to finish because Zoe abruptly rose up on her tiptoes and kissed him hard.

"Are you mad?" she said breathlessly when she'd finished. "You really think I'd pick some stranger for a roommate over you?" The crease had gone from between her brows and she was flushed. "But are you sure, Gideon? Royal's been so important to you for so long."

He let out a breath, wishing the journey had already ended and they were in the apartment he'd picked for them a week or so earlier. Where he could lay her down in the bright new bedroom with the extra-large king-size bed, show her what was *really* important to him. Because the decision had been an easy one to make. He needed to be wherever she was, simple as that.

"Home is where you are, Zoe," he said quietly. "Always has been."

She got a little misty-eyed at that, not saying a word, but kissing him instead. Which was totally fine by him.

A minute or so later, both of them breathless, he finally let her go and turned to his Harley, the saddlebags already packed. The removal guys would be here soon to deal with packing up the apartment, but it would take a few days before the place in Ann Arbor would be ready. So he'd planned on taking Zoe for a road trip first.

"By the way," he said casually, as he helped her onto the massive bike. "I hope you brought your swimsuit."

"Uh, no. Why?"

"Because we're going to Ann Arbor by way of Cape Cod."

Her eyes went wide, her mouth dropping open. "What?"

"You saw the sea in LA. But I haven't. Thought you might wanna show it to me."

The joy in her face reached right inside him, wrapped itself around his heart. "Oh my God, of course I would!" She flapped her hands at him. "Get on the goddamn bike and let's get out of here!"

He laughed and got on the goddamn bike.

And when she put her arms around him, holding on tight as they left Royal, he didn't look behind him.

He didn't need to.

Acknowledgments

Once again to my editor, Martin Biro, and my agent, Helen Breitwieser, thanks so much for your hard work with this series. And to all the folks at Kensington for theirs.

Also to my three best ladies. You know who you are.

If you enjoyed *Sin for Me,* be sure you
don't miss the first book in Jackie Ashenden's
scorching Motor City Royals series

WRONG FOR ME

After eight years in prison, Levi Rush is finally out and back
on the gritty streets of Detroit to claim the future he was owed.
A future that includes the one woman he's wanted for years—
his former best friend, Rachel. She's the reason he went inside,
and if getting her to do what he wants means buying the building that houses her tattoo studio and using it as leverage, then
that's what he'll do. Because if there's one thing he's learned inside, it's that if you want to win, you have to play dirty.

Rachel Hamilton is a tattoo artist and one hell of a tough
girl. Detroit is her home, and she's determined to make it a better place. But her plans are threatened when her old friend Levi
reappears and gives her an ultimatum: She gives herself to him
body and soul, or else she and her business are out on the street.
Levi's got no room in his heart for anything but anger and the
lust he's been carrying around for so long. But the only thing
stronger than the secrets of their shared past is their fiery at-
traction to each other. . . .

Keep reading for a special excerpt.

A Kensington trade paperback and e-book on sale now!

Chapter 1

Rachel Hamilton came to a stop outside the battered metal roller door that was the entrance to Black's Vintage Repair and Restoration, the motorcycle repair shop owned by her friend Gideon Black. She took a breath.

The acid eating a hole in her gut wasn't from fear.

It didn't have anything to do with the fact that Levi was back.

It was only because she hadn't felt like breakfast that morning and hadn't eaten anything. Perfectly understandable and explainable. Nothing whatsoever to do with how sick she'd felt, how her stomach kept turning over and over like a gymnast doing a complicated floor routine whenever she thought about Levi getting out of jail.

Nope. Nothing whatsoever to do with that.

Her palms were damp, but that was because it was hot. Same with her dry mouth. She should have had some water or something.

But you didn't because you would have thrown it up.

Rachel closed her eyes.

No fear. None. That's what had gotten her through life so far, and that's what would get her through this. She just had to pull her armor on, pretend she gave no fucks whatsoever. It was the only way to protect herself. It was the only way to deal with the man who'd been inside for eight years.

The man she'd put there herself.

Her former best friend.

Oh Jesus. She was shaking.

Okay, so perhaps she shouldn't think about that. She should think about how many fucks she gave instead. Which was none at all.

But naturally all the pep talks in the entire universe weren't going to help, and, when she opened her eyes, the nausea was still sitting right there and she was still shaking like a leaf.

Get. Yourself. The. Hell. Together.

Mentally she put herself in her usual snarky, sarcastic armor, the one specially designed to keep the world at bay, as she dug her nails into the palms of her hands. Her nails were nice and long these days, so they hurt biting into her skin. But that was good, and she welcomed the pain. It helped her focus, helped her center herself.

Taking another breath, she pushed open the small metal door inset into the big roller one, and stepped into Gideon's garage.

For a second she paused, trying to normalize her breathing, letting the familiarity of the garage settle her. It had always been a safe place for her, somewhere to go when she needed company, a good friend, a sympathetic ear. Gideon had gathered together a small group of kids from the Royal Road Outreach Center years ago, kids who were alone in the world, and even now, a decade later, they remained close friends. Gideon, Zoe, Zee and Levi. They were still there for one another, still looked out for one another.

Except you didn't. You weren't there when Levi needed you most.

Rachel swallowed, ignoring the thought. She couldn't afford to be thinking that kind of shit, not now. Not when she was barely holding it together as it was.

The smell of engine grease and oil filled her lungs. It was a comforting smell. There was a big metal shelf and a classic Cadillac up on a hoist blocking her vision, but she could hear the sound of voices. Gideon's, deep and rough, and Zoe's lighter tones. And then someone else's . . .

Rachel stilled, the sound going through her, painful as a sliver of glass pushed beneath her skin.

A masculine voice. One that used to be deep and rich, full of laughter and bright with optimism. A warm, encouraging, friendly voice. One that used to make her heart feel lighter whenever she heard it. But now . . . now it sounded dark, with a roughness that hadn't been there before. Like the voice of someone unused to speaking aloud.

Levi.

A shiver ran the entire length of her body.

He was here, only a few feet away. After eight years.

Come on. You have to do this. Stop being such a fucking coward.

She forced herself to move forward, past the metal shelf, heading down toward the end of the garage where a long workshop counter was positioned against the wall beneath a massive row of grimy windows, some with different colored panes of glass.

The summer sun was shining through those windows, illuminating Zoe, small and slender, her black hair pulled back in a ponytail, sitting on the counter with her legs dangling. Beside her was Gideon in his blue overalls, all shaggy black hair and heavily muscled shoulders, leaning back with his arms folded.

Another man stood with his back to her. He was as tall as Gideon, which was pretty goddamn tall at nearly six four, and built just as massively. The cotton of his black T-shirt stretched over shoulders that would have done a gladiator proud, while his jeans hung low on his lean hips. The combination of sun through the dirty windows and harsh fluorescent lighting of the garage drew out shades of tawny and deep gold in his shaggy dark hair.

Her heart twisted painfully hard.

She remembered those shoulders, that lean waist, that dark hair turning gold in some lights. Except he'd been . . . not quite as built back then. He'd been thinner, more greyhound than Rottweiler, and his hair had been cut short.

He's changed.

Well, of course he had. No one went to prison for eight years and came out the same person.

Perhaps if you'd even gone to see him once in all that time . . .

She blinked hard, digging her nails deeper, using the pain to focus once more.

And maybe she'd made a sound of some kind, an inadvertent gasp or the soles of her platform motorcycle boots scraping on the rough concrete floor, because suddenly, the man standing there with his back to her swung around.

She stopped dead, as if that sliver of glass had finally reached her heart.

Levi looked the same. Exactly the same. Still shockingly handsome with the strong line of his jaw, now rough with deep gold stubble, and high, sculpted cheekbones. Straight nose and long, deeply sensual mouth. Silver-blue eyes that . . .

Her breath caught, glass cutting straight through her heart and out the other side.

No. She was wrong. He didn't look the same. Not at all. There were lines around his mouth and eyes, lines that hadn't been there before, and that wasn't due to age. That was something more. There was a ring piercing one straight, dark eyebrow, and beneath that it looked like his eye had turned completely black, his pupil huge, a thin ring of silver blue circling it.

She couldn't stop looking, couldn't stop staring, the shock of seeing him hitting her like a wrecking ball. And then there were more shocks, more blows, as the differences in him began to filter through her consciousness.

The piercing. That one dark eye. The width of his shoulders and the way his T-shirt molded over a chest and stomach ridged with hard muscle. And his arms . . . Jesus, his tattoos. Around each powerful arm was a series of black bands, each one decreasing in width until the bands around his wrists were merely black lines. They were simple, beautiful, highlighting the strength of biceps, forearms, and wrists, and the deep, dark gold of his skin.

When the hell had he gotten those? Levi had never wanted tattoos, no matter how much she'd told him they'd suit him. She'd even teased him about being afraid of the pain, though she had known that wasn't the reason. Levi hadn't wanted the tattoos because he hadn't wanted anything to get in the way of his dreams of escape.

Escape from their shitty Royal Road neighborhood. Escape from Detroit.

He'd planned to get money enough to leave, get a good job in a high-flying company. Have an apartment that didn't have dealers lurking on the stairs and drunks on the sidewalk out front. Build a life that was about more than mere subsistence and struggle. A life that didn't include tattoos.

Looked like he didn't give a shit about that now.

You can't get a high-flying job with tattoos on your arms. You can't get one with a record either.

The acid in her gut roiled, and she had no idea what to say.

Levi didn't break the heavy, impossible silence, and he didn't smile. He just stared at her as if she were an insect he'd found crushed under the heel of his boot.

Say something, you idiot.

But her voice seemed to have deserted her entirely. All she could do was stare back at him, this man who'd once been her best friend. Whose dreams used to help her believe that there was more to life than existing on her grandma's Social Security checks and hiding from the child protection agencies that wanted to take her away and put her in a foster home. More to hope for than a crummy job in the local diner or behind the counter at the 7-Eleven.

But that friend had once been Levi Rush.

She didn't know who this man was, with his pierced eyebrow, tattoos, and aura of leashed violence and menace. A man like all the other thugs who seemed to infest Royal Road.

And then, as suddenly as he'd swung around to stare at her, the quality of his strangely asymmetrical stare changed. Became focused, intensifying on her the way a sniper locks onto a target.

It was unnerving. Frightening. And Levi had *never* frightened her before.

He looked even less like her friend than ever before. More like a general about to conquer a city. With her being the city.

Her protective mechanisms, ones she'd built up over a lifetime of being on her own, kicked in with a vengeance, and she'd lifted her chin almost before she'd had a chance to think about whether being prickly really was the best way to handle this.

Eight years ago she would have launched herself into his arms for a hug.

But it wasn't eight years ago. It was now. And she'd made so many mistakes already, what was one more?

"Hey, Levi," she said, her voice sounding pathetic and scratchy in the echoing space of the garage. "Long time no see."

Connect with U(s)

Visit us online at
KensingtonBooks.com
to read more from your favorite authors, see books
by series, view reading group guides, and more.

Join us on social media

for sneak peeks, chances to win books and prize packs,
and to share your thoughts with other readers.

facebook.com/kensingtonpublishing
twitter.com/kensingtonbooks

Tell us what you think!

To share your thoughts, submit a review,
or sign up for our eNewsletters, please visit:
KensingtonBooks.com/TellUs.

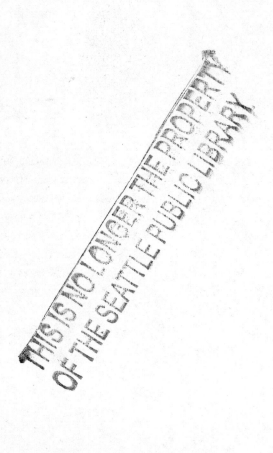